NEVER THE SAME LOVE TWICE

JENNIFER BEASLEY

To the power of Prescott

"THERE ARE ALL KINDS OF
LOVE IN THIS WORLD
BUT NEVER THE SAME LOVE TWICE."

— *F. Scott Fitzgerald*

PART I

JUNE 2016

CHAPTER 1

PEERING DOWN AT MY DESK, I read through the medical report once more, searching for anything else that might be of interest to the parents of my patient-to-be. I'd now repeated the same diagnosis over and over for Wendy and Jason Webinson's unborn baby, and as my eyes shuffled from the medical report to the couple, all I could see in their doe-eyed stares were equal parts hope and despair. I tried to fill the silence with empathy.

"So, again, I'm sorry to be giving you such solemn news," I said as I gestured to the papers in front of me, lab reports and ultrasounds indicating that their unborn baby would have serious complications once born. I'd been sitting with the parents for almost an hour, listening to them talk over and around the diagnosis I had shared because no parents want to talk about anything but, of course, how unfortunate the prognosis is.

Here I was, the one in the white coat, bearing bad news for yet another family awaiting their first child. On this day, it was a twisted bowel in utero. Last month, a brain hemorrhage, and next month, perhaps a genetic abnormality. I became a neonatologist to help shepherd tiny humans through their courageous fights, yet all I did lately was deliver damning news to idealistic parents.

"If our baby is born in August, she'll be home with us by Thanksgiving, right?" the mother, Wendy, asked as she squirmed uncomfortably in the chair opposite my desk. She was trying to make eye contact with me, but her eyes started to shift as soon as I spoke.

"Unfortunately, we won't know the extent of the intestinal atresia until after the surgery," I said, "at which point we'll then assess the recovery period for your baby."

First time parents all seemed to be cut from the same cloth, thinking about themselves first. Thinking about the idyllic holiday season and their baby's role within their perfect little lives. Not knowing that soon enough, after seeing their baby hooked up to breathing tubes and heart rate monitors, the idea of celebrating a holiday would be nothing but a cruel joke.

"But you mentioned that the recovery time is six weeks for our baby's surgery, right?" Wendy inquired as she leaned even further forward in her chair.

I was accustomed to parents hearing my words and feeding them back to me to bargain a better prognosis. And so, to add emphasis, I leaned back in my chair, tilted my chin up, and replied in the most basic terms possible, "We'll have to see how your baby does. Six weeks is the standard."

After they'd heard another round of my generic non-answers, Jason and Wendy were ready to leave. As they stood, I added, "Before you go, I'd like to tell you about the surgeon who will be performing your baby's surgery. His name is Dr. Alexander Smi—" then I got cut off.

"Is he here? Can we meet him?" Wendy asked innocently.

A small smirk drew across my face, which I'd hope would pass as a smile. "Dr. Smithton is one of the leading pediatric surgeons in the country. He anchors a large practice up at Cleveland Clinic, and whenever there is a complex infant surgery in a 100-mile radius, we often call on his team," I explained. "Since this surgery will undoubtedly be complex due to the bowel obstruction and the likely prematurity from that bowel obstruction, Dr. Smithton himself will perform the surgery. This hospital has seen this large of bowel obstruction only twice before, and Dr. Smithton—"

I got cut off again.

"Will we be able to meet him soon?" Wendy asked eagerly.

I sighed. As if Alexander would even want to talk to these parents.

"I'm hoping we can do a conference call," I said encouragingly, though my thoughts trailed off to how I would broach that subject with Alexander. "I'll reach out to Dr. Smithton again on your case and ask to have a pre-birth meeting."

That was only a half-truth, as I hadn't even asked Alexander about this case yet.

"So, he's all the way up in Cleveland? He doesn't live here in Jacobs?" Wendy asked as if Cleveland was a million miles away, as opposed to the actual sixty miles. "What if I go into labor, and have the baby, and then Dr. Smith can't get to us in time because of campaign traffic or something?"

"Smithton. Dr. Smithton," I corrected. I couldn't help it.

"What if Dr. Smithton can't get here because one of the candidates is campaigning here that day?" Wendy looked both worried and like she were a senior political strategist for the 2016 election.

"Yeah," said Jason, who, up until this point had let his wife do most of the talking.

I didn't know anything about the traffic patterns of the battleground counties in this swing state, but I knew I had to get this conversation back on track.

"Don't worry," I said. "Dr. Smithton always takes a helicopter when he has an emergency surgery." I waved my finger gently in the air for demonstration. "No traffic up there." I put my hand on Wendy's shoulder and led her toward my office door. "But please, don't worry; it's our jobs as doctors to make this work. Please, Wendy and Jason, just focus on being healthy and growing your baby. This will all be here before you know it."

And with that, the parents-to-be quietly left my office.

I plopped back down at my desk, exhausted with the knowledge that this baby would soon be in my NICU, and in my care. Her case was going to be complex. I leaned back in my chair and rubbed my temples. *These poor parents.* Had my words landed on them like a velvet hammer? They simply had no idea what was coming for them.

I stared at the Monet painting on my wall. Most doctor's

offices have these types of paintings hung to comfort patients. I was sure it did nothing for Wendy and Jason, but as I stared at the water lilies, my mind shifted to Alexander. What if he didn't want to perform the surgery? What if he wasn't available that day? And when should I call him? I would normally follow up with medical professionals directly after a patient meeting. Like, within thirty seconds of the patient appointment ending. Yet, I spent the next fifteen minutes mindlessly scrolling Instagram and checking my email repeatedly. Why was I procrastinating?

I took a deep breath. All right, *let's call him*. Closing my Instagram app, I dialed his number. Suddenly, my husband's picture pop up. My husband was calling at the same time. I got flustered and let out a shriek. I answered but then quickly hung up. *Wait, did the call go through to Alexander though? Did it look like I hung up on him too?* I went to my sent calls. Whew, no.

I called my husband back.

"Did you hang up on me?" Billy asked, confused.

"Sorry, I accidentally hung up...I meant to take your call... it's been a day!" I said too enthusiastically. "How are you doing?"

He got right into it. "You asked me to call you about the bathroom remodel. They put in the marble today. When they carried it in, I realized it's a lot thicker and the color matches—"

"Babe," I interrupted, "did he say if he was going to reimburse us for the toilet crack though? I know it's barely visible, but it makes me upset that we have to pay for something with a crack on the side."

Since we'd started our spare bathroom renovation a few weeks ago, the crew had dropped the new toilet and put a crack into the drywall when they were installing it. It wasn't horrible, just kind of annoying.

"I didn't ask," Billy said. "I don't want to be confrontational with him and honestly, I could fix it. It's so small you'll forget about—"

"Will you make sure you watch while they install all the heavy and expensive pieces?"

"Yeah, I'll be the foreman," he replied, not giving me any indication if he was joking or serious.

We talked a bit more about the unexpected timeline for the remaining fixtures to be installed, then reviewed our schedules on our joint Google calendar, including the upcoming activities for our seven-year-old son, William. As I hung up, I wondered if I had exerted too much rigidness with the Webinson family just moments prior, and now again with my own husband.

I decided to head to the NICU to get my mind focused. It seemed to be the only place where I could feel like myself anymore, like I belonged. There was such a dichotomy between the way the NICU made parents anxious and my own joyful feelings. For them, it was a place where their baby was under duress, but for neonatologist Lauren? Well, it was my happy place. A place where I could make a difference, a place where I could see growth and vitality, a place that made me hopeful for the future. And it was mine. As the only neonatologist at the hospital, I steered my own ship in the NICU, the captain of the sea, and I appreciated the opportunity.

As I got off on the floor and started my rounds, it seemed like everything was under control. Honestly, most days were like this: normal. With the maximum occupancy of just ninety-nine hospital beds, we only had nine NICU rooms. And most of the year, we didn't even have 100% census; it hovered between six to seven babies at any given time.

The fact that the hospital was so small was always a point of embarrassment for me. All outside doctors were the same; they always asked me about occupancy and census, trying to size up how much responsibility I really had. And I always had to answer, "Nine NICU rooms." With other hospitals at 100 NICU rooms, I continuously feared that other doctors thought my job was laughable. And perhaps it was. Even though I was forty-one, I only had five years' experience as a physician. I'd not completed my route to medical school at the lightning pace that most doctors had. Maybe I wasn't esteemed enough to work at a prestigious hospital in a metropolis.

After making my rounds and prepping the nurse practitioner on treatment for the twenty-six weeker we'd admitted in our NICU the day prior, I walked down the hall a final time, peering into the rooms on both the left and right. No matter what other doctors from my med school program said, I was so lucky to be at this hospital. We were a small town in Jacobs, Ohio. Over an hour outside of Cleveland, we were never considered a true suburb as the town was rather limited. Jacobs was more of a farming community than big-city suburbia. This hospital, while not modern, was a chance for me to really be my own boss.

Sometimes, when I saw pictures of state-of the-art hospitals that my med school friends texted me, I had to remind myself that they were no happier just because they practiced at large hospitals in big cities. Where they were, they were just considered a number. Here, at Covenant Medical, I could 'own' my career. Sure, I wasn't making loads of money, but I made enough, and I was in charge of my unit.

"Dr. Leonard," I heard a nurse say behind me as I was rounding a corner. "Dr. Leonard, do you want little Madison to get the blood draw tomorrow morning once we get a good blood pressure? Or do you prefer we do it tonight after we get a weight on her?"

"Let's wait until the morning. The labs won't even look at it tonight if we do it now," I replied.

I debated staying in the NICU for another couple hours. It wasn't my night; my shift was technically over, and our nurse practitioner had already started her shift. But I just felt so welcome within my little home of the hospital. The thought of seeing my son felt even better, so I decided to head home for the night. Plus, if I went home now, I could put off calling Alexander for another day.

*****

"Mom! Oh my God, Mom, remember how you said that I probably wouldn't see anybody that's running for president?"

I had just walked in from the garage to the smell of spaghetti sauce and the sound of drilling in the guest bathroom. My son William immediately came running up to me.

"Remember how you said that the president people only go to adult places? Well, my principal said today that Bill Clinton is going to come to our school! He used to be a president before I was born! The President people are going to come!"

I smiled. William calling everyone 'President people' was so adorable. I was that mom, like all moms, that found sheer and utter joy from listening to my kid talk.

"Principal Tim wants all the parents to come too, and he said that Bill Clinton is going to speak in the cafeteria or in the gym!" William was so excited and talking so fast.

Letting out a laugh, I said, "Okay buddy, give me a hug! That's awesome news! Did you do anything cool at school today?"

"I found out that the President people are going to come to my school," William deadpanned in the way only a little boy could.

"I guess that's pretty cool, I'm happy for you, bud!" I tried to sound encouraging. "Did Principal Tim say anything else?"

"He said that after, we'll have goetta sausage in the cafeteria because that's Ohio food."

I laughed, probably my first laugh of the day.

I gently unwrapped William's hands from around my waist. He darted into the living room to play with his toys as I walked over to Billy in the kitchen. I leaned into him and placed my forehead close to his face. He looked at me awkwardly before finally kissing me on the forehead.

"The construction guys are almost done," he said, attempting to live up to his foreman comment.

"Oh, that's good," I replied. "Work went well today. The 26-weeker is having a hard time swallowing, but other than that, the babies were pretty tame."

I always felt like I gave Billy such broad-brush descriptions of my job because I never had the energy to unload my day on him. It wouldn't be fair to him, and he never understood anyway. Likewise, Billy never really talked much about his work, other than general updates about having a big upcoming meeting or going into the office. Billy worked for a large IT company, helping with implementations of different systems, and most days, he worked from home.

Billy enjoyed his job, and he was good at it; he made the same salary I did. Together, we were a bit of a power couple, but no one saw us that way. Everyone saw us as the non-traditional couple, where the wife was the breadwinner (which wasn't true), the husband worked from home and didn't work very hard (also wasn't true), and that we only had one child because we wanted to focus on our careers (perhaps mildly true).

Billy was quiet, the textbook definition of an introvert, and although I felt that I was an extrovert who shined, being married to Billy over the years had made me quieter, more complacent, and more muted. I chalked it up to being in my forties now, with a demanding career. My many responsibilities had made me rather robotic. Still though, sometimes I really wanted Billy and me to have a big night out, to be loud and sing at a concert together or dance in a dive bar or yell at a baseball game. But that rarely, if ever, happened anymore. It used to, but we were so far removed from the lovey-dovey couple of our twenties that we forgot those people might still exist within us. Yet occasionally, like tonight, my heart remembered.

Standing together in the kitchen, I picked up the spatula on the stove and started stirring the spaghetti sauce.

"I made that from scratch," Billy said.

I lifted the spatula to my mouth, my other hand hovering below it so the sauce wouldn't drip onto my clothes. It tasted like every other sauce, nothing special.

"Wow, it's really good," I lied.

"Yeah, I make it to William's taste. He seems to like it a bit sweet," Billy said quietly as he cut up a few mushrooms and gently released them in the sauce. "Hey William, you might want to put your toys away because dinner is going to be ready soon."

William, now deep into his Lego pieces in the living room, nodded and started tidying up his play area.

"I'm just going to take a quick shower," I said as I backed away from the kitchen, not even waiting for a response from Billy. I felt equal parts grateful for this well-oiled machine that Billy and William called the evening routine yet wistful that I wasn't always a part of it. Sometimes, like tonight, I was home by 6:00 pm and eating dinner with the family and acting like a normal mom. I was responsible for helping William with his homework, ensuring he took his bath, and completing the bedtime routine. After a long day seeing patients at the hospital, this parental duty felt like another full-time job. But then other days, I was at the hospital throughout the night, missing my life at home. Missing Billy's cooking, missing William's soccer games, missing William's cute word choice, missing my Kindle.

*****

After dinner, after the remodelers left the house for the final time, and after William's bath in the brand-new 'fancy' bathroom as he called it, I snuggled with William in his bed. He asked me question after question. "Do you think the President people are in the Army? Will the President people come over to our house? How long will the President people be at our school? Maybe two days?"

"I don't know, kiddo," I said softly as I rubbed William's back. "I bet the President people are excited to see you though."

"Do you think the President people will meet our school hamster Benny?" William asked, looking at me intently.

"Yes," I said with a laugh. "It's going to be great. Now let's lay quietly for a couple minutes and close our eyes."

After yet another question-and-answer session, my son drifted off to sleep, and I sat up in his bed and just stared over him. Such a healthy, vibrant boy. I didn't deserve him.

As I walked out to the living room, Billy was focused on watching some show on restoring antique cars. "How did he do?" Billy asked as he kept his eyes directed toward the TV.

"He's really excited about Clinton speaking at his school. He asked if we were going to go...." my voice trailed off.

This was a common conversation. Not Bill Clinton speaking at our son's school but deciding which parent would represent William at his school events. Soccer games, school assemblies, heck, even Parents' Day wasn't a given for either of us. It was all based on our work schedules, and with Billy's job allowing him to work from home most days, the lion's share of the school activities rested with him.

"Am I going to be the only guy at yet another one of William's class events?" Billy asked, his eyes now turned toward me.

"Well," I said as I sat down on the ottoman in our living room and politely folded my hands in my lap for emphasis, "don't you think a lot of men are going to be there since this event involves a former president? It's not the hamster show-and-tell like last month." For my final point, I leaned forward. "Also, you know I have a 24-hour shift tomorrow. I had no idea Bill Clinton was going to come to William's school."

"I bet Clinton didn't either." Billy smirked. "He's probably just told where to go like a little lamb."

"So, you'll go?" I asked to get Billy to confirm it out loud.

"Yes, Lauren. It's my day to take William to school, so I'll do that, come home, and take my 10:00 a.m. conference call, then go to the rally....is that what it's called? Is this like a real rally?"

"Thanks, babe," I said as I moved from the ottoman to him on the couch.

Even though it felt unnatural, I put his arm around me and snuggled into him, making my body submissive under his gangly arms and chest. We rarely showed physical affection. And me being wrapped around him was such a juxtaposition to our conversation. In our conversation, we were equals, or perhaps I even had the upper hand, telling him where to go and when. And now, curling up in his body and having his arms around me, I was submitting my body to silently convey that he was still "The Man." Billy sat there, uncomfortably, letting me curl up in him. It felt cumbersome.

As we sat for a moment, staring forward at the TV,

pretending to watch an antique car get a fresh coat of ruby red paint, I wondered if Billy was happy in our marriage. I knew I wasn't, but I had no idea what happiness should look like for me. Yes, I wanted to go out and have fun with Billy, but did the absence of that mean that I was in a bad marriage? Perhaps I was just overreacting.

Still, the more I would try to suppress my thoughts or downplay them, the more they haunted me. *Can't we talk more about us and not just William? Couldn't I have asked him how his workday went? Couldn't he have thanked me for putting William to bed? Can't I enjoy being curled up in him right now? Is this how it is for all couples?* It wasn't unusual for my thoughts to spiral like this when I thought about our relationship.

"I think I'm going to get ready for bed," I whispered in his ear. Billy turned his head and looked into my eyes, and immediately I regretted the whisper. *Shit, he thinks I'm asking for sex.*

"Oh, yeah?" he asked nervously. I could see in his eyes that he didn't want to have to deal with us attempting to have sex. We hadn't had sex in so long that it felt like such an effort to even contemplate it now.

"Yeah, I'm pretty tired," I said quickly, "and want to get to bed early for my shift tomorrow."

"Oh, okay," Billy said, sounding relieved. "Good night."

I walked out of the living room, into my bedroom, my solace, and ultimately, my loneliness.

CHAPTER 2

A FEW DAYS PASSED before I felt confident enough to call Alexander. The fact that I had waited this long was risky. If Wendy Webinson went into labor right now, I'd be scrambling to find an available pediatric surgeon, calling Alexander in a rush. And the last thing I wanted to do was look like I was scrambling in front of Alexander.

Dr. Alexander Smithton had it all together. He was renowned in the area of pediatric trauma, and I wanted to match his professional stamina.

I played our initial conversation over and over in my head, planning what I was going to say. I wanted to, of course, focus on the baby's condition. I wanted to express the problem statement that Covenant Medical had a need for this type of surgeon, as our hospital didn't have anyone close to his type of expertise on staff. I wanted him to know that I had done my research, that I knew he had surgically resolved this condition before. I wanted to emphasize the pre-term labor odds of the mother, and how time was of the essence regarding his agreeing to perform the surgery. Finally, I wanted to stress my role as the overarching physician responsible for the baby's recovery and my ultimate accountability for the baby's growth and development while in the neonatal ICU.

It was so important to me to show my worth, to show that we would be equal partners in the care of this patient.

That was a lot for one call. There wasn't time to introduce our personal lives, and I really hoped he shied away from asking me about my life. So much had happened since we met all those years ago, and right now, the patient's successful surgery and subsequent treatment was my goal.

As I sat at my desk, still not dialing his number, I wondered what was I so afraid of? We had seen each other a year prior at a Cleveland Clinic neonatal conference. He had been the keynote speaker, and I'd been so jealous of what seemed to be his throngs of groupies constantly surrounding him. So many people approaching him near the stage after his speech, congratulating him one at a time on being master of the universe.

But I remembered way back when, when he was a nobody. Part of me felt comfort from knowing he wasn't always the ringleader of a major hospital system, and the other part of me was happy that he knew I had this knowledge. He knew little Dr. Lauren Leonard remembered him not as the white knight physician, but as the young adult with acne.

So why hadn't I called sooner? Again, I had put the baby at risk by not securing Alexander to perform the surgery already. Wendy could give birth any day with her odds of pre-term labor, and I was just sitting on securing the surgeon! Was I nervous that Alexander would blow me off? Not see me as 'worth it?' Or maybe he would look down on our little hospital in Jacobs. If other doctors made fun of where I worked, surely Alexander might think the same. He had never been to the hospital before, as far as I knew. Would he even have an appetite for performing a surgery in our little sleeper of a town?

As I sat with myself for a moment, my phone in my lap, I admitted to myself why I was nervous. I didn't want the past to become the present. Alexander was going to inquire about my family. About Billy. So then was I supposed to politely inquire into his life, awkwardly sounding surprised when he revealed things to me that I already knew from stalking him on Google? Was I supposed to ask if his divorce had calmed down at all, trying to be respectful while also not letting on that every nurse around Cleveland was talking about it? If Alexander asked about little William, was I supposed to gloss over my life as a mom because Alexander wasn't a father? Or maybe get a leg up by praising parenthood, to make Alexander feel a bit deflated and make me look like I had it all?

God, why couldn't I just call him?

Biting my lip, I dialed his number.

"Laur-en Leon-ard," Alexander said, overtly enunciating my name as soon as he picked up. Using a singsong voice, and sounding like he was smiling, he no doubt wanted to make sure *he* was setting the tone for this call. He must have had my number preprogrammed in his phone, a nod to the group text thread we were on a couple years ago regarding an academic journal entry he wrote.

"Alexander! Hi! Hey, it's Lauren, how are you?" I rolled my eyes, realizing I'd just fucking introduced myself after he had already said my name. *Great job,* I thought.

"Doing well. It's crazy here. You know we had MIT and Mayo in earlier last week, right? A symposium that we sponsored on fetal heart rate decline within uterine babies of opioid addicts."

He dove right into giving me his resume. Talking fast, he caught me up on his entire last year, traveling here, there, and everywhere for speaking engagements on pediatric surgery. His study was being published in the American Medical Association journal, and without asking, he started offering up tidbits on his personal life. He even talked about parts of his life I didn't know about, including his buying of a new condo in downtown Cleveland after moving out of the house that he and his now ex-wife had shared.

"What about you, kid?" he finally asked. "How's the bustling metropolis of Jacobs, Ohio treating you?"

For a moment, I was quiet. He had just given me two insults in two sentences. Using the word 'kid?' Although he always acted older, we were only one year apart in age. Was he cutting me down to size? Or was I being overly sensitive? And why the rude comment about the town I lived in? Sure, it wasn't as fast paced as where he lived in Cleveland, but the way I saw it, we were both in Ohio, both in the Midwest. I kept my annoyance close to the chest as I wanted to make sure that again, I kept this call focused and professional.

After I finished catching him up on my work focused on lung treatments for infants testing positive for cystic fibrosis but not yet posing symptoms, he seemed really interested. I offered that I hoped to share my findings with him once finished with the analysis. We talked shop a bit more, and I got the sense that Alexander could have talked like this all day with me. But I needed to get down to business.

"So, Alexander, the reason for my call is related to a surgery that Covenant Medical will have to undertake, and we're hoping to secure you for that surgery." He was silent, so I continued. "It's a bowel obstruction that looks, at least through the mother's ultrasound, that it's going to be an atresia. The ultrasounds can't give us the exact story, but the obstruction is dilated too much for this to be a meconium plug. The mother is almost 30 weeks pregnant, and the hope is that when she delivers, you could fly in to perform the surgery."

He was quiet. Was he going to say no? I continued, now straying from my original talking points, and started to lay it on thick.

"Covenant Medical understands your tenure and experience make you in demand not just for neonatal surgeries but also for leadership of your teams at Cleveland Clinic. I understand your schedule is already very full. Our hospital thought you could really make a difference here, because without your expertise and—"

Finally, he cut me off. "Oh, of course, oh yeah, I understand,

I'll do it," he said gently. "Sorry, Lauren. You caught me off-guard. I thought you were just calling to catch up. But yeah, I mean, how far along did you say the mother was? Did you already send the ultrasounds to my office, or should I request those? How much does the baby weigh in utero right now?"

We talked about the medical case in detail and his larger-than-life attitude began to fade away. For a moment, he was the student and I was the teacher. *I* was bringing *him* up-to-speed on his newest surgical case. Knowing that I wasn't calling to flirt with him calibrated him enough to focus on our new patient.

I even mentioned that the parents might want to meet with him.

"Lauren, you can let the parents know that I'm available for a call, so they can get to know my history of similar surgeries. But as you know, it's not going to help me. I'm just going to need to open that baby up and dig in to get any answers."

I nodded, even though he couldn't see me, and wondered if he talked like that because he had no kids himself or because what he was saying was simply true.

Before I could reply, he continued, "That said, maybe you and I could meet prior to review the ultrasound and get a game plan together for the baby's care post-surgery."

"Sure, do you want me to include the OBGYN? I don't think you know her; her name is—"

"Let's do it, just me and you. Fewer cooks in the kitchen," Alexander said bluntly.

I couldn't disagree, and selfishly, I didn't want to share him when it came to this case.

But I didn't know what Alexander meant by meeting prior. Was the big man on campus going to leave Cleveland Clinic for the day and come to Jacobs? To Covenant Medical? Did he want me to tackle all that Cleveland traffic and come to him? Were we going to meet somewhere in the middle, in one of those innocuous Pleasantville suburbs?

"Maybe we could meet halfway or something," he said, verbalizing the third option I had in my head. "Does Friday work for you?"

Wow, this was really real. We were going to meet, just the two of us.

"Um, actually, it does. I have that day off," I said, glancing at the Google calendar Billy and I shared. I'd pulled up on my laptop. Looking at that day, I had notes in there that I stupidly communicated to Alexander. "We remodeled our bathroom, so I was planning on picking paint colors to start the repainting, but I can reschedule that," I babbled.

Jesus, I sounded so trite. This guy was a renowned surgeon, suggesting a meeting to discuss my patient, and here I was advertising that I would need to switch bathroom paint appointments.

"Wow, Leonard, an HGTV bathroom remodel? A doctor and a designer...a woman of so many talents!" I could hear the smile in his voice, and he had to know I was smiling on the other end.

All right, so this conversation was going to end on a flirty note.

"Why don't I text you where we can meet?"

"Sounds good. And thanks, Alexander, for agreeing to perform the surgery. Covenant is really thankful." *Keep it focused on the hospital, not me,* I thought.

"Happy to do it. Looking forward to seeing you and catching up. I'll text you...all right, talk with you soon. All right, bye."

I hung up.

I had to get up out of my office chair and see my babies in the NICU.

If I didn't, I would just sit and obsess over the phone call. I didn't want to overanalyze every word he said. Yet, as I walked down the stairs from my office to the NICU, behind the back corridor and past the OR, I couldn't help but indulge myself... was Alexander excited to see me? And where the hell were we going to meet to discuss the surgery? What hospital between Cleveland and Jacobs was going to allow us to be squatters in their facility? Was Billy going to ask a million questions about this? Was he going to be mad that I wasn't going to be there to pick out paint colors?

Was I really doing this?

Was I really going to see Alexander again?

CHAPTER 3

When I woke up on Friday morning, it felt just like the day I took my medical boards. That sense of dread that everything could come crashing down around me, coupled with the feeling of promise, altering my life forever, with no going back. My nervousness started to get the best of me as I crawled out of bed, knowing that most of the day was just passing the time until my meeting with Alexander. I had to remind myself that this was a meeting to discuss a patient, nothing more. To my credit, perhaps this was less of me being self-conscious and more of Alexander having an intimidating effect on everyone.

He'd texted me not even twelve hours after our call. He'd asked if we could meet closer to Cleveland—but away from Cleveland Clinic—in the suburb of Norins, Ohio. Known for its money, the Village of Norins was always where people wanted to see and be seen. Residents in that suburb, with their red brick mansions and their white Range Rovers, were equal parts high-energy hot and smooth-talking cool.

Although I'd lived in Ohio my entire life, I'd always gathered that 'acting cool' in the Midwest was such an oxymoron. Acting rich and beautiful and important and suave in such a junior-varsity environment seemed ridiculous compared to actual hot spots like Manhattan or Silicon Valley, where brilliance, art, and individuality intersected. Yet Norins, Ohio was a city of salt-of-the-earth Midwesterners pretending to be something they weren't with the knowledge that they only looked shiny against the mundane backdrop of the Middle West.

Alexander texted for us to meet at Morton's Steakhouse, which seemed both professional and sexy, and fit the theme of the Village of Norins. I didn't know what to make of Alexander choosing such an expensive restaurant for dinner. As the hours of the day ticked by and it got closer to when I needed to head upstate, I still hadn't decided what I was going to wear. Procrastinating, I decided to pick my outfit last, distracting myself first with hair and makeup.

I began watching a YouTube makeup tutorial on how to contour my face. After using bronzer to brush below my cheek bone, I wasn't confident that it made a difference. I FaceTimed my best friend Steele to see if she thought I looked any better. Steele, who probably had better things to do than grade my makeup application, subsequently did not answer her phone.

As I was curling my hair, little William trotted into my bathroom, now home from school and sweaty from playing outside.

"What are you doing, Mom?" he said, his furrowed stare in the direction of my curling iron. It was only then that I realized I rarely, if ever, curled my hair. I was always trying to keep my hair off my face. Traditionally, I pulled my long, thick, highlighted brunette hair back into a low bun when at the hospital. At home, I usually twisted my hair into a top knot.

But as William was looking up at me, I sighed and realized that my son was already recognizing something I failed to see. I was trying to look more polished than usual. "What's that?" William inquired, pointing at my ceramic curling wand that I'd bought from Sephora and barely knew how to use.

"Mommy's just curling her hair," I said with a smile, trying to be as generic as possible.

"Can you curl my hair?" William asked innocently.

I laughed. "No, sweetie," I said. "It's really hot. Be careful not to touch it, okay?"

Billy walked into the bathroom, and now the entire family was huddled in our small master bathroom. It had also been remodeled the year before, now a spa-like setting with the heated floor. I held my breath. Would Billy find it odd that I was paying so much attention to my hair?

But instead, he just glanced briefly at me, then turned his attention to William. "Do you want to go practice soccer in the yard?" he asked.

William, never one to leave me hanging, yelled, "Bye Mommy!" Then he followed Billy out of the bathroom, and I heard the garage door open as they headed out into the yard.

As William's salutation echoed in my head, I put down the curling iron and stared at myself in the mirror. Why was I trying so hard with my appearance tonight? If I was honest with myself, I knew I was a little starved for attention. I simply wanted Alexander to think that although I was decades older than the first time we met, I still 'had it.'

With my makeup and hair done, I had to tackle what to wear. Monochromatic was easy and foolproof. I chose a black turtleneck, black pants, and basic black flats. Even though I wanted to wear teardrop earrings or a statement necklace, I stopped short of jewelry. I wanted to hide the impression that I was trying too hard. The hair and makeup were more than enough. And I didn't want to get any questions from Billy as I left.

I'd told Billy about the dinner but not that it was with Alexander. Half of me felt guilty, but the other half of me didn't see the point of mentioning his name. Billy knew, of course, who Alexander was. But I didn't want the disappointment of Billy simply not caring that I was meeting with Alexander. Most men are competitive, especially with each other, and especially for their wife. But over the years, I'd learned that Billy just wasn't built with that particular man chip.

After I got ready, I walked through the garage to the front lawn, where I saw Billy and William kicking the soccer ball. Instantly, I felt so separated from them. Nights out for me were with the family, piling in the car together to grab pizza, not going to expensive steakhouses with successful doctors.

"Okay guys, wish Mommy luck at her meeting!" I yelled,

but Billy and William seemed much more interested in their game than they did in wishing me luck. I started my car for the hour drive ahead, and as I pulled away from the house, William gave me a big wave. He smiled and kicked the ball into the mesh soccer goal in our yard.

A myriad of emotions washed over me as I eased my car on the road: hope for the surgery, concern in measuring up to Alexander, guilt for not being with Billy and little William on a Friday night, disappointment in myself telling them this was just a 'meeting' when it was more than that for me, and finally annoyance. My irritation came 10 minutes into the drive, when I encountered a political motorcade blocking I-71 for miles.

I picked up my phone and googled who was in town. Apparently, both Trump's campaign and Clinton's campaign were holding rallies at some point during the weekend, but I couldn't figure out who was holding me up from arriving on time to this important dinner. I unlocked my phone to text Alexander.

(Me) Hey, looks like I ran into campaign traffic! I might be a few minutes late.

I sent it with an American flag emoji for good measure.

(Alexander) "I'll only forgive you if you get Trump's autograph.

I rolled my eyes and laughed. I felt a certain guiltless power in texting him. Part of me felt that as long as I didn't speak the words, whatever I wrote and suggested were permissible to my conscience.

(Me) Oh, actually, I'm talking with Hillary right now on her tour bus. She wants to know why you're making me drive all the way up to Norins to see you.

The 'to see you' part was a bit daring, but I smiled as I sent it. My phone chimed with the next message.

(Alexander) Hillary and I both know you'll look for any excuse to leave Jacobs.

My heart sank. I'd been expecting a flirty reply from him. Was he insulting me by insulting where I lived? Again? First the initial call, and now this text. How come Alexander was giving himself permission to throw these quips my way, inevitably making me feel insecure about myself? Was that his intention? Or was he being benign while I was being overly sensitive? I knew it was the latter, but it was easier to lean into Alexander being an egotist.

Why the hell are you even making this trip? I wondered. *You should have emailed his assistant the ultrasounds and medical notes and called it a day.*

Alexander must have sensed that I was not taking the text well because he shortly followed it up with: *But then again, you're too good for Cleveland, too.*

I kept my phone out of sight for the rest of the drive, except to glance at Google maps as I got closer to the destination. As I arrived at Morton's, I pulled into the valet lane and immediately saw Alexander get out of a massive white Cadillac Escalade. A smile drew across my face because when my son saw things like that, he always asked, "How come short people drive tall cars? Why don't short people drive little cars and tall people drive big cars?"

Alexander was 5'7", and I was 5'9". I usually slouched a bit when I was around him. And tonight, I had made sure to wear flats. It wasn't that he was short; he was just short compared to me. Alexander was confident in who he was, and I had always admired that he never let his height nag at him. Still, a part of me wanted to play the role of the submissive tiny girl. I wasn't sure that's even what he wanted, but I really had a penchant for trying to please him.

I let Alexander walk inside the restaurant instead of greeting him by the valet stand. I wanted to make sure I could make my entrance. Also, I still had to apply my lip gloss, which was a sheer pink to contrast all the black I was wearing. While I waited in my car, I watched two girls in their twenties in tight black dresses and Louboutin heels head inside the restaurant. I wanted to see if Alexander would notice them. He didn't, and I let out a little sigh of relief.

As I walked into the restaurant lobby maybe two minutes later, I pulled my hair in front of my body to make sure my soft curls laid perfectly. The Friday night crowd had started to rally as the bar was packed and loud. Everyone was dressed in business casual, the corporate crowd continuing to linger after happy hour. I spotted Alexander, already on his phone. He saw me and waved me over to where he was standing. As I walked over, I heard him say, "Can you email me the report and I'll call you back?"

I stood before him adjacent to the floor-to-ceiling wine cellar, and he mouthed "Sorry," as he pointed at his phone and promptly ended the call. "Hey! Give me a hug," he said enthusiastically.

We embraced. It felt a bit awkward to me, as our bodies touched and I wondered if he felt awkward, too. Was he confident, or clueless?

"So, you got stuck in traffic, huh? You made it here on time. I just got here myself," he said casually, which of course, I already knew.

We continued small talk and luckily, he had made reservations, so we were led back to our table right away. We ordered drinks, and the conversation stayed very professional. It felt a bit funny, the mixture of alcohol and ultrasounds. I decided to dive right into talking about our patient and asking his thoughts about the impending surgery. At first, I felt like a killjoy, continuously pulling out small X-rays and reports, which I had brought in a secured manila envelope. Yet I appreciated the opportunity to have Alexander's complete attention and talk through the blueprint for our patient's recovery. I felt comfortable in this role as the doctor with the knowledge, educating Alexander on our patient. The more I talked, the more

I hit my stride, showcasing my medical chops.

By the time our starters arrived, we had a thorough game plan for the surgery and aftercare. The conversation then drifted to the parents and how much handholding they would need during this months-long process.

"I guess they named the baby already," I said in between bites of my Caesar salad. "Emma."

"That's a nice name," he said blankly.

"Wendy's an interesting mom," I said. "I'm not sure she understands the severity of Emma's condition. I think Wendy is banking the recovery time will only be six weeks and then—"

"Well, let's see what I can do with the atresia. Don't go putting time stamps on me, Leonard," Alexander said both cutely and correctly, then took a swig of his imported bottled beer.

Our conversation floated from our patient to discussing more broad topics, including the recent organizational changes at Cleveland Clinic that made him head of his department, as well as some new pediatric studies that had been released in the past few months. We briefly chatted about the healthcare reform policies of both candidates and joked for a bit that we should join the campaign trail.

The dinner was going surprisingly well. My biggest concern was being washed away, as it felt like we were indeed equals and that he was seeing me as a real doctor. He was accepting me in this new (to him) role. *I don't know what I was afraid of,* I thought. I was keeping Alexander on his toes, and he wasn't asking me too many personal questions.

I hadn't anticipated how light, free, and fun it would be to see Alexander, and to be out on a Friday night. I rarely got to eat at a steakhouse, and if I did, I was preoccupied with making sure that William was behaving. And usually he wasn't, which meant I gave into his pleas to let him play on his iPad, resulting in rude stares from parents at adjacent tables. Billy and I used to have date nights, but we seemed to not have much to talk about, and so inevitably our dates became less and less of a priority for us. We would joke that we preferred to be in our sweats eating Chinese food together on the couch, instead of getting all gussied up and going to a fancy restaurant. But if I was honest with myself, we preferred it that way because we felt more comfortable spending time letting a TV talk to us than us talking with each other.

But here, with Alexander, I felt enlivened. Perhaps it was the wine, or the expertly prepared salmon, or maybe just that he was asking me softball questions.

And then, what felt like all at once, it got deeper.

"Lauren, I've always been meaning to ask you," Alexander said. "I think I know the answer, but just to hear it from you, why did you decide to become a neonatologist?"

I froze. He was right. He did know. Was he asking me to talk about the past? I didn't feel comfortable being vulnerable right now, or perhaps ever, so I gave the answer all neonatologists give to explain why we chose our area of medicine.

"You know better than anyone, Alexander. Working with newborns is the best gig in the world. They grow and heal so quickly, and they don't talk back. They're perfect patients," I said convincingly.

He nodded while he looked deep into my eyes, almost

wistfully. Was he hoping I would talk about the real why?

"I wanted to be able to help babies whose bodies couldn't help themselves," I concluded. "No more resilient fighters in the world than those tiny humans."

We were quiet for a moment, and then he replied. "That's how I feel too, in a way," he said, now looking down at the table. "I guess for me, I like working with babies and children because I don't have kids of my own. I've always wondered if it was the chicken or the egg; if I never had kids because I was a busy doctor who wasn't able to fit in a family, or because in not having a family, I could dive head-first into my profession."

"Well, you could still have children," I said as my fingers slowly moved up and down the stem of my wine glass. I didn't know how Alexander felt about being early-to-mid-forties and finding a significant other, having a child, and becoming a family man. Part of my asking was due to our history, part pure curiosity, but mostly I was testing him a bit, doing the exact opposite of what I wanted him to do to me during this dinner.

Alexander nodded, then sat up in his chair and pushed his shoulders back. "I think I'm pretty set on how my life is now. I'm proud of the practice I lead at Cleveland Clinic. Everyone tells me I'm too young to have this much responsibility, and that fatherhood would make me happier, but I just don't see how I'm missing too much, you know? I'm on the pulse of life, literally."

It was both sad and relieving to hear him say that about not having children. Sad that the young fantasy I had built in my head never came, but relieved that in real life, Alexander was happy.

"How about you, though?" Alexander said, obviously ready

to be off the hot seat. "You have to be ecstatic about your little boy. After everything you went through."

I was stunned. He *was* going to bring it up, a past that I had not yet made peace with. I tried not to fidget in my seat. My heart started beating quickly, and I could feel myself starting to sweat. Perhaps Alexander didn't know how intrusive he was being. But to talk through my past right now would be overwhelming. I crossed my arms in front of my chest.

I let silence fill the air, and then Alexander asked the same question of me, if I saw myself having another child.

On the surface, I really enjoyed that we were asking these questions of one another, in our early forties. Most people in their forties can't talk conceiving without mentioning their age, the difficulty, and the odds against them, thinking they were running out of time. Being in the medical community, we knew better. We got to see first-hand that there were perfect babies born to mothers and fathers in their fifties. But I struggled with my answer to his question. Did I want another child? I knew my planned answer, which was that I was so over-the-moon with my son that I wanted a million more babies like him.

But thinking about my life right now, did I really want another child? No. I wasn't emotionally in a place where I would feel comfortable embarking upon parenthood a second time with my husband. But I couldn't tell Alexander about my shortcomings with Billy. That would have felt sloppy. I decided to focus on logistics, not on me.

"I, um, I think that..." I stammered. "I think that with one child, it's manageable, and it's definitely an easier path than having multiple children. I think I have it pretty easy. William is a great child."

What I wasn't saying to Alexander was the guilt I felt, almost daily, that William was indeed an only child. Growing up as an only child myself, I'd always longed for that relationship my friends had with their siblings. I knew I was putting William in the same tough spot I was put in as a child. William would be on his own when Billy and I passed away. I didn't want to be a burden on my son, and in a more perfect world, I wish I would have given my son the greatest gift you can give a child: a sibling. But saying all that to Alexander felt superfluous.

"William really is a great child," I repeated, my voice cracking as I thought about my son.

"No," Alexander said, looking into my eyes with his shoulders turned toward me. "It's you. I mean sure your child is great, but it's because he came from you. You're a powerhouse, Lauren. You're able to lead an entire hospital department, be a parent who is available to her child, rehab a house, and find a way to come up here on a Friday night to discuss a patient when I know there is probably a basketball game or piano recital that you're missing." And then, as a zinger, he leaned back and quietly, almost to himself, added, "And you're beautiful while doing it all, which is no easy feat."

The wine was now hitting hard. He carried on a bit more, saying how true his words were, and I continued to thank him for his efforts to come to Covenant Medical to do the surgery. On the outside, I was playing it cool, brushing off his compliments and focusing on the hospital, but deep inside my soul, I felt validated. His words affirmed what I thought about myself but never heard from my own husband, or anyone else really. Alexander understood the multi-dimensional life I led, and he was applauding me for it. Him articulating how I felt about myself made me feel like I belonged.

From there, we didn't talk much more about work or our personal lives. Instead, we started discussing the restaurant and the crowd, trying to stay in the moment and keep things lighthearted.

The server approached soon after, waving a dessert menu. "Oh, no thanks," I said as the server smiled and kept walking past. Alexander turned into me a bit more, like he wanted to share a secret with me.

With his voice lowered, he said, "Hey, let's go out for ice cream. Let's go get some Graeter's."

"Now?" I asked. Graeter's was THE best ice cream on the planet, an Ohio institution. I was even sure Morton's Steakhouse had Graeter's in their freezer right now if Alexander wanted to satiate this instant craving of his.

"Yeah, how about we go grab some ice cream, and we can talk more about the surgery on the drive," Alexander suggested.

I replied by nodding and soon after, the bill came. I really wanted to pay half, but Alexander insisted on paying. I looked closely to see if he would pull out a corporate credit card, having Cleveland Clinic fund this night out. I smiled as I saw him retrieve his personal credit card from his wallet. It made me even more sure that he wanted to be here with me.

As we got up from the table, I could feel the wine. Thank

goodness I wasn't about to get behind the wheel. I started walking to the door and Alexander walked behind, placing his hand on the small of my back. His touch was slight, and yet it was the sexiest touch I'd felt in months. Hell, a year. Years? It felt so good and for some reason, I allowed it. Maybe he was trying to be a gentleman? Maybe it was habit? Maybe I was starved for attention? Yet it felt so comfortable, and so natural, with his hand on my body.

Outside the restaurant, Alexander and I waited for his vehicle in silence. The late June weather was scorching even at 9:00 p.m. and made Alexander perspire around his hairline. Although he was balding, he still had an outline of hair that looked like it had been trimmed quite recently. Had he gotten his hair cut in anticipation of our dinner?

As the valet attendant pulled his car up, Alexander again placed his hand on the small of my back, and again I let him. He then walked past me to the driver's side, and I headed toward the passenger side and climbed into his massive SUV. With three valet attendants watching, I tried to be as graceful as possible while hoisting myself up into his Cadillac Escalade, which felt enormous compared to my Toyota Prius. As I sat in the car, looking forward at his massive dashboard, I couldn't help but feel like our cars were a bit of a metaphor for who we were as people. I was a Toyota Prius: thoughtful, practical, and unassuming. Alexander was a Cadillac Escalade: commanding and captivating.

As we drove away, I realized that in being together in his car, we were alone, just the two of us, for the first time in decades.

"It's really good to see you," Alexander said, not wasting any time and looking over at me briefly before shifting his eyes to the road He must have realized, just as I did, that we hadn't been alone together in what felt like a lifetime. Perhaps he too had feelings he wanted to express.

"I was hoping that we could reconnect, albeit professionally..." His voice trailed off, and silence filled the car for a few heartbeats. "I thought about you over the years. I always checked up on you here and there. Social media, hospital newsletters, colleague discussion, that sort of thing. I'm really happy for you, all that you've accomplished, and everything you turned into. It's great that you're a doctor, too, now. Who would've thought, both of us now working together on a patient?"

I had, for so long, fantasized about hearing those words from him. Alexander recognizing my place as a physician and being proud of how I chose to script my life. I looked over and grinned to let him know I appreciated his words.

We pulled into the Graeter's parking lot, and Alexander parked his vehicle facing away from the ice cream shop toward the adjacent park. It was completely dark by now, and there was barely enough light to see his face. At first, I thought we were going to get out of the car and head in, which would help me wear off some of the alcohol I was feeling. But Alexander kept the car running, leaning forward with his hands on the steering wheel and soothing classical music piping through the speakers.

Something was about to happen. I turned my head to look at him, my heart now beating out of my chest. He turned to look at me, hands still on the steering wheel.

"Lauren, I just want you to know, I really have thought about you over the years." He continued in this manner, saying every single damn word I'd wanted to hear my entire adult life.

And then, with hands now off the steering wheel, he leaned over and cupped my face. I was still, his surgeon hands feeling so warm and familiar. He leaned closer. My mind went blank. He was waiting for me to say something, do something, for me to move closer or pull away. He was waiting for a sign. But as our dynamic dictated, he was going to have to take the lead and I was going to be there to follow, like a little puppy dog.

Our eyes met. He must have taken that as permission because he leaned all the way in to kiss me. It was a gentle, quiet kiss, with his lips on mine for what felt like a suspension of time. While my outside body was still, inside I felt a jolt, from the top of my head to the bottom of my toes. I stayed in his embrace, his lips and tongue moving on mine, my cheeks in his hands, until finally I pulled away.

"Alexander," I said as I put my fingers over my lips.

He leaned back in his driver's seat, staring ahead. He wasn't about to apologize, and I wasn't about to talk about how I was married, and how this was wrong. In our silence, that narrative was playing in our heads; there was no need to also verbalize it.

And then, it was my turn to be honest with him.

"I think I did this to myself," I said as I, too, sat back in my seat, glancing briefly at him then looking out toward the desolate park. "I think I wanted this tonight. You thinking I was smart and pretty, giving me attention. I created this. For me, this was more than discussing a patient."

"But I invited you to dinner, and I asked you to come all the way up here," Alexander replied, half sweetly and half competitively. It was as if we were in a contest for who could be the most deceptive, and who wanted who more.

"Well, Emma, our new patient, will be arriving within the month," I said. "I'm sure we'll be seeing each other again soon, and we know to keep it professional."

"Professional," Alexander echoed with a nod.

"It's getting late," I said after a stretch of silence. "I should start heading back." What I didn't add was that I was going to have a hell of a time explaining why I was in Norins after 10:00 p.m. for a work meeting.

We never went in for the ice cream.

Alexander drove me back to Morton's in silence. We said our goodbyes, and I retreated to what now felt like my pathetic little Prius.

As I pulled onto the highway to start my drive back to Jacobs, I started crying. I didn't want to get involved with Alexander. But I knew I wanted his attention. I didn't want to be a big-shot neonatologist at a large hospital. But I knew I wanted Alexander to think I was a fantastic doctor. I didn't want a crappy marriage with Billy. But why did I just *know* that Billy wasn't even going to be concerned that I'd been gone so long?

There was no foundation under me, no safety net that I could rest on, and I could see the writing on the wall: my personal life and my work life were beginning to collide.

*****

An hour later, I tiptoed into our house through the garage, thinking how unneeded it was to be quiet. I knew in my bones that Billy was fast asleep, not concerned about his wife being out late. As I changed into my pajamas, took a shower, and brushed my teeth, Billy never stirred.

Only when I crawled into bed did Billy, laying on his back with his eyes closed, say groggily, "The Google calendar has you taking William to soccer practice tomorrow."

"Okay," I replied plainly. And then I added, "I'll let you know how practice goes."

Billy then rolled over, his back to me. I turned my back, too, and tried to fall asleep.

CHAPTER 4

FOR A FEW WEEKS AFTER MY DINNER WITH ALEXANDER, I felt distracted and lonely. All because of one dinner and one tiny kiss, I couldn't seem to look my husband in the eye. I had trouble being in the moment with my son. I was annoyed with my patients, and I was tethered to my phone, glancing at it every ten seconds to see if Alexander would text or call, or worse, stay silent. Thus far, he was choosing the latter and hadn't reached out.

Going to dinner with Alexander and allowing that kiss was a wrong turn. I was mixing my work and my personal life, which we all struggle with, but I knew I was playing with fire. I was a wife, one of my most important roles. And although Billy didn't know it, I was hurting him and creating a problem in our marriage that might not be able to be repaired.

As much as I should have leaned into Billy and our subpar

marriage, as much as I should have tried to find a fix, I chose to focus on Alexander. *Maybe I'll send him a text, thanking him for the dinner?* I thought. *Or a quick call to confirm, yet one more time, his availability for the Webinson's baby's surgery? Do I tackle the kiss head on and apologize to him? Flirt with him?*

Not only was I at a loss of what to do, but I hadn't made peace with how I felt about the kiss. A part of me needed validation from Alexander after all this time, and having him kiss me, well, the kiss was the piece of affirmation that I needed. How he felt about me was shown with his desire. I held onto the kiss as evidence that he desired me, and he felt I was good enough. I replayed the kiss in my mind, daydreaming about the kiss turning into something more.

Oppositely, the kiss made my life messy. Say what you will about a boring life in a small Midwestern town, but it's a calm, quiet, organized way to live. I had my cookie cutter life: a husband, a son, a house, a career, a running path, and a church. My job was the only part of my life that had any variability to it, but even being a doctor at the local hospital was somewhat regimented and organized. And so, with one tiny kiss, and with one humongous crush on Alexander, my life was becoming tangled, and I could feel the straight lines were about to zig zag even more.

I went through the routine at work. Even though I was disengaged, I was able to keep the NICU in a good spot. Luckily, our census was low, and I was only caring for five babies. Wendy Webinson hadn't gone into labor yet, and I knew this quiet time at work was going to be my calm before my storm. And with my final shift before three consecutive days off, I assumed that I could fix myself while away from my job.

Part of fixing myself was confiding in someone. And I knew that if anyone was going to help me get my head on straight, it had to be Steele. My friend since high school, Steele Torsney knew me when I was just a lanky teenager trying out for cheerleading. Steele, of course, with her naturally blonde hair and petite frame, was not only captain of the cheerleaders but did her best campaigning to make me part of the squad. But even 5'1" giants of persuasion have their limits, and I never made the team. Still, Steele had been looking out for me every day since we were thirteen, and as a mom and wife herself, she got me.

And now, more than twenty-five years after we first became friends, my form of therapy was our monthly happy hour meetups, where we talked everything from celebrities to ailing parents. I knew I was going to need to be honest with her at this particular happy hour.

As I pulled up to the small wine bar near her house, I saw her sitting on the patio, smiling as she spoke with the waiter. *That's Steele*, I thought. A stranger to no one, so attracting and kind. She was a vision in her bright pink Lily Pulitzer dress and bouncing blonde hair, pointing to something on the menu and looking back and forth between the menu and the server. Steele always had a great sense of style. In Jacobs, there are only a couple boutique clothing stores, and our mall was rather small, so Steele bought all her clothes online and made monthly trips up to Beachwood outside of Cleveland to shop at Nordstrom.

As I got out of my car, I could feel the July humidity on my skin.

"Lauren!" Steele said as she waved me over to the table. "Hey girl!" She stood up and embraced me in a hug. With our height difference, I had to lean down low, like I always did when I was hugging my son. "How are you? Is this table okay? I ordered us a bottle of white because it's so hot outside, is that okay?"

Before I could answer any of her rapid-fire questions, her phone rang. We both looked down to see who was calling.

"If I get one more FUCKING election call," Steele said as she sat back down. "I swear to God, Lauren, at this point I don't even care who wins! I just want my phone to quit ringing!"

"You could turn your phone on silent?"

"Well then I wouldn't be able to pick up and find out who I should vote for," she deadpanned with a wink.

As the wine came and we each got a glass in, we both started commiserating about life. Steele was feeling unappreciated at work, and although it was supposed to be part-time, she was actually pulling full-time hours working at the school her children attended. She felt torn between needing to set boundaries while still ensuring her job got done. For my part, I told Steele about the Bill Clinton event at William's school and how Billy guilted me about him being the only father to attend. I told her how I felt insecure in my gender role.

I was waiting for the right time to talk about what I really wanted to talk about. As we headed into starting our second glass of Chardonnay, I mustered up the strength to broach the topic of Alexander.

"So, Steele," I said as I leaned forward in my seat, staring her in the eye through her designer sunglasses, "I have something to tell you."

"Okay," she said, fidgeting with her hair.

I decided to go the long route, telling her the backstory with the Webinson's baby and how there had to be a duality of medical care, both from a pediatric surgeon as well as a neonatologist.

"Let me guess who the pediatric surgeon is," she said with a smirk.

"Yes, bingo," I said, knowing that Steele would be invested in this. "So, he and I talked on the phone about the surgical case, and then I met him for dinner to review the ultrasounds and get a plan together for the baby's recovery," I said as I looked down in my lap, careful not to say his name aloud yet.

"Wait, you met for dinner?" Steele said as she leaned forward in her seat. "What did Billy say? Were you nervous? Did you guys talk about anything besides the patient? What did you wear?" And then, as a finishing touch to the round of questions, Steele leaned back and empathized, "Wow, I would have been nervous to see him again."

I explained how my nerves did get the best of me anticipating the dinner with Alexander and how she didn't pick up when I tried FaceTiming her after my contour makeup application. I also casually mentioned to her that I didn't tell Billy who I was meeting for dinner.

"You just left and didn't tell him?" Steele asked incredulously.

"Well, of course I told him that I was going up toward Cleveland Clinic to discuss a surgery, and that it was a dinner meeting. Billy knows about the patient and how the meeting was surgery related. I just didn't tell Billy who the surgeon was."

"Only the most important part," Steele said sharply.

"I know, but you know Billy, he probably would have been like, 'O sure, how's that guy doing?'" I said in a low voice to mimic how Billy sounded. "Steele, you know Billy. The guy doesn't show emotion or get involved in caring about things like that."

"Yeah, that's the problem..." Steele said, her voice trailing off. She picked up her glass and just before taking a sip asked, "So, what was it like? Did you enjoy talking with him again?"

"Let's put it this way," I said as I started to become bolder, the wine now making me a bit cloudy. "It started with me seeing his 5'7" frame get out of a massive Cadillac Escalade and ended with him kissing me in the dark three hours later in that same Cadillac Escalade." Like in the movies, Steele nearly spit out her wine. As she struggled to swallow so that she could speak, I concluded with, "So yeah, for the past few weeks, I've been a mess! Because all I can do is think of him and the kiss."

"Wow," was all Steele could muster at first. "Damn girl, look at you getting some action on a Friday night!" We both busted out laughing.

For just a moment, I was in this innocent place where I was able to laugh with a friend about what happened, knowing that it didn't go any further than a kiss.

As I sat back in my chair, now slouched a little holding my glass of wine, I looked at Steele. I knew what came next. Steele was going to ask me the hard questions. *How do I work with Alexander in a professional way? How do I put this behind me? How do*

I forget about it?

But that's not at all what she said.

"I think the next couple months are going to be tough, Lauren. Being around Alexander, I think the temptation of having an affair will be ever-present. You'll have to decide what you want to do."

And with that, her cell phone rang, inevitably another election robocall, and she cursed again quietly as she took my advice and turned her phone on silent.

I was stunned with Steele's analysis, that I had a choice here of what I wanted to do. I was forty-one years old: a mother, a wife, a doctor. I didn't have any choices. I had to play the roles I had built for myself over the years. And I wasn't just 'playing' or acting my way through these roles; I was living them. Billy and I had been married ten years. I had never cheated on him. He had never cheated on me. Billy needed me to be faithful. We had a son together. My son needed me to put him first. I was a doctor. My patients needed my full attention, and I could never compromise their health by having inappropriate relationships with another doctor.

The answer about how I should proceed with my life was clear.

And then, the internal black and white assessment slowly turned to gray as Steele asked, "Lauren, when Alexander kissed you, did it remind you of the past?"

I didn't want to look back or assess the past and what role it was now playing in my life. Steele had lived that past with me; she knew what I went through, and we spent years analyzing what it meant for my life, and my destiny. So now I was only concerned with the present, and what life could be in the future. On the surface, I had the best life and did not want one kiss with Alexander to be a rethinking of my life choices and my past traumas. But I couldn't escape her question, so I answered honestly.

"Alexander makes me feel like home," I told Steele, my voice quivering. I was answering her question, but I was also trying to convey why I was drawn to him, and why I knew that if I was honest with myself, I'd always be drawn to him. "When I was with him…he just gets me, you know? And he's proud of me. He sees me as this girl that just really made it on her own, grew up to be a woman, and has a certain power to her. Since he knows my past, he knows my resilience. He sees me as beautiful, he actually told me that, which I know doesn't matter, but damn, it made me feel good."

"Do you feel that Billy doesn't feel that way about you?" Steele asked.

"We both know that Billy loves me," I answered sternly. "But Billy doesn't pontificate or express with words how proud he is of me. You know better than anyone, Steele. That's just not him."

"Maybe you should talk with him about it, you know, like tell him that you are missing that in your marriage and that you'd like him to provide pep talks and praise you more for all that you are."

This is where Steele, although well intentioned, didn't get it. She didn't understand that Billy and I were just too different. He was very involved in the house, very involved with our child, and very involved with his job, but he did not want to be very involved with his wife and who I was as a person. The idea that Billy would 'provide pep talks' was inconceivable.

And the more he didn't appreciate my uniqueness, the more I went through life drowsy, stifling myself to make him feel comfortable. There was no individuality, and there was no passion. And Billy wasn't going to change; praise and passion may have been part of our relationship once upon a time, but I had to admit that our fire was long gone.

The sun was setting, and the Ohio mosquitos were starting to bite. I checked my cell phone and realized that while sitting with Steele for almost three hours over a bottle of wine and pizza, I hadn't gotten a single text or call from Billy. It reinforced exactly what I was trying to convey to Steele. Knowing that Billy wasn't thinking of me and having gone now weeks without Alexander reaching out after our kiss, I felt so alone. I was in the presence of my best friend and yet, I still felt so alone.

These feelings inside of me, and the way I had answered Steele's questions, steered me toward believing that I was on a precipice of something big. I was moving to the next level in my life, and I was feeling that in a way, that I didn't want to bring Billy with me. I wanted, even just for a day, to be me, be myself, and not think about the consequences of what my life was about to turn into.

Steele and I hugged as we made our way to our cars. As she slid into her vintage truck that her husband had bought at an auction, she said, low enough for just us to hear, "Well, Lauren, just be kind and gentle to yourself, and don't overthink that dinner. It was just a kiss. A kiss won't change anything. If you start overthinking it, give me a call." And with that, she closed her driver's side door, and she was off.

I stayed in the parking lot, thinking over her parting words. As much as Steele 'got' me, she didn't understand where I was emotionally. To me, this was not just a kiss. This was me diving into a fantasy of Alexander. This was me escaping the organized, muted, boring life I'd been living for so many years. This was me reclaiming my past, as much as I may have been trying to block it out. Perhaps the fantasy was all in my head, and the kiss was just a small, tangible piece I could hold onto, but to me the kiss was a catalyst for something more, something bigger.

Just as I was about to drive home, I thought about texting Alexander. I started to draft him a text because I was missing him, and I wanted instant gratification that he was indeed, missing me too. All this talk about him and the kiss made me want to hear his voice, read his words, and be close to him.

But I reminded myself, *You are a wife, a mother, and a doctor.* I deleted the words on my screen, put my phone in my purse, and started the drive home.

When I got home, I tried not to unfairly be angry at Billy. After all, I had just spent the evening out for drinks with a friend. But still, although I knew I couldn't admit this aloud to my friend, I was mad at my husband. Mad that right now, he stood in the way between me and Alexander. What if I got to be with Alexander, really be with him...sleep with him and have dinner with him without having to feel guilty. What if we could go lay by the beach together in Mexico. What if we....

And then Billy came into the garage as I was getting out of my car. He walked over to his toolbox and without looking at me, said, "Hey."

"Hi Billy," I said. "It was great catching up with Steele. How did William do tonight?"

"Well, he wasn't interested in doing his homework, but he ate a big dinner, and we played a lot of soccer outside. He was tuckered out and went to bed pretty easily." Billy grabbed his screwdriver from the tool chest and headed back into the house, not looking at me once.

I was accustomed to feeling invisible. Billy just oftentimes saw right past me.

And of course, instead of saying something in the moment and working on the actual relationship I was in, I stayed quiet, letting my thoughts return to the imaginary beach in Mexico.

CHAPTER 5

THE NEXT MORNING AROUND SEVEN O'CLOCK, my cell phone rang. I was still sleeping. I'd just started my three consecutive days off, and on this Friday morning, Billy was going to take William to school. I thought I had a lazy morning ahead of me, which is rare for a doctor, or a mother, and almost impossible when you're both.

I raised my head to glance down at my phone. It was Dr. Margaret Roseburg, Wendy Webinson's OBGYN. Wendy must be in labor. I immediately picked up the phone.

"Your patient's mother, Wendy Webinson, is in labor," Margaret said without hesitation. "I've got a long day of scheduled cesareans ahead of me, but I'm going to squeeze in her cesarean around 3:00 p.m. If you and the NICU team could be on standby starting at 2:00 p.m., then I'll need the group in the operating room with me right around time for surgery, and Lauren, I'm really hoping that this goes routine. I'll keep you posted on Wendy's labor." And without missing a beat, she abruptly hung up.

I sat up. All at once, I felt the weight of the world. I thought about Wendy, having her first baby, not yet truly aware of the roller coaster she was about to ride as a parent of a sick newborn. I thought of Dr. Roseberg and her busy day and the enormity of having to administer a cesarean where the baby would potentially present failing vitals. I thought about myself. *Fuck, my NICU is adding a really sick baby*. I thought about Alexander, and how even though we didn't discuss the kiss, I was going to have to call him immediately. He needed to fly down to Jacobs tonight to perform the surgery.

While still in bed and with Billy and William already out the door for the day, I dialed Alexander's cell. It felt odd to be calling him from my bed, in my pajamas, and as his phone was ringing, I grabbed my glasses from my nightstand.

"Well, this is an early call," Alexander said flirtatiously as he picked up the phone.

"And it's likely going to be a late night, Alexander," I said sternly. "Looks like the Webinson baby is going to be born today."

Alexander didn't answer and seemed distracted.

"Wendy Webinson is in labor," I continued, "and the OB is going to deliver the baby late afternoon. I suspect the baby will be prepped for surgery around 5:00 p.m. or so. That will give the hospital time to monitor her vitals and take X-rays for you to evaluate. How does that timing look for your schedule?"

Alexander was quiet. Then a moment later he replied, "Ah, damn, it looks terrible schedule-wise but that's okay." He was on his speaker phone now, "I'm in the car, on my way to work, looking at my surgery schedule on my phone." He didn't speak for a few moments, then added, "I've got a handful of surgeries starting later this morning, and hopefully the hospital doesn't receive any pediatric ER cases that come in at the last minute. After I hang up with you, I'm going to call the clinic to make sure they have a helicopter reserved for me. I'll keep you updated."

"All right, great, likewise," I said matter-of-factly.

We said our goodbyes, and for a moment I sat there in bed, thinking into the future. Not years from now, but rather months. I tried to manifest myself bringing this baby back to health. I closed my eyes and imagined the surgery going successfully. I saw two proud, happy parents, peering over the incubator to witness their baby continuing to breathe. I imagined Emma dressed up, put in her car seat, discharged from the hospital.

I slowly opened my eyes and sighed. There was so much work ahead of us to get Emma to that discharge.

I decided not to go into the hospital until right before the birth. I didn't want to go into the NICU and step on the toes of the nurse practitioner, Mary, who had planned on being solely in charge for the next three days. I also didn't want to speculate yet one more time with the Webinson family. There was no crystal ball at this point, and so I decided to follow my old med school routine.

Climbing out of bed, I went to my dresser and pulled out a set of workout clothes, then cleaned up the bathroom. My plan was to spend the morning going for a run, taking a long shower, and clearing my head. The combination of breaking a sweat, feeling the hot water in the shower, blow drying my hair, and listening to music had always kept my body busy and helped me center myself so I could focus on what was ahead of me.

As I made my way out of the bedroom, headphones in one hand and phone in the other, I heard the garage door open. Billy was already home from the school run. We met in the kitchen.

"Hey," I said. "William was okay at drop off?"

"Yup." Billy walked past me and went to the fridge.

"Thanks for taking him. Do you have a lot of meetings today?" I asked.

Billy closed the fridge, a can of soda in his hand. It was his version of a morning coffee. "Yeah."

"Oh, okay." I'd hoped he might tell me more, that he might try to connect with me on some level, but my husband was keen on using single-syllable words these days. "I actually need to go into the NICU today. One of my patients is about to be born, the one who needs the atresia surgery," I said. "You remember, right? Her mother just went into labor."

Billy mumbled something to the effect of 'Hmm,' but I couldn't make out what exactly he said. I pressed my lips together and set my headphones on the counter as he cracked open his soda.

"So, I'll be going to the hospital early afternoon," I continued. "I'm not sure when I'll be home, but probably not until after dinner, so I can make sure the baby is okay after the surgery."

"Okay," he said, brushing past me to go toward his home

office.

As Billy closed his office door behind him, I grabbed my headphones and closed my eyes, willing my tears away. This was *exactly* what I'd been trying to tell Steele. He didn't even try to take an interest in my career or what was going on at my job, and he apparently had no desire to elaborate on his own work either.

I popped in my ear buds, scrolling through my phone to find my running playlist as I headed out the door. I didn't have the energy for this, not today. I needed to focus on helping baby Emma.

*****

I was in a calm headspace as I drove to Covenant Medical. At this moment, my job was bringing together an entire team of medical professionals. I badged into the second floor NICU. After scrubbing in, I saw Mary, the NICU's nurse practitioner.

"Oh, hi, Dr. Leonard," she said, surprised. A quiet girl of only twenty-eight, Mary seemed startled that I was there and looked at me as if I was going to spend the day micromanaging her.

"The patient with the bowel obstruction, she's going to be born within the hour," I explained.

We spent some time going through the NICU admittance checklist and deciding where the baby should be placed. I finally decided on the middle room to ensure that enough nurses' eyes were on her during all hours of the day. With that decision made, I hurried up to the seventh floor, where the hospital performed the cesarean surgeries.

As I got off the physician elevator, I saw Dr. Roseberg and walked briskly toward her. Shoulders back and matching her quick clip sentences, I looked her straight in the eye. "Looks like you're headed in now. I'll join you in surgery," I said. "I have Mary heading up the NICU. I'd like to incubate the patient once you've provided the Apgar score. Once incubated, I'd like to immediately take the patient to the NICU for admittance. We'll administer a PICC line for her fluids and proteins. Dr. Alexander Smithton from Cleveland Clinic will be here early evening to perform the surgery." And then, more gently, I finished with, "He's happy to update your patient Wendy unless you would like to stay tonight to monitor her."

"Let's see how this goes," Dr. Roseberg said as she pointed to the surgery room, "and I'll let you know."

With that, Dr. Roseberg headed into the operating room, and I followed her. I let her scrub in first, then I stepped toward the sink. I said a silent prayer for Emma as I washed my hands and forearms, making sure I got under my nails, too. Then, I stepped into the operating room.

It was a cold, sterile room, with bright lights and stainless steel everything. I had vast experience in these rooms as most of my NICU patients were premature, and we quickly had to usher the baby from the delivery room into the NICU once born. No time for the mom and baby to bond. No congratulations, all business.

I caught a glimpse of Wendy as a few of the other medical professionals in the room were taking her vitals. Her epidural had kicked in, but she looked nervous. Jason was near her head, and he looked equally scared. I smiled at him, and he nodded.

As the procedure finally started, Wendy followed all the doctors' instructions. When Dr. Roseberg began the incision, Wendy didn't ask for more pain maintenance. The first few minutes into the surgery, I was surprised by how calm the room was. *Maybe this is going to be smoother than we anticipated,* I thought.

About ten minutes in, it was time to lift the baby. As Dr. Roseberg scooped the baby, now my real-life patient, up out of Wendy's womb, Emma started crying hysterically. A great sign, as it told the medical staff there was no fluid backed up in her lungs. Our first win.

Once the team could see the infant, a collective "Awwww" echoed throughout the room.

"Emma!" Wendy shouted, undoubtedly reacting to Emma's bold cry. Jason finally smiled, and although they couldn't see their daughter through the surgery partition, they could hear her, and that was enough.

The beautiful wail carried throughout the room, and it was important that I now take over. I immediately grabbed the baby and brought her over to the infant station. Since Emma was full-term, the good news was that her weight was a healthy 7.4 lbs. The bad news was staring us in the face: Her stomach was purple. A massive distended lower belly, in which she was likely retaining water, and her weight would most certainly drop after the surgery.

Seeing Emma's stomach, my heart sank. This poor little baby. But I simply didn't have the time to get emotional; I had to be all business.

I placed little Emma onto the medical-grade bassinet under a warmer, while one of the most tenured NICU nurses began attaching wires to Emma's chest to monitor her vitals.

"Wendy, before we hook her up, would you like to see Emma?" I asked.

Now, both Emma and Wendy were crying, Emma's screams drowning out her mother's weeping.

"Hi baby girl, Mommy loves you," Wendy said through tears as I brought Emma close to her. Wendy was still getting stitched up, and it was almost poetic how soon enough, Emma would have stitches in the same place on her stomach from her surgery in a few hours.

"Mommy loves you," Wendy repeated and as she spoke, Emma immediately stopped crying. They locked eyes. It was as if time stood still in that moment. And then, as quickly as we rushed into the surgery, we rushed Emma down to the NICU.

On the way down the elevator, I called Alexander. He answered right away, and I launched into giving him Emma's stats. He was pleased with the heart rate, though very concerned with the distended stomach. He knew he didn't have as much time as we had originally planned.

"I'm going to board the helicopter in the next ten minutes to make it down there in time," he said in a determined voice.

Over the course of the next couple hours, I met with my NICU team, a great group of day-nurses and of course Mary. I called the fentanyl pain medication into the pharmacy, all 0.058 ml of it for a seven-pound baby. I called in the proteins, fluids, and all other applicable intravenous medications.

Alexander had arrived and was prepping for surgery. I didn't have time to meet him on the tarmac, but just outside of the operating room, we spoke about what he saw on the X-rays that we had taken of Emma's bowels.

"So, the images of Emma's intestine from the X-rays look different than the ultrasound pictures I saw from Wendy," Alexander said as he was scrubbing in, washing his hands aggressively. "I don't think this is going to be a routine bowel obstruction surgery." He didn't say any more, leaving me hanging on what he thought was unique about this case.

The nurses brought Emma to the operating room. I watched as Alexander began his surgery. It was the first time I had ever seen him operate. I was in the corner, observing Emma as she was given drugs to make her unconscious. We listened as her persistent cry faded with the anesthesia given.

While I had stayed in the moment the entire day, the next minute or so I was transported back to the past. I was watching Alexander's hands move, listening to him call out instructions, yet all I could see was him sitting at my parents' kitchen table.

I decided it wasn't prudent to stay in the operating room, considering I was having trouble focusing. I said a quick prayer, then left. My time would be best spent talking to Emma's parents versus staring at Alexander while he performed the surgery.

I made my way to Wendy's recovery room. It was a full house in this small room, with Wendy, Jason, and Jason's parents all huddled in the room. Wendy lay motionless in her hospital bed. She was experiencing the worries of a new mom coupled with the fogginess from a series of heavy-duty painkillers. I explained that Emma was now in surgery and that Dr. Smithton was going to update us once the surgery ended. Wendy started to perk up, talking about her cesarean, and giving a play-by-play of what went through her mind during the surgery. The conversation was upbeat, and we hadn't been talking even thirty minutes when Alexander rushed in Wendy's hospital room.

"Dr. Smithton!" Wendy said, her eyes widening. I turned around. There was Alexander, practically running in, almost out of breath. I could not believe I was seeing him already. The surgery must have, well, not happened at all.

He looked at all of us, catching his breath and nodding his head at the new grandparents, and then focused on Wendy. "Emma is fine, she is now out of surgery," Alexander said as he gave a black and white update for all the color commentary that was inevitably about to follow.

"Before the surgery, I thought I saw something in Emma's X-rays, and when we got into her stomach, the X-rays proved to be true. When we were able to get in there," Alexander said as he touched his own stomach, using his hands for emphasis, "it was more complex than we thought. Her bowel obstruction, it burst in utero. Think of a garden hose, twisted. That's her small intestine. It twists and after a while, with the pressure of that 'hose,' it bursts." His hands flew up over his head.

I always appreciated how Alexander used layman's terms instead of medical terms when speaking about health and medicine. It made him so good at connecting with the parents of his patients.

"When it burst while you were still pregnant," Alexander

continued, "it appears that Emma's body built a pseudocyst around the burst bowel." Alexander's left hand was in a fist position, and he used his right hand to cover it, demonstrating the pseudocyst. "Honestly, guys, it saved Emma's life inside your womb," he said, now motioning toward Wendy's stomach. "It's really miraculous."

Wendy and Jason looked relieved, but I knew what was coming next.

"But it's messy," Alexander, now talking slowly and deliberately, relayed to the parents. "There were feces all over her abdominal wall, and while I got most of the pseudocyst material and feces out, her body is not at a place where we can sew the bowels back together. I wasn't able to do the actual surgery."

The room was quiet.

"So then, I created an ileostomy," Alexander continued. "Think of this as part of the small intestine coming out of the stomach, onto the skin, and Emma will poop from there. Once Emma heals from this initial surgery, once she grows a bit and her bowels mature, we can go in and do the surgery we wanted to do, which is sew the bowels back together. 'Hook up the hose' if you will. That will be around eight weeks from now."

The Webinsons and Alexander talked a bit more, with Wendy fading in and out of the conversation, her surgery painkillers likely making her drowsy. After shaking Jason's hand and verbalizing his commitment to Emma's health, Alexander departed with a few of his nurses. I joined him for the walk back to the NICU, where Emma was now resting comfortably.

"It's a one in 50,000 chance that the bowel would burst and

cause that much of a mess," Alexander said to me.

"And it's probably even more rare to have Emma survive it in utero," I added.

"Yep."

We talked a bit more about this presentation within Emma's intestine, trying to identify a cause. I always felt doctors needed a cause, or a reason why. Why did Emma have a bowel obstruction in utero? We didn't have that answer, and we might never know. And it might never matter. For the moment, we just needed to keep Emma healthy and march toward that second surgery.

As Alexander and I walked into Emma's NICU room, the nurses had Emma in her heated incubator. It was so quiet except for the occasional beep from the medical equipment. It was just him, me, and a sleeping Emma. We stared at Emma, in her incubator, then glanced to the LCD screen to read her vitals. Then back to her. Then back to the vitals. We both realized, at about the exact same second, that her vitals looked promising. We let out a collective sigh.

All of the adrenaline from the day had faded. My body felt lighter, and my breathing slowed. It felt so natural to be with Emma and Alexander and have just us in a room. Finally, Alexander spoke, still staring down at Emma in her incubator.

"Lauren, I want to apologize for a couple weeks back. I think I was just excited to see you; you know you represent an important time in my life, you 'knew me when,' so-to-speak, and I think…I got carried away. I'm sorry." He then looked into my eyes, and my chest tightened.

For a moment, I couldn't speak. I was ready to cry. Having

him here at my work, watching me at my job, with this beautiful baby girl in between us, was a full circle moment for me. I had at one time wished for a picture that looked exactly like this. My heart longed for those days when we were so young and our whole lives were out in front of us. It was just us, two young adults who could only imagine what their lives might become.

"Thanks for saying that," was all I could muster. As we locked eyes for a few seconds, the mental picture of Alexander at my parents' kitchen table came back to me, but our gaze naturally fell back to Emma. The quietness in the room made everything feel like it was happening in slow motion.

We stayed in her room together, watching her sleep for what felt like forever. Emma's vitals stayed consistent and there was no reason for us to continue monitoring her so closely. Yet, neither of us wanted to leave. I could sense from Alexander lingering that he appreciated being here with me and Emma, as every so often he would touch Emma's incubator as she stirred. He would then glance at me from the corner of his eye and smile softly.

"I guess I better head back up to the rooftop," he said, his voice wistful. "Let's have those weekly calls about Emma's nutrients and bloodwork. Please keep me posted on any daily changes in her condition."

We continued to stare at Emma as time felt frozen. A dizzying day ending in the most peaceful way, the life of this beautiful baby girl.

CHAPTER 6

IN THE DAYS AND WEEKS THAT FOLLOWED, our most precious patient Emma Webinson seemed to settle into her new role as homecoming queen of the NICU. Traditionally, all my NICU babies were preemies, but since Emma was full-term, she was bigger and had more personality. She smiled and laughed at her overhead mobile, moving her arms and legs like she was a little fitness model. She was named the princess of the NICU because Wendy would dress her up in frilly skirts, being careful to bypass all the wires and the enormous ileostomy on Emma's stomach.

I was proud of Emma's parents and how well they were adjusting to parenthood in the NICU. They spent about twelve hours a day in her room, reading her books and singing songs. They tried their best under heart-wrenching circumstances. Both Jason and Wendy did get frustrated that their little one had to endure so much, and so they asked me the same questions every day. 'When will we be able to take Emma home? Do you think they would do the surgery any earlier? Is Emma going to develop properly if we can't hold her?'

One of the most common misconceptions about the NICU is that babies won't develop properly if not held by the parent. Since oftentimes the babies are so tiny and fragile and their vitals so tumultuous, it is not always advised for parents to hold the baby. In the case of Emma, it was ill-advised to hold her as she had the ileostomy on her stomach and wires everywhere, thereby making it nearly impossible to cradle her. Still, parents always lamented not being able to hold their child as a detriment to their growth and development. Some NICU's even fed into that misconception, having 'snuggle' volunteers who would hold the babies on behalf of parents who were not available. I never accepted that silly narrative that a baby would not develop without being held. In fact, I would encourage my parents that even though their baby could not be held, the baby knew the parent was close by, and communication was just as important as physical touch.

Jason and Wendy were lucky that Emma was healthy enough to upgrade to lying in an open hospital-grade crib. Each time Emma's parents would worry about her emotional and mental development, I would try to be empathetic, encouraging them to lean into what they *could* do, which was sing to Emma, and encourage their baby to look at her hanging mobile while she was on her back, and talk with her and make silly faces.

With Emma's condition, the days dragged on and on. We

were simply waiting for her body to recover from the first surgery, trying to prepare for the next surgery that would resect rejoin the bowels.

But when the parents would leave at night, against my own orders, I would hold Emma. This bond I began with Emma started right after her birth, and it only grew with power and significance as the weeks carried on. By her fourth week in the NICU, I knew I was spending too much time at the hospital and too much time with Emma. And on this particular Thursday night, I was waiting impatiently for Wendy and Jason to head out, so that I could spend time with Emma, just her and I.

Finally, when I saw Wendy grab her purse, my heart fluttered because I knew I could have my alone time.

"Good night, Dr. Leonard," Wendy said as she and Jason waved and turned the corner down the NICU hall.

I badged out of the nurses' station computer and entered Emma's room. Emma lay there so peacefully, and a month in, I no longer saw the wires and breathing tubes and monitors. I just saw the angelic face of what felt like my daughter.

I picked her up gently, ensuring her swaddle was intact. I delicately held all her wires, making sure they were connected and straight, and then I sat down in the rocking chair, moving slowly forward and back.

With Emma still sleeping, I quietly began to sing, *I see the moon and the moon sees me. The moon sees somebody I'd like to see. Down at the edge of the deep blue sea, the moon shines brightly down on me.*

Emma stirred, and I could feel in my soul that she loved our bond, and she yearned for my singing to her. And I yearned for this attachment, too. As I was holding her, I felt not just close to Emma, but also close to Alexander. The idea that Emma was both my patient and also his, and that this baby was the way that Alexander and I were brought back together made me tear up while I was holding her. Looking over her button nose and cherubic cheeks, I saw myself and Alexander in her. And beyond the physical, holding her was bringing me so much comfort, her presence righting the wrongs of my past.

I continued holding her and singing quietly until my arm started to lose feeling and I knew I had to head home. In the moment, it was so hard to leave Emma. I knew I had my life, my job, and my son, but placing Emma back in her crib and walking out of the room, and away from that euphoric moment, never got easier.

I went back out to the nurses' station, my real life resuming, and input notes and pharmacy orders into the computer for the nurses on the upcoming shift.

"Dr. Leonard, why do you hold Emma each night once the parents leave?" Ginelle, our tenured nurse asked me as I was finishing typing my orders. Ginelle, having been in the operating room when Emma was born, had also grown attached to her, but she kept it much more under control than I did.

"I'm trying to assess gross motor skills and identify potential cognitive deficiencies stemming from the total parenteral nutrition," I answered, trying to sound convincing but obviously lying. Ginelle was smarter than that, but she simply raised an eyebrow at me, then shrugged and continued restocking the

NICU linen closet.

I believed what I said, that in essence I could objectively treat Emma. I could still be her doctor while having this overarching emotional attachment to her.

And I was still able to be a mom to my actual child, William. In fact, as I left the hospital and headed home, I was even more eager to see my son. As I came in through the garage, I could tell that Billy was downstairs, likely watching TV, and William had been upstairs playing with his toys. We tried to work with William on boundaries and allowing him to be in places of the house by himself. But still, as William ran to me and gave me a hug, I didn't hear Billy coming up the stairs.

I bent down and enveloped my son, immediately noticing the enormous size difference between Emma and William.

"Hi sweetheart! Can Mommy hold you! Let me hold you like when you were a little baby," I said with a smile.

William laughed and yelled, "I'm a big kid!" He wiggled free of the embrace, then ran to the living room to show me how tall he built his Legos.

My heart grew in my chest, peace bubbling up in me. I felt even closer to William because I sensed my heart opening up more now that Emma was born. But it widened even more now that Alexander had, albeit sparingly, come back into my life.

*****

As July turned into August and August started to near its end, my life felt in line. My son was about to start his new school year,

I was proud of my NICU babies, I had Emma to brighten my day, and, if I was honest with myself, I enjoyed fantasizing about Alexander. I was still ignoring the continued troubling signs of my marriage, which, as of late, had included Billy choosing to be in the basement each night playing video games and not interacting with either me or William. So, with my heart lusting after Alexander, and my mind focused on my patients, I settled into a new season.

I was updating Alexander on Emma's bloodwork every few days, and we did so by email, his work email to my work email. It carried on like that for some time until one night, while I was at work, he called my cell.

"Hello?" I said as I picked up, even though I already knew who it was.

"Hey, Leonard," Alexander said. "I'm thinking I'll stop by Covenant Medical tomorrow. Things are light here at the clinic, and I'd like to see Emma start taking a ten-milliliter feeding about every four hours. I want to be there during her first feeding. Do you think it's a good idea for Emma to start taking food?"

"Oh." When I'd seen his number light up on my phone, I hadn't been expecting that question. I wasn't sure what I'd been expecting, but it wasn't about feedings, and it certainly wasn't that he was going to come to Jacobs the next day. "Uh, sure, that sounds reasonable. I think she's ready."

We decided on a particular pharmacy-grade formula, and I entered the orders for it while we were still on the call.

"Will you be there for the feeding?" he asked.

"Yeah," I said. "I'll be here, I'm on shift for the next couple of days."

"Great!" Alexander's voice went up an octave, his excitement obvious. "When does she eat, 8:00 p.m.? How about I stop by around then."

"That works well," I said. "See you tomorrow."

As I hung up the call, all at once, my mind was off to the races. I thought about how I got off at eleven tomorrow night. About how I could just tell Billy that I had to work a twenty-four-hour shift. About how Alexander and I could spend the night in the back of his Escalade. And how, just for a night, he and I could be together.

CHAPTER 7

THE NEXT MORNING, I woke up early to make pancakes for William. Although my son preferred the easy-to-make toasted Eggo waffles, occasionally I would make him homemade buttermilk pancakes and draw smiley faces with fruit and whipped cream, much to his delight. This morning, William squealed as I placed a pancake in front of him with two strawberries for the eyes, a dot of whipped cream for the nose, and a half moon of blueberries for the mouth.

Cooking these pancake breakfasts was one of my favorite activities to share with my William. It surprised me that I took so much joy in this particular activity, because before I had a child, I was never really a breakfast eater, and I'd never been a cook. Yet last night I gleefully set my alarm for 5:30 a.m. to get up and make my child breakfast.

More surprising than my enjoyment of making breakfast for my sun was my love of motherhood. I'd always known I wanted to be a mother, and for a long time growing up, I thought my only role in life would be being a mother. My mom didn't work, and her mom didn't work, and so on. I broke the mold, being the first girl in my family to go to college. Even so, I didn't have faith in myself to actually graduate, much less have a career. In my mind, I had anticipated my life looking like the lineage of generations before me, which was to be a mom and be a mom only, and to do that one thing extremely well.

There was no larger stratification than coming from a family of stay-at-home moms, and then little ole' me becoming a doctor. I had no idea how I was going to be able to parent with the career I had. My only example of what a good mom looked like was my mom, who was with her child at all times. All I knew growing up was that parenthood equaled time with your child. And I got all my parents' attention since I was an only child. My parents had me and then a year later had another baby, but he died of SIDS a few months after he was born. All I remember of my mom was after my brother died, but my dad once told me that she was never really the same after that tragic death.

I think my mom ultimately spent so much time with me growing up because she was afraid of losing me too. I inherited the mindset that motherhood was constantly being with your child, and I'd inherited her anxiety within my first year of having William, afraid I would befall the same fate as my own mother.

On this morning, sitting across from me at the kitchen table was this beautiful little boy, full of energy before his first full day of the school year. And his day didn't end there, as he had his after-school soccer practice, a quick dinner in the car scarfing down protein bars, and then finally swim team practice that went, in my opinion, way too late into the night.

"Mom, if I eat the pancake nose right now, can I have more whipped cream?" William asked sweetly.

I laughed. "Well," I said leaning close to his face, "how about you eat the strawberry eyes and blueberry mouth and then I'll redraw the whole face in whipped cream!"

William started laughing and popped a blueberry in his mouth for emphasis.

We sat there together, at 6:30 a.m., smiling and chatting in our pajamas and with bed heads, as if we were in a dream. Like most households, our mornings were usually chaotic, the duality of grogginess and a race against the clock, but this morning felt like a little gift from above.

Billy came out of the bedroom and walked into the kitchen, smiling in William's direction as he saw us sitting at the table. He had showered already and was wearing his favorite jeans that he'd had for almost a decade. He came over to the table, leaned his head down, and kissed William on the top of his head. Billy didn't say anything to either one of us, just laid his lips to William's head and then walked past both of us to his office, presumably to check some work emails that did not need to be answered—or even read—this early in the workday.

This was pretty routine in our house, for Billy and me to not interact much in the mornings, as we had our family Google calendar that filled our silence. Billy knew I was going to be up early to make William breakfast. He also knew that I had to work late tonight which would mean he would be picking up William from soccer practice, feeding him dinner, and shuffling him to and from swim lessons. I knew that Billy, for his part, was going to be on conference calls most of the day.

But there was so much that our Google calendar didn't say, so much that I wished it did. I wanted much more for our lives than just going through the motions of familial logistics. I wanted Billy to come into the kitchen this morning, look me in the eye, and engage with me the way everyone else in my life did. I wanted Billy to show some personality, perhaps take the whipped cream can, spray it in his mouth, and have both William and I mock-scold him. I wanted Billy to come kiss my head, like he did William's, and whisper good morning, and ask me how I slept.

And for my part, I wanted to see Billy walking toward us in the kitchen, and I would pop up out of my seat to give him a kiss, coffee breath and all, and offer to make him a pancake. I wanted to be so in love with him that I wanted to please him, any way I could, even with a pancake so early in the morning.

Instead, William and I turned our heads as we watched Billy walk past us to his office, simultaneously opening his laptop while closing his office door.

*****

As I dropped William off at school, it felt bittersweet. I loved this little boy so much. The thought that I was failing in my marriage and that I was craving another guy made me feel like I was failing William.

As I turned toward the backseat, both of us still in our seatbelts, I said, "Okay buddy, have a great day. Remember what we always say?"

In unison, we declared, "Dear God, let us always be safe, always be healthy, and always be loved. Amen."

And with that, he unbuckled his seatbelt, hopped out of the car, and ran into school, his backpack shuffling left to right with his strides.

Back home I showered, meticulously applied my makeup, curled my hair, and stood in front of the mirror, asking myself if anyone would correlate my looks that day with Alexander coming to the hospital. Would nurses think I was trying to look cute for him? Would they see right through me?

As I was packing up my work bag, I called Covenant Medical to speak with Mary. Fumbling through my work bag for my car keys, I put Mary on speaker. She updated me on most of the patients, who seemed to be doing well today. She didn't mention Emma.

"Oh, that's great," I replied. "So, you know Emma's surgeon, Dr. Smithton? He's going to arrive at the beginning of the overnight shift. I think he'll be at Covenant a little after eight o'clock tonight, and we are going to attempt the first feeding. We'll see how it goes."

Mary and I discussed a couple other patients and then said our goodbyes. As I was about to leave, I walked toward Billy's office. I wanted him to see me looking pretty, or at least prettier than I normally looked.

Adjacent to the kitchen, his office was a small room at the front of the house that had glass French doors, so you could see in even with the doors shut. I decided I needed to walk into the office, and give him a kiss, or rub his back, or do something to connect with him. I didn't want to go to the hospital and see Alexander knowing I had not said one word to my husband that day.

I looked through the glass doors, giving a small wave as Billy glanced up at me. I smiled at him, and he looked into my eyes for less than a second, then gazed back down to his laptop and started typing. He wasn't angry, and I didn't think he was even trying to be mean. He was just careless.

As I stood in the hallway in front of his office, holding back tears, I felt invisible. And angry. And ready to be careless myself.

CHAPTER 8

I WAS IN A MELANCHOLY MOOD when I arrived at the hospital, my euphoria from William's pancake breakfast having subsided. Perhaps it was feeling slighted by Billy, or feeling nervous to see Alexander again, but likely it was that Emma's health seemed to be getting worse and worse by the day.

Some days, a patient's health can normalize, and as a doctor, you feel you got really lucky. Today was not one of those days. It seemed to be problem after problem for Emma; the first issue stemming from her initial surgery and subsequent placement of the stoma. The intestine twisted in an awkward way on her stomach and as such, Emma's ileostomy bag would not stay on. The wound care nurse tried to adhere a new bag, but inevitably it would quickly wear away, exposing Emma's intestine and she would cry out in pain, as the surrounding epidermis was deteriorating and causing a skin infection.

While treating that issue, Emma's morning bloodwork came back and her T-cell counts were dropping so low that soon, she would have to undergo a blood transfusion. And whether it was due to being poked and prodded all day or maybe due to just being a baby, it was becoming quite evident that Emma was developing colic, spending what felt like hours on end crying, to no avail.

We needed Emma in a good spot medically in order to administer the first feeding tonight. Jason and Wendy Webinson were elated, so excited to finally be able to feed their little girl for the first time. It had been a month since she was born, and the stress on Wendy prohibited her breast milk from coming in, as is the case with many NICU mothers. Tonight, Emma was going to try ten milliliters of pharmacy-made formula, recommended by Alexander. With ten milliliters being roughly about the size of two teaspoons, this feeding was less about the food and more about testing the small intestine to ensure it could move fluid through properly.

I didn't want to tell Jason and Wendy that Alexander would be joining the first feeding until just beforehand. I didn't want to rattle them. Around 7:00 that night, I came into Emma's room and peered over her crib.

"Tonight's the big night! Are you excited, little girl?" I cooed at Emma sweetly as both parents sat in his-and-hers rocking chairs by her crib, separated only by all the wires and hospital equipment.

"She's ready! I don't know if I am though." Wendy laughed.

"I understand," I said, still peering over Emma's crib and looking down at her. "But we'll just try ten milliliters. With such a small amount, if she vomits it up or dumps it, it won't hurt her health."

"What do you mean, 'dump it?'" Jason asked.

"Oh, that's when the fluid isn't broken down in the stomach, and so literally you'd see Emma swallow the formula, and immediately you'd see it come out undigested into her ileostomy bag," I explained. "We don't want that result because it would indicate that there are additional concerns with her digestion and absorption of nutrients."

Both parents now looked completely terrified.

"Don't worry, I promise it's going to be fine," I replied as I put my hand to my chest for emphasis. "Ten milliliters is a conservative amount to try with Emma. This is the normal course of action after four weeks of only intravenous nutrients."

Their faces seemed to soften, their eyebrows no longer raised, as they waited for me to go on.

"Dr. Smithton, the surgeon from Cleveland Clinic, remember him?" I said, hoping I sounded casual. "He's coming in tonight to watch Emma take this bottle, and he and I will be meeting after to prepare a feeding schedule for Emma for the next few weeks until her second surgery."

"He's coming here? Tonight?" Wendy asked suspiciously. "Why, is he nervous about her taking her bottle?"

"Wendy, Jason," I said calmly, "this feeding should be exciting, not worrisome, and Dr. Smithton and I collaborating together for prescribing a feeding schedule is standard protocol.

We'll continue working together even after the second surgery and until Emma is discharged."

Emma's parents nodded yet now I was the one that was getting nervous. All at once I realized how much more interaction I was going to have with Alexander. As my heart started to beat a little faster, my cell phone rang faintly in my white coat pocket, so I excused myself from Emma's room and took the call. It was Alexander, and right away, he seemed flustered.

"Ugh, damn Lauren, what time did you say the feeding was for our patient? Eight o'clock? Is there any way to push it to 9:00 p.m.?"

He offered no initial reason, so I started doing the math in my head. On the one hand, Emma had never eaten before in her life, still being fed entirely intravenously, so it wouldn't matter to the patient one bit when she ate. But then I thought of the two anxious parents I had just spoken with. "Well, you know Emma's parents are already apprehensive about feeding her, so I'd recommend we keep the original time frame. Why, are you unable to make it?" I asked, already a bit disappointed.

"No, but I haven't been able to get on the road yet. We found out late this afternoon that there was some vice-presidential photo op for Tim Kaine at Cleveland Clinic. I guess he toured our facilities, and they wanted the senior physicians to meet with him to discuss healthcare reform. So I got dragged into that."

"No worries," I said dumbly.

"So yeah, I'll likely get to Covenant Medical around, well, maybe around nine o'clock. Go ahead with the feeding, it was only ten milliliters that we decided, right? I don't want to stress the intestines any more than that. And then after, you and I can still meet though to go over the feeding plan. Want me to come straight to the hospital?"

Although I wanted him assessing Emma, I wanted Emma to have her first feeding before she became too sleepy. "Let me feed Emma as planned, assess the intestinal reaction, and then meet you out somewhere." That felt like a rather definitive response, and I was shocked that it had just come out of my mouth.

"Oh, uh, okay," Alexander said. "Just tell me where."

Suddenly, I was in control when it came to Alexander and his plans. It felt so...foreign. But I took the reins and said, "Let's meet at the Applebee's on Oak Street. If I'm there late, just have a drink to get started."

"Applebee's! The finest restaurant in Jacobs, Ohio. Sounds good," he said with a laugh. "See you soon, Leonard." And with that, we hung up, and my night got started.

*****

Emma's first feeding went well. Her body was able to sustain and properly digest the formula. Jason and Wendy both sighed with relief as Emma was able to suck, swallow, burp, and digest all ten milliliters.

It was a good sign for Emma. It meant she was healing from her pseudocyst and her body was preparing for the second bowel surgery. It was also good news for me as a neonatologist, knowing that Emma was improving despite the ups and downs in her bloodwork and skin infection. I felt more confident and hopeful for Emma's recovery than I had at the beginning of this shift. And of course, this was also a win for Alexander. I was excited to be able to detail all of this to him.

I was supposed to work until 11:00 that night, but since Alexander was going to be at Applebee's by 9:00, I needed to leave early.

All six babies, including Emma, were asleep for the night, and none of them were due to wake up until midnight for their next feedings. All of the parents had gone home, so it was just the three night nurses and me. They were a strong team and didn't need me micromanaging them.

"Hey, Tracy," I said as I stopped by the nurses' station. "I'm going to be off-property for the last couple hours of my shift, so please put me on-call and know that I can get back quickly if you need me."

"Sure," said Tracy. "We'll call if we need you."

As I walked back to my office, I vacillated about whether I should call Billy. In theory, I had until 11:30 p.m. to make any contact. Traditionally when my shift ended at 11:00 p.m., I would make it home within a half hour. It wouldn't be unusual for me to text him late in my shift if I was going to get held up at work.

Yet this was not usual, this was not normal, and I was definitely not being held up at work. I was playing with fire, but I was only at the tinder spark, where you think you can dance around the fire and never feel the burn.

With the NICU team all set and my proposed feeding recommendations for Emma secured neatly in a folder, I headed to my office bathroom and changed from my white doctor's coat and khakis into tight skinny jeans and a tighter black t-shirt. I looked pretty Midwestern casual, so I decided to put on some statement earrings and some cute summer heels that I had under my desk. I took a look in the mirror, and I didn't look bad. I also didn't look like I was trying too hard.

I hopped into my Prius and before starting the car, I dug for my makeup buried at the bottom of my work bag. Illuminated by the horrendous lighting in my car, which made me look washed out, I applied two different mascaras: one for lengthening and one for volume. I then tried, rather unsuccessfully, to create a dramatic smokey-eye with my eyeshadow palette and the flimsy brush that came with it. I'm not sure if it made me look better or worse, but it certainly helped me feel sexier. Finally, I applied some sheer lip gloss that was also supposed to plump up my lips. The immediate tingle from the gloss felt good, and at once I wondered about Alexander. If we kissed again, would he feel the lip gloss tingle too? Would his lips plump up in size? I laughed at the thought.

As I pulled out of the hospital parking garage and made my way onto the highway, a massive wave of guilt washed over me. I thought of myself, with all this makeup on, driving to meet a man who wasn't my husband. And my husband didn't even know about it. I thought of William, asleep in his bed. My eyes welled up with tears. I tried not to cry, reminding myself about the eye makeup I had just applied.

But I couldn't help it. I felt so lonely, knowing that the only man who wanted to have dinner with me was a man who I couldn't have. And as sexy and empowering as that could have been, I didn't think of myself as anyone with power. I felt powerless, both in my failed marriage and in my attraction to Alexander. I felt like I didn't have any choices here. All I knew was that I could not let it happen.

As I pulled into the Applebee's parking lot, I made a silent promise to myself. *This is just going to be dinner. You are a doctor, talking with another doctor about a patient's medical plan. You want his attention, and you want him to want you, but you can't lean into it. You don't have any choices here, Lauren. You are going to do the right thing.*

I walked in with my medical folders cradled in my arm and looked around the restaurant nervously. Not for Alexander, but for anyone else I might know. Jacobs is a small town, and it would be extremely obvious if someone who knew me saw me meeting some strange guy at the bar. At nine o'clock at night.

Luckily, the restaurant was dead, as I imagined it would be this late on a weeknight. I saw Alexander in the corner at the bar, hunched over and staring straight into his cell phone. He looked so small sitting on the bar stool. As soon as I saw him, my rigid demeanor softened. It was such a kind gesture for him to drive all the way to Jacobs, even if he couldn't make it in time to see our patient.

I made my way to the bar, and he looked up. I still had my game-face on, my non-sexy demeanor, and he stood up awkwardly out of his bar stool to give me a hug. But apparently he thought better of it because he sat back down and gestured for me to sit beside him.

I breathed in the scent of his cologne, and it was amazing. *Damn,* I thought. Perfume, that was the one thing I forgot.

After we exchanged hellos, he immediately asked about Emma's feeding. I gave him the play-by-play of how well she did, and how I felt her intestines were working enough to sustain the continuation of formula feedings.

"Should I show you the X-rays that were taken directly after the feeding? I've also got a proposed feeding plan here." I patted my hand to the folder that now sat between us at the bar. "We got a few looks at her bowel gas patterns. I think you'll be pleased."

"Uh, sure, but first, it's been a long day for both of us, do you want a drink?" he asked, simultaneously looking at me while motioning the bartender over. Because we were two of the only customers in the restaurant, the bartender came right over and asked me what I wanted.

"How about a vodka soda?" Alexander answered for me, staring straight at the bartender. The bartender shifted his eyes from Alexander to me, for me to confirm the drink choice.

"Sure." I smiled.

"You used to like those, right?" Alexander asked innocently as the sound of the bartender scooping my glass through the ice tub echoed throughout the bar. I nodded.

As my drink came and I took my first sip, I knew that the contents in that glass were, hours later, going to allow me to behave in ways that I had sworn off. Cooler heads prevailed when alcohol was not a factor. But for so many of us, me included, we decide to use alcohol to provide us permission to let go.

I already knew I was in trouble.

CHAPTER 9

Would I change my mind over and over again tonight? Despite the promise I'd made to myself twenty minutes before in the car, I could see a new option: Allow the alcohol to be my tour guide. The alcohol coaxed me to remain in the moment. It let me forget both the short-term promise I made myself and the larger, more long term promise I made to Billy in our wedding vows.

Even sober right now, I knew alcohol had to be my crutch. If I was going to have the courage to explore, I needed alcohol. I didn't have the guts to make that conscious choice. Maybe it was the Midwestern girl in me, or the Presbyterian upbringing, but I could not bring myself to have an affair with Alexander while sober. I had to leverage alcohol to flirt, to feel sexy, to feel equal to Alexander, and to give him a sign of permission to act in those exact same ways toward me.

He must have appreciated the way I was opening up, because as my drink got low, he proceeded to order me another vodka soda. There wasn't a discussion about what was to come next or where the night was going to go. All I could infer was that in ordering me another drink, Alexander liked where this was heading.

We started talking about the Cleveland Cavaliers championship from earlier in the summer, vacillating about LeBron James's legacy in our state. We needed to talk about Emma's feeding plan, but I was enjoying the casualness of our conversation and realized how rare it was to talk to a man for fun. An hour into our time together, we still hadn't ordered food, and I was feeling the two drinks I had finished.

"Would you split some mozzarella cheese sticks with me?" I asked, smiling as Alexander started looking over the menu.

"Ah, the fried cheese, an Applebee's delicacy," Alexander joked. "That sounds like a deal. I gotta eat something. I can feel this whiskey."

Even with my two vodka sodas, I knew we couldn't keep ignoring our patient. I pulled out my proposed daily feeding guideline from its folder and pushed it aggressively his way. Alexander glanced at me.

"Here are some of Emma's stats around her sleeping patterns and her weight gain, and I've tried to provide some recommendations here of how we might want to proceed with her new feeding plan," I said, pointing to the materials I had drawn up only hours earlier, my brain now foggy from the vodka.

Alexander didn't speak. He leaned to his right side—leaned

into *me*—and pulled a pen out of his left jeans pocket. He began to mark up the feeding plan, surprisingly increasing the suggested amount by 15% more than I had proposed but also scaling back the times of the feedings to every five hours. Instead of reviewing the changes together and talking over the X-rays with me, he made a few more scribbles of notes on the document and handed it back to me.

Alexander smiled. "All done."

So that was it. Our work took all of ninety seconds and now how were we going to fill the rest of our time tonight?

We decided on some appetizers for dinner, as there was a late-night happy hour and appetizers were half off. Eating potato skins and mozzarella cheese sticks with him was lighthearted. Our dinner at Morton's had been buttoned up and highbrow, and with our inexpensive late-night meal at the bar of an Applebee's, we were laughing, relaxing.

"Oh my God, Alexander, you just spilled ketchup on your shirt," I said, leaning in further. I started dabbing his shirt with my napkin.

"This always happens to me," he said as he stared down, his arms at his sides, allowing me to get in his space.

"You need steadier hands," I joked, a punchline many surgeons hear.

"I'll show you how steady my hands are," he shot back, one hand gripping my thigh.

And with those words and his hands on my body, a spark went through my body. Was Alexander feeling the same way I was? Did he know what he was doing to me? Did he know I hadn't felt this aroused in so long?

Alexander stood, and my muscles tightened again.

"Hey, I'll be right back," he said. "I just need to use the restroom."

"Oh, sure."

After Alexander walked away, I raised my hand, catching the bartender's attention. "Could I get another vodka soda, please," I said, and he nodded.

"You got it."

I was on my way to being drunk, and I knew in that moment that if I wanted to keep my behavior going, I needed to keep drinking.

I pulled my phone out of my purse. It was almost eleven. I wanted to be mentally sound when I texted Billy. Opening our texting thread, I typed: *It looks like I'm going to have to continue work. I'll be home in time to take William to school at 7:30 tomorrow morning.* I purposefully kept it vague, ensuring that I committed to being home in the morning to take William to school. After all, the Google calendar indicated that it was my day to take William, and we both lived and died by that calendar. I was sober enough to still understand our family dynamic.

I'd bought myself all of the night's hours. Billy wouldn't even read the text until the next morning. He was likely asleep for the night.

"Hey," Alexander said, his hand rubbing my shoulder as he sat back down next to me.

I smiled at him just as the bartender returned with my drink. "You want anything else?" he asked Alexander. "It's last call."

For some reason, as Alexander ordered his last drink, he ordered me another one too. I drank my last two drinks in what felt like twenty minutes. I didn't know what was going to happen from here, but with my brain now dazed, I didn't have any inhibitions about asking Alexander about his plans for the night.

"So, do you have to drive home now? Do you work early tomorrow?" I asked, hoping he wasn't going to say yes.

"I actually called on my way to Jacobs and got a hotel room for the night, at the Courtyard, Marriott. I think it's like ten minutes from here," Alexander said after taking a sip of his 'nightcap,' which was straight bourbon.

I was silent. So, he did have a master plan. Was I that obvious? Did he already know how tonight would end?

"I'd like you to come back with me, Lauren," Alexander said, his hand now again on my leg, rubbing it slowly. "If you'd like we can just sit up and talk. We can do our pushup competition like the old days."

I closed my eyes and smiled. He remembered. Eyes still closed, I ran my fingers through my hair and nodded. I couldn't verbalize anything at this point. I was afraid any words that would come out of my mouth would speak words of wisdom, and I would decline his offer.

As we silently made our pact and left the restaurant, there was the issue of the two cars. I didn't want my car sitting in the Applebee's parking lot all night, ripe for someone to see it and wonder about where I was, but I didn't want it sitting at the hotel, either. I also couldn't get behind the wheel with my drinking.

Shit. You already fucked this up, Lauren.

I looked at Alexander for direction.

"Let's drive your car to the hospital," he proposed. "We'll drop it off in the parking garage and get an Uber back to Applebee's. Then we'll take my Cadillac to the hotel."

I laughed. "Alexander, this is Jacobs. We don't even have Uber."

"Okay, I guess I'm driving a Prius then, and parking it in a secret spot at the hotel," Alexander said with a bit of condescension.

I stood there, my brain still foggy but concluding that this was the best option. I handed him my keys and he got in the driver's side. As we buckled in and started for the hotel, seeing him drive my car reminded me of Billy. Usually, Billy drove when we went out together, so that I could give my attention to William. And then I turned over my left shoulder, looking back at one of William's soccer balls rolling around in the back seat. The wave of guilt washed over me again.

As we got to the hotel, we parked in an undisclosed spot that no one could see from any roads. Alexander asked that I wait in the car while he checked in. About five minutes later, he texted me to come to room 531.

> (Alexander) It's an omen. May 31st is my birthday.
> (Me) I remember.

I made my way into the lobby, and the harsh bright lights reminded me that what I was about to do was very, very real. With the hotel lights blinding, the lobby TV blaring the day's election coverage, and the front desk agent typing away on her keyboard, it was sensory overload and a reminder that the rest of the world was clearheaded, even if I wasn't.

I got up to the room and knocked on the door. My heart was beating out of its chest. I'd let the alcohol make my choices for me, and now here I was, at a Courtyard hotel on a work night.

A moment later, Alexander opened the door slowly, and I all but tackled him, the door closing fast behind me. I playfully pinned Alexander up against a wall, and I pressed my body into him as he started kissing me. He quickly turned me around by my waist, pushing me up against the door, and with my left hand, I dropped my purse to the ground and shut off the lights. It was now dark again, and I felt better.

We were both breathing heavily as Alexander's hands started to move along the sides of my body. I moaned. Everything felt so sexual, and I knew I was encouraging him to do more. With that cue, he slowly raised my shirt over my head, exposing my bra. He cupped my breasts and stared at my body, admiring me for a few moments.

Even though we were both early forties, we had pretty good bodies. We weren't supermodels, but both mildly fit, and I could tell he wasn't disappointed by what he saw. He guided me to the bed, and in a quick burst, he used all his force to push me down. My body flopped onto the bed like a little kid. I bounced a bit and laughed.

Bouncing like that on the bed reminded me of William, and how we always used to sing, "Five little monkeys jumping on the bed" when he was a toddler.

Was this what the fleeting moments before an affair felt

like? The juxtaposition of lust and despair? An equal coupling of passion and shame? Did most women think about their child while in the middle of having a new man undress them?

Alexander was still standing over me, and I snapped myself back into the moment. "Wow, that was quite a push," I teased.

"Wanted to show you those steady hands," he said, his voice now considerably lower and sexier.

He pushed me up toward the pillows and while on top of me, took off my pants. Alexander had undressed me down to only my bra and underwear, while he was still completely dressed.

I pointed at myself, then him. "This clothes ratio feels rather unfair," I said coyly.

He obeyed my covert command and proceeded to take off his clothes, including his boxers. He pressed himself to my underwear, and I began to moan even louder. My body hadn't felt like this in so long, and it felt so right. My vodka soda brain was telling me that all that mattered was tonight, and my Alexander, and our patient Emma. That the rest of the world should fade away because tonight was just for us.

Soon, I was naked, and Alexander got up, went to his jacket, pulled out a condom, and put it on. He walked back to the bed, got on top of me and asked, "Are you okay with this?"

"No," I said, that question immediately bringing me to tears. It was a rare moment of vulnerability with Alexander. With myself. I was not okay with what I was about to do. And I needed Alexander to know that I wasn't taking what I was about to do lightly.

I wasn't okay with it, but I needed it to happen.

"I want it so badly, though," I whispered. "I want you, Alexander."

That was what he needed to hear. Just like that, we were having sex. We were having an affair. I was really doing it. I had made a choice. I had taken a path. There was no turning back now.

Alexander thrusting into me was heavenly, and he kept commenting on how good I felt, how good I looked. We fit so well together, like our bodies were made for only one another. My moans grew louder and louder, and I opened my eyes, staring directly into his. A slight opening of the drapes gave the tiniest bit of light, the moon illuminating our faces.

I put my hand to his cheek as I said, "Oh, Alexy."

It was the name I used to call him.

He put his arms under my back and pressed harder into me, whispering, "I've missed you so much."

Only a few minutes later, we laid motionless together, side by side, in the afterglow, the tenderness overshadowing what we had just done.

CHAPTER 10

I LAID IN ALEXANDER'S ARMS, feeling like I'd just run a marathon. Though my body was completely exhausted, there was an inexhaustible comfort in our bodies being intertwined. He was spooning me as I was laying on my right side, and he kept whispering sweet things in my ear.

"You're still so sexy," he whispered as he ran his hand up and down my left thigh. Our bodies emanated heat, and I loved feeling his naked body resting with mine. Yet I wondered if what he was telling me was true. Did he actually think I was sexy, with this forty-one-year-old body he was seeing naked, or was it just words? We fell asleep only briefly, maybe an hour or two, as my mind would not allow for a deep slumber.

As the hours passed by, I was slowly starting to sober up. The alcohol weakened as my crutch, now playing less of a supporting role to justify my actions. There was a linear correlation between sobering up and the rush of guilt. My chest began to tighten, and I knew any moment now that the guilt would bubble so high in me that I might explode.

Still lying motionless, I tried to be as calm as possible. "Alexander, I have to get back to the hospital," I said softly, not even knowing if Alexander was awake because my back was to him as he cradled me.

"Shhh, stay," he whispered in my ear.

Had he anticipated that I would fall asleep, spend the night, and have a casual morning with him? I couldn't be that surprised by the assumption. After all, Alexander had the luxury of not having to live the double life that I was now about to embark upon. I had to go home to my husband and son, who were unknowingly now members of a broken family.

"I have to get back to the hospital," I repeated, this time a little louder. "You know, for what it's worth, I don't do this. I've never had an affair. I've never slept with someone outside of my marriage to Billy."

It was the first time I had said my husband's name to Alexander, and I wondered if saying my husband's name made him as uncomfortable as it made me.

"Don't worry, I know who you are," Alexander replied, whispering in my ear, hugging his arms around me a little tighter.

"Then you know that this is unlike me," I said, now uncomfortable with lying in bed with him. "I feel the alcohol got the best of me tonight. I'm married, I have a son, and my job...." my voice trailed off. "You know I became a neonatologist later, so I only have five years' experience. You're at a different place in your career than I am."

"Doctors of different tenure can still have feelings for each other," he whispered as we spooned.

He wasn't understanding the point I was trying to make. Maybe I wasn't either. I just knew that I had to get back to the hospital; I had to see Emma.

I got out of the bed, quietly got dressed and was about to leave. I saw Alexander climb out of bed and get dressed as well. I looked at him, perplexed, and he said, "What? You have to take me back to my car, remember."

Our drive was quiet. As he drove my Prius we held hands, and to fill the silence I reiterated how I never do this. I wanted Alexander to know that I thought he was special, and in some sick way, I needed him to know that I was saving my one affair just for him. There was a hidden significance that I had not slept with many men in my life, and no men outside my marriage. Alexander was the 'chosen one' in a way, and perhaps it meant that we were chosen for one another. And as I verbalized that, he listened and just silently nodded, undoubtedly unsure how to respond.

We pulled into the parking lot at Applebee's, which now felt like the setting for my final hours of innocence. Alexander's massive Escalade was the only vehicle in the parking lot, and he pulled up my Prius beside it.

"Are you okay to drive?" he asked gently.

That question made me start to cry, as yes, I was sober now and okay to drive. But was I 'okay' to live my life? Was I 'okay' to go home to my husband, who I had just betrayed? Was I 'okay' to just go on with my daily routines, not obsessively thinking about Alexander every five seconds and hoping for the next time we could meet?

"I think driving a car is about the only thing I'm okay to do," I said, voice cracking.

"Lauren, what we did back there at the hotel…it was amazing. Don't be too hard on yourself. You're an amazing person. Thank you for being you."

His kind words hit in the wrong way, as I couldn't reconcile the stratification of Alexander thinking I'm amazing, and Billy, certainly after finding out about the affair, thinking I'm criminal. I decided not to say much more to Alexander and so he kissed me on the cheek and then left my car, plunging me into my racing thoughts and further realizations of what I had just done.

I made my way quickly to Covenant Medical. I parked in my same spot in the parking garage and made my way into the NICU, stopping first at my office to throw my white coat over my skinny jeans. Now around three in the morning, the nurses were extremely surprised to see me. Likely it was the smudged mascara and messy hair, that I tried unsuccessfully to fix in my office mirror. They didn't ask any questions though, and I didn't offer anything up.

Making my way straight for Emma's room, I peered into her crib as she slept, keeping most of the lights off to not stir her. I wrote the new feeding plan that Alexander had edited on the whiteboard and made sure to include all his notations. Back at the computer station, I badged into the computer system and electronically entered Emma's feeding guidelines, ensuring a consistent feed every five hours.

"We have another blood draw for Emma in a couple hours," Ashley, the night nurse, mentioned to me. "Would you like me to do that now so that you can see the numbers?"

"No, let's hold off poking her. I'm going to go back into her room for a while."

As much as I had the desire to have sex with Alexander earlier, I had an even greater aching now to be with Emma. As I walked back into her room, hearing her lightly snore, my heart expanded in a way I've only experienced a couple times in my life. I gently bent over her crib and laid the palm of my hand on her forehead. She didn't even stir. She was the most beautiful baby, wires and nose plugs and all.

This little baby was letting me live again. For so many years, I had been going through the motions, keeping score of my life through a Google calendar and now here, I felt I was falling in love twice in one night. With Emma and with Alexander. Alexander saying, 'Thank you for being you,' made me feel finally that I was enough. I was getting validation for the first time in so long, and it made me feel alive. And here Emma was, the angelic link between us. I was caring for her and she was improving, and I felt that she, too, must have felt that I was enough.

There had to be a reason that Emma was born with her condition. There had to be a reason that she showed up in my NICU. And there had to be a reason that Alexander was the top doctor for Emma's surgery, and I had chosen him. What reason other than fate? We were a family, in a way. Living out this beautiful blessing that fused us three together.

Chapter 11

I HAD ALWAYS SEEN MYSELF AS SOMEONE WITH HIGH MORALS.
Once, when I wasn't even ten years old, my mom allowed me to
go up to the grocery store by myself with my friend. Back then in
Jacobs, the grocery store was 'the place to be' for us kids, so my
friend and I went to Fisher Foods, on the hunt for an after-school
snack. While we walked all over the store, we always wound up
selecting the leftover donuts in the clear case, which were half off
past two o'clock.

One specific day, after delicately placing the donuts into
the plastic baggies and heading toward the checkout, I pulled
out the two one-dollar bills my mom gave me. As I did so, from
the corner of eye, I saw my friend take a Tiger Beat magazine
and put it under her shirt. I was in shock as she did it, and even
more shocked that the magazine laid perfectly upright, nestled

between her stomach and her shirt, defying gravity. The cashier never saw it, and I never talked to my friend after that day.

I never forgot what it felt like to see my friend steal. *Cheat. Lie. Deceive.* From that day when I was ten years old, I chose to be a values-driven person. As I aged , my values were guided by my Christian faith and by those Midwestern values my parents instilled in me. And even now, as an adult, I was led by the Hippocratic oath I took as a doctor.

One thing was sure, I spent most of my life waking up every day being able to look myself in the mirror. I knew who I was, and I could live with myself free of shame.

But in the days after being with Alexander, everything I was as a person was crumbling. After sleeping with him, I wasn't me anymore. I was a new person. Not new as in better, but new as in unrecognizable. Every time I looked in the mirror, I couldn't feel the person that was staring back at me. The girl in the mirror looked confident, loving, and kind. But that was not me. I was cruel, selfish, and careless. I felt so embarrassed to be in my own body, having done what I did, and there was the unshakable feeling of loneliness. I missed me.

I hadn't anticipated the contrast that now laid before me: In combating loneliness by having an affair, the affair actually made me feel more withdrawn and lonelier than I had ever been before. I could not believe that it worked in the opposite way I'd intended. It was a heartbreaking dichotomy that plunged me further into anxiety and fear about who I was and what my future held. I thought Alexander and I having sex would validate me. But having sex with a man who wasn't my husband invalidated the very core of who I was. My confidence now replaced with guilt. My steadfast nature now replaced with risk. My ideals now replaced with carelessness.

How was I supposed to teach my son the value of honesty when I was ultimately not truthful with his father? How was I supposed to talk with Billy about what was missing in our marriage without staking claim to being the one that was tearing the marriage apart? And finally, how was I supposed to uphold the American Medical Association oaths that were the bedrock of my profession, while compromising Emma's care by having a sexual relationship with her other doctor?

I felt so far away from Billy, William, my NICU babies, and especially Emma. I had failed them all in different ways. There was no way for me to show up for them in the way they needed me to. They needed a strong, confident Lauren. What they got was me spending my first few days after the affair either crying quietly in my car, berating myself in front of a mirror, or sitting at my desk feeling nauseous at the thought of the affair becoming public.

As the days passed, my shame was usurped by only one thing: Emma's declining health. Emma was now presenting such low blood cell counts that we were going to have to give her a blood transfusion. We knew it was coming, but I hadn't anticipated it coming so soon. I put in the orders for the blood, which would take a few days.

As I spent a few minutes in Emma's room one day, I leaned over her crib to touch the palm of my hand to her forehead, gently pressing down to calm her stirring from pain when she awoke. I stared into Emma's eyes, now gray and sunken in, not knowing where my guilt about the affair ended and my grief about Emma's health started.

At home, the biggest marked difference about me was that I couldn't make eye contact with Billy and William. They both felt so pure and so innocent; they had no concept that the woman in their house wasn't the person they thought she was. William continued to be upbeat and relied on me for so much: cleaning his room, doing his laundry, and cooking his meals. William never missed a beat, staying true to his gregarious nature, even if my demeanor had completely changed. I found myself doing more of the household chores than I normally did, at first thinking it was a way to keep myself busy. But I quickly realized that being super-mom and super-wife was an attempt at penance for the affair. Every time Billy asked about our Google calendar or William hugged me, I did one more chore to silently tell them I was sorry.

Billy didn't seem to suspect anything though, which I thought he might, given my appearance. My eyes were always puffy, and my shoulders were always hunched over. When I was around Billy, I avoided talking with him. I wished that he would ask me what was wrong, to give me an opening to tell him. But he never seemed to pick up on my grief, which I found profoundly sad. I didn't have a right to feel sad about it, but Billy always seemed to look right past me, so I guess he felt comfortable with me keeping my distance from him.

After a week of me feeling sorry for myself and Billy seemingly hiding out all day in his office and all night in the basement, I got up the courage one day off to knock on his office door. He looked up from his laptop and didn't motion for me to come in. He didn't say anything either. He just waited for me to invite myself in, so I did.

"Hey there," I said casually, trying to hide the pain I felt in my heart. "I know that we haven't seen much of each other lately, with work and all, so I thought maybe we could go out for a drink or something."

This wasn't uncharacteristic of me. I used to appeal to Billy all the time to go out on dates. Up until last year even, I was nudging him for us to have regular Thursday night date nights. But he never wanted to compromise William's soccer practice schedule, which I understood. But today, standing at the door of his office, I was suggesting a date with the knowledge that I had just slept with someone else. I figured, if we went out for drinks, would I tell him? Would I have one drink, become vulnerable, start crying, and spill the beans? I didn't know, but I did know that Billy and I at least had to talk with one another. A marriage can't be sustainable, even in the short term, without any communication.

Billy thought for a few moments. "Maybe we could go out next month, during Octoberfest. We could go to that downtown brewery stand. My buddy at work said that Jacobs is going to bring in two beer vendors for the Octoberfest night." He stopped talking, picking up his phone from his desk and began typing in what I could only imagine was a Google search about the beer vendors.

"Well, we just…we haven't been able to spend any alone time

together. I just thought maybe we could do something, like even tonight. I have the day off!" I said, a little too enthusiastically. I could tell that Billy didn't feel any sense of urgency to spend time with me. "Don't you want to spend time together?"

"Lauren," Billy said softly. "Sure, you know that I want to spend time with you." And then, the long excuse came, just as it always did. "We're both so busy. You're a physician running a hospital department. I told you my company just got that State of Ohio polling location technology contract. Each night we have William's soccer, or swimming, or both." He continued for a bit longer, gently voicing the running list of all our family Google calendar entries.

I didn't answer. Was he trying to make our schedules an excuse for not spending time together? Or did he legitimately feel that our lives were too busy to cultivate our relationship? I wasn't asking for us to vacation in Greece. Was I really asking too much? My brain was so slow and my body so lethargic that I didn't have the energy to fight him on this. I was the one that had an affair. I had no right to make any demands. Still, I found myself bringing out a voice of reason into my words.

"But...I miss you," I said as I stepped into his office, no longer at the door but now right next to his desk. "We used to go out and do things together and talk. I just feel like we haven't spent time together in so long. All we have to do is go out for dinner," I said, letting him off the hook for sex. "I think it would be nice to reconnect."

"Lauren," he said, looking me in the eye and using my name again, "we were *never* the couple that went out all the time drinking and dancing and living it up. Maybe next month we can go out together. We know we love each other; we don't have to show it 24/7 to know it."

I was very plainly and very overtly being denied. I wasn't going to keep begging for a dinner date, but I wasn't going to leave his office without him knowing how sad and lonely I was. Even if I didn't have a right to be sad and lonely, I still felt so detached from him.

"I feel so distant from you."

"I'm right here," Billy said softly yet apathetically. He then looked down at his laptop as a new email chimed on his computer, and the discussion was complete.

As I walked out of Billy's office, past the kitchen, and into my bedroom, I proceeded to fall right into my bed. It was barely afternoon, but I had no physical or emotional energy left to give. As I fell onto the bed, I bounced a bit, and it reminded me of how Alexander playfully pushed me onto the bed just before we started having sex.

The thought of Alexander paying so much attention to me when I wasn't supposed to receive it contrasted with Billy not interacting with me sent me over the edge. I started sobbing. I could not control myself anymore. I curled up in a fetal position under the covers so that Billy wouldn't hear my cries.

I cried for what felt like an hour. I was grieving bringing a man back into my life that I wasn't supposed to be with. I was grieving Emma's deteriorating health. And most of all, I was grieving a husband that did not want to be with me. I had never in my life felt more alone and never felt more confused about what lay ahead.

CHAPTER 12

"DR. LEONARD, THE LAB REPORTS aren't giving us anything we want to see."

A couple days later I was back at the hospital, sitting at my office desk, having just spoken with another set of parents of a baby-to-be, when I got a call from Ashley, Emma's night nurse.

"Give me a second to look," I said.

Right away, I logged into Emma's account on my laptop to assess the latest bloodwork results. Her red blood cell count was dropping rapidly, and the hospital was still washing the blood for the blood transfusion. We probably couldn't give her the blood transfusion for a couple hours, since the antibiotic I'd prescribed for Emma to take in anticipation of the blood transfusion was wreaking havoc on her gut flora, good bacteria in the stomach that often deteriorates when countered by an antibiotic. Emma had also developed a cough and labored breathing, which I feared she got from one of the visitors or staff having a virus and passing it to her.

"I'm looking at her numbers right now, Ashley, and you know what I think this might be?" I stopped to both pause for emphasis but also to see if Ashley wanted to showcase her skills and correctly diagnose Emma.

"You think it's unrelated to the intestines?" she asked.

"I think it's pneumonia. We're going to start seeing this more and more as it's the virus season, and we'll continue to see it throughout the winter. I'm going to order a chest X-ray. I'll come down to meet with the radiology team when they take the X-ray. Based on what they initially see, I may halt the blood transfusion for tonight."

I quickly hung up with Ashley and put in orders for radiology. I continued to assess Emma's vitals and bloodwork from my laptop, and the more numbers I read, the more I knew, this did not look good. If Emma had pneumonia, then the blood transfusion would be risky. But if we didn't do the blood transfusion, Emma's pneumonia would get worse and her anemia would progress. I thought about consulting Dr. Wang, the pediatric physician at Covenant Medical. But I knew that the only other physician that should definitively weigh in on Emma's health should be her surgeon, Alexander.

Alexander hadn't called or texted since that night, now a week ago. I tried not to let that eat away at me. I felt so alone, and his silence was making it worse. At the same time, his silence was a gift, allowing me to draw away from him a bit and focus on my grief, on what I had done, and in a way, focus on normal life.

But here was my normal life, making medical decisions for patients, intersecting with my loneliness and my desire to have Alexander contact me. I knew I had to call him, and I knew I didn't have any time to waste.

As I dialed his cell, my heart was beating out of my chest. Luckily, when he answered, he seemed like me, melancholy.

"Hey there, kiddo," he said gently.

Usually, I would be frustrated with that greeting, but today, his nickname for me just felt like a hug.

"Hi Alexander. I know we haven't talked since last Thursday night," I said, somewhat laying things out in the open. "But I really wanted to reach out to talk about Emma Webinson. Her health is deteriorating."

"What?" Alexander said rather loudly. "What do you mean? Is she vomiting up her formula? Is it green vile? Is she dumping?"

I updated Alexander on how Emma's health was presenting, and that we had the double-edged sword of the blood transfusion.

"Wow, I can't believe this. I just had a conversation with the Harvard Medical Review society yesterday about this case," Alexander muttered. "I was going to do a speaking engagement there in a month about atresias that burst in utero and the effects of a pseudocyst. I was going to use Emma's surgery as the case study."

This had absolutely nothing to do with why I called. My stomach churned as I realized Alexander was focusing on his career versus focusing on his patient, who at the moment, was very sick.

"Okay, Alexander," I said. "My question is, based upon what you saw with the atresia when you performed the surgery, do you have any advice on medical care for the next 72 hours? I'm thinking the next few days are going to be critical to getting Emma back on course."

"Stop all feedings," he said. "Do not administer formula, breast milk, Pedialyte, or any liquid to her mouth. Administer the proteins through the IV only and ensure that her ileostomy bag is changed every two hours to avoid risking additional infection to the epidermis."

His medical orders were declarative, and I agreed. We were quiet again for a moment. And then he spoke.

"How are you doing?" Alexander asked, sounding genuinely concerned.

My voice choked up, and I started crying. "It's been a bad week," I said as I wiped away my tears. "I feel extremely guilty for what we did, and now with Emma so sick, I'm scared."

I didn't tell him anything related to how I felt Emma was, in a way, my child. Our child. And how, in a way, our conversation right now mirrored any conversation that worried parents have about their child, whether it's that their child is sick, or being bullied, or even misbehaving.

"I'm scared because I don't want to lose this child, and I don't want to lose my family, and I don't want to lose my job, and I feel like all of that is on the line right now."

"Lauren," Alexander replied, now extremely serious. "This isn't the end for you. Everything will be repaired. Everything will work out because you are strong, and you will piece everything back together. Don't be scared. I've seen you be strong before, and I know you can be strong again."

"Okay," I said, giving a non-answer because I didn't have the energy to continue the conversation. I had so many thoughts about Alexander, but right now, all of them needed to be suppressed in order to care for Emma.

"How about we talk tomorrow? Let me know how Emma's doing. I've got to get back to Harvard on if I should still do that seminar."

"Okay," I replied, wanting to scream into his ear that Emma was more than a fucking speaking opportunity.

We said our goodbyes, and an hour later, I was down in the NICU by Emma's bedside. Jason and Wendy were in their rocking chairs, silent as they watched me walk in and lean against Emma's crib.

"Emma's bloodwork shows that she likely has pneumonia," I said. "This isn't uncommon for babies, but this is coming at a bad time because she needs a blood transfusion. But that's too risky for her right now."

Emma's parents looked concerned, their faces already haggard from a lack of sleep and constant worry.

"So, what do we do?" Jason asked, reaching out to hold his wife's hand.

"I'm giving Emma a steroid to see if that can raise her vitals," I explained. "I'm hoping that in the morning, she'll be stabilized enough to do the blood transfusion."

"Okay," Wendy said, giving the same non-answer I had given Alexander an hour ago. I was silent for a moment, waiting for Wendy to pepper me with her usual litany of questions, to bring up the holidays again and if Emma would be discharged by then. But 'Okay' was all I got. And what else was there to say really, to this upsetting news?

"My shift is about to end, and Dr. Wang, the pediatric physician, is on rounds in the NICU tonight. I've already written notes to her in Emma's electronic chart. Do you think you'll head out soon for dinner or stay? If you want to stay, I'll ask Dr. Wang to come down from the pediatric floor and introduce herself."

Wendy looked numb. Staring at Emma, she replied without a hint of energy, "We'll probably head home soon." Jason nodded, silently acknowledging that their presence in Emma's room did not provide any guarantees.

As I left Emma's room, I debated staying the night in the NICU. It wasn't my shift, but I didn't want to leave Emma. But I also knew better than anyone that we needed to let the steroid work its magic, which was going to take time. Plus, it was my night to pick William up from after-school soccer and take him to swim practice. I needed to see my son, to know that I wasn't completely failing him, too.

*****

I got to William's soccer practice right as he was starting to look for my car. I'd been crying, so I leaned up into the rear-view mirror and wiped the mascara that had been dripping down my cheeks. Looking barely presentable, I got out of the car and walked briskly over to William.

He started walking toward me and a smile flashed across his face. I smiled back, the first time I had smiled all day. The way my mouth curved up and my cheeks raised felt so foreign. For just a moment, my brows weren't furrowed, and I wasn't swimming in a sea of shame and guilt and worry. In this moment, I was walking toward the light, toward the sun, my son, and it was the best part of a horrible day.

"Mommy, guess what!" William exclaimed. "Coach Jamal says I get to play goalie at the next practice because I'm really good."

I knelt down to William's eye level and gave him a hug. He hugged me back, obviously thinking that I was embracing him because of his new soccer position.

"Isn't it great?" William asked, now yelling in my ear as we hugged.

"I'm so proud of you, baby," I said, now tearing up again.

I held tight to William as he tried to wiggle out of my arms. Nothing about me felt normal or right, but hugging my son gave me a sense of myself again. It gave me a sense of belonging, and perhaps most importantly, a sense of pureness.

CHAPTER 13

WILLIAM AND I MADE OUR WAY THROUGH THE BACK ROADS, me taxiing my son from one extracurricular activity to the next. As we got out of the car and I lugged his swimming bag up the stairs into the Jacobs Aquatic Centre—which I always thought was a very fancy name for the only non-hotel indoor pool in Jacobs—I looked down at William.

"Do you need any help changing out of your soccer uniform and into your swim trunks?" I asked.

"No, Mom!" he replied loudly, and I sensed his embarrassment of me having to go into the boys' locker room with him. We made a plan for him to change by himself and then for him to wave at me before he dove into the pool with his coach.

I decided tonight to sit in the bleachers and watch William

swim back and forth, hopefully being hypnotized by his stroke. The facility was miserably humid, contrasted against the outside autumn evening. With the cool breeze and the leaves rustling in the trees, it was the perfect weather to be outdoors. I debated using the hour to walk around outside, taking in the crisp air to clear my head, but for some reason, I felt I needed to be close to William. I stayed put in the bleachers.

As I watched my son dive into the pool with his friends, my mind slowly drifted away from the present environment and onto thinking about Alexander. I couldn't believe the call I had with him today had to be about a deteriorating Emma. I missed him so much, and I just wanted to see him again. Even with these layers of guilt, I missed being close to him. Did I make him feel bad by insinuating that I was upset with my choice of sleeping with him? Was he now mad at me?

Get it together, Lauren. Stop making life harder on yourself, echoed in my head as I decided to occupy my mind and lose myself in social media. At first, I started scrolling through Twitter, but it was all election coverage. I moved onto Facebook, but I felt a sting every time I scrolled through pics of my college friends with their husbands, out and about on vacation and loving each other. My eyes began welling up with tears, and I was about to chuck my phone in the pool when I heard someone approach me.

"God, you don't look good, are you okay?"

I looked up. It was Steele. I'd forgotten that her daughter had diving practice at the same time as William's swim practice. Traditionally, I never stayed when I dropped William off for his swim practice, usually choosing to go home for an hour or head back to the NICU to answer work emails. But tonight, neither my home nor my little NICU nook felt much like a safe haven.

The aquatic center became my temporary purgatory, my suspension of time, but at least now I had my best friend to join me.

Steele sat down next to me, straddling the bleacher bench so that her body could face me. Dressed in skinny jeans and a bright pink top, she looked everything that I was not: cheerful, confident, and capable. I couldn't look her in the eye and instead kept my head down, with my arms resting on my legs and my shoulders hunched over.

"What's wrong, girl? You usually aren't here. Is everything okay with William?" Steele glanced over to the pool and then back at me.

"William is the only thing in my life that is okay," I replied, wondering if I was being dramatic. I began to tell Steele about Emma's health, trying to convey Emma's condition without violating HIPAA, the health privacy law. As I spoke, my voice started to choke up, and my hands started to shake. Steele put her hand on my back and rubbed it lightly.

"I'm so sorry to hear this," she said.

Although she was feeling sorry for me, I actually felt sorry for Steele because she believed my grief and bewilderment stemmed just from my patient. I knew this was probably the moment to share my affair aloud and confide in someone.

"Also, something happened," I said, rather cryptically. I rubbed my hands together to stop the shaking. "It's really bad, and I'm just devastated." I fell silent, hoping Steele would guess it so that I wouldn't have to say the words out loud.

She didn't guess, so I spent what felt like most of the swim practice explaining to her about Alexander coming to Jacobs, our euphoric high that Emma was able to digest her formula, our flirtatious dinner at Applebee's, and ultimately our decision to go back to his hotel. I relayed every detail about how sexy I felt that night, how rebellious I wanted to be, and how much it meant to me that Alexander desired me. I admitted that my game plan that night was to let the alcohol be my guide and submit to whatever wound up happening.

With every breath, it felt cathartic to finally get it out and tell the world what happened, even if I was just telling Steele. I continued, detailing my myriad of feelings, feeling spellbound while having sex with Alexander, and how that quickly turned to deep despair, and how I vacillated between these mood swings, feeling anything but myself.

Steele didn't condemn me. She kept her hand on my back, rubbing it gently as I poured my heart out to her, my tears falling between the bleachers twenty feet to the ground.

"Lauren, you need to talk to Billy," Steele said as she leaned forward toward me. "You need to repair your relationship. This affair isn't about Alexander, not really."

"Then what's it about?" I asked, sniffling.

"This is about how you are unhappy in your marriage. You don't have to tell Billy about the affair, but you need to repair what has been torn apart in your relationship."

"Steele, you don't understand," I said impatiently, now

wiping my eyes and using my hands to gesture. "I tried to tell him how much I missed him, and how much I wanted to spend time with him. I tried that literally a few days ago in his office. He doesn't get it. He doesn't even want to go out to dinner with me. I slept with Alexander because I know that I won't be getting a loving relationship from Billy. I've tried, I'm trying now, and I'll continue to try, knowing that Billy doesn't truly love me."

"Sure he does," Steele said encouragingly.

Now I was angry.

"No, he doesn't!" I snapped. "I know it's difficult for couples with healthy relationships to understand this. You're in that group, Steele; you simply don't understand. But let me tell you what it's like with a husband who isn't concerned about having a loving relationship: Billy does not care what my needs are. I could take your advice and talk to him until I was blue in the face about bettering our relationship and it would not matter."

Steele was quiet, and she looked surprised by this sweeping indictment of Billy's and my marriage. I continued.

"Billy doesn't have any desire to change anything. He's content living in a D+ marriage." And then, for additional emphasis, I turned the tables on Steele. "Imagine if Adam just didn't listen to what you needed. Imagine if you wanted to talk about work or a problem you were having, and Adam was just silent, barely engaging with you. Not even looking you in the eye."

"I would…"

I didn't let her finish.

"Imagine if you tried and tried but you were just so lonely.

And after not being able to get back to a fulfilling relationship, you realized you had to just accept it and be lonely, knowing you wouldn't have sex, or emotional support, or even share a laugh with your husband. And then as you've finally come to accept that, someone comes in your life who understands you, who doesn't make you feel lonely anymore, who listens to your problems and wants to see you and have sex with you. Imagine if that happened to you."

"I probably would have had an affair," Steele mumbled quietly, not looking me in the eye but validating my feelings. Would Steele really have made the same decision I had? Probably not, but it felt good to know that she said she would have.

Steele let out a big sigh, then looked at me intently. "Look, Lauren, you have three crises in your life right now. You've got a crumbling marriage, you're having an affair with someone you have a history with, and you have a very ill patient. You have so much to solve, but right now, I hear you on not solving Billy, so just solve for your grief and heal through your son. Just do exactly what you're doing right now. Watch your son swim and spend time with him, and know that no matter what, no matter what happens, your son is your most important priority. Let William guide you through your crises."

As I listened to Steele reiterate my need to be a good mom, I saw some type of foreshadowing. Would Billy, Alexander, and Emma uproot my life even more than they were now? Was I on the brink of losing everything and knowing that the only constant in my life was my little boy?

"You started this conversation saying William was the only

thing that was going well in your life, and I say, keep savoring that," Steele declared.

I nodded in agreement, and we talked a bit more about how I felt. The sounds of water splashing and whistles blowing were echoing throughout the building. As our conversation ended, we both watched silently as Steele's daughter took a breathtaking dive off the three-meter platform. Little Ruby looked like an angel, descending from heaven, right into the diving well without a trace of a splash.

"If at first you don't succeed, make babies and have them succeed," Steele said with a wink as we watched Ruby climb out of the diving well.

William was floating on his kickboard, and he looked up at me and smiled. Steele was spot on. I needed William to be my guide. I had to focus on how, as a mother, I could fulfill his needs. I could bring myself back to life through him.

As swim practice ended and William was in the back of the car, recounting to me each minute of his time in the pool, my phone rang. I looked up. It was the hospital. We were less than five minutes from home, so I declined the call. Dr. Wang was the attending physician, and I had faith in her. She was a great doctor. Emma had a heavy-duty steroid that was going to pacify her for the night, and I was trying to take Steele's advice and focus on being present for my son.

Back at the house, William was exhausted from his multisport evening, and he went to bed very easily. I kept checking my phone, expecting to see a voicemail from the hospital. I also thought Alexander might call to check on Emma's condition. I debated for a moment about going back to the NICU. *Was I irresponsible?* I wondered. *Maybe I shouldn't have prioritized William's swim practice over Emma.*

I walked past Billy's office to see if he was there, and he wasn't, which meant he was playing video games in the basement. I cleaned up the living room and kitchen a bit and was surprised to hear Billy walking up the stairs from the basement.

"Hey," he said casually, like I was a roommate who had just walked in the apartment door.

"Hi," I replied.

"How was soccer and swimming?" Billy asked.

"It went well. I guess William gets to play goalie next week."

"What! Are you serious! That's awesome, so Jamal really feels he's ready, huh? Wow. So proud of our little guy," Billy exclaimed with a huge smile on his face.

"Yeah, and I was watching him tonight at swimming, his backstroke has really improved. He doesn't have trouble floating on his back anymore because his kicking helps him propel his arms," I said as I mimicked someone doing backstroke.

"William is just such a natural athlete," Billy replied, still smiling and shaking his head, almost in amazement. I could hear the adoration in Billy's voice for our son. He was eager to stay in the conversation with me here because we were talking about William. He was looking me in the eye, smiling.

I started to feel nauseous as Billy and I continued to talk. I couldn't believe this was happening, but I was starting to feel jealous of my own child. Billy was so animated and proud of everything William did, and I desperately wanted Billy to see me like that. I wanted Billy's eyes to light up when he talked about me and my accolades.

I decided to try again. "You know, good news we found out at work," I said. "Our hospital might get more funding from the county to hire nursing positions. And that funding may be the prelude to getting the new heart institute wing built."

I paused as Billy just nodded and walked past me in the kitchen to the refrigerator to grab a La Croix. I hadn't even touched on Emma's health yet.

As I heard the can open, Billy said, "Just popped up to get a soda. I've got a lot of meetings tomorrow, so I'll be to bed in the next hour or so."

"Okay."

This was exactly what I tried to explain to Steele, I thought as I watched him walk out of the kitchen and back down to the basement.

Feeling so completely defeated, I went to my room, crawled in bed with my scrubs on and my mascara staining my white pillowcase, and I fell asleep.

*****

My cell phone rang, waking me from a deep sleep. Billy stirred next to me, and with my eyes still closed, I reached for my cell phone on my nightstand.

"Hello," I said groggily. I knew it was the hospital.

"Dr. Leonard, it's Ashley. I called earlier in the evening, around 8:30 p.m., because Emma was developing a severe stridor and her labored breathing has increased overnight. But now her blood pressure is rising, and her heart rate is dropping, and I think you need to come in."

"Give Emma another dose of the beta-lactam antibiotic and roll her on her stomach," I said as I started to sit up. "Ensure you're monitoring her heart rate while she's on her stomach. I'll get dressed and come in."

We hung up, and I crawled out of bed. I walked around the other side of the bed in the dark, and I leaned down to Billy.

"I'm going to the hospital," I whispered. The phone call didn't seem to wake him up, so I figured I would text him early in the morning. I went into my closet and peeled off my scrubs that I fell asleep in, then put on a fresh pair of the exact same scrubs. I slipped on my medical clogs, and I headed for the hospital.

*****

As I parked my car in the hospital parking garage, my phone started ringing again. I grabbed my tote bag and answered the phone as I got out of the car. I headed toward the garage crosswalk into the seventh floor of the hospital.

"Dr. Leonard," Ashley said, her voice both fearful and raised, "Emma's heart quit beating just now. I can't find a pulse on her. I think Emma's oxygen levels are too low to start—"

"I'll be right there." I hung up.

I threw my tote over my shoulder as I began running as fast as I could. As I dashed through the crosswalk, I couldn't think about anything but getting to Emma's room as soon as possible. The crosswalk ended and I came to the seventh floor of the hospital, immediately bypassing the elevator for the stairs. I jetted down five flights of stairs in a flurry, skipping stairs and breathing heavy. My mind and my heart were racing.

When I got to the NICU, I didn't scrub in or even wash my hands. I charged through all the doors and security checkpoints and raced right to Emma's room. All three night nurses and Dr. Wang were in her room standing over the crib.

Everyone turned toward me as I entered the room. I put one foot in front of the other, approaching Emma's crib. I looked briefly at Emma, who had turned a miserable shade of yellow, and my eyes darted straight for her vital signs on the LCD screen above the crib. I could hear the flat line echo throughout the room.

No one was talking. Two of the nurses were crying. Dr. Wang looked at me as I leaned over the crib and gently put my hand on Emma.

She was dead.

CHAPTER 14

IT TOOK ONLY FIVE MINUTES to unhook Emma from her tubes and wires. As the nurses stood behind me, watching every move I made, I slowly removed Emma's ileostomy bag and cleaned her stoma, then carried on with cleaning the rest of her body with a warm washcloth. I tried my best to be emotionally numb as I did this, treating Emma just like the expired patients that came before her. And ensuring that I was, to the best of my ability, putting on a show of the stoic physician for the nurses that worked for me.

As I finished cleaning Emma, I turned to Dr. Wang and the nurses. "Would you mind leaving the room for a few minutes?" I asked, my voice steady. "I want to say my goodbye."

Part of me expected them to judge me for even this tiny show of attachment to Emma, but they all looked as upset as I felt. We'd all grown attached to this bright and beautiful baby girl.

"Of course," Dr. Wang said, and the nurses murmured their agreement as they all headed out the door.

As soon as they shut the hospital room door, I broke down. I looked at Emma's lifeless body before me, and it felt as if I myself had died right along with her. I began to sob, half despondent and half angry that Emma was leaving me. My tears were starting to fall on her naked body as I leaned over her crib, rubbing her tiny arm.

I couldn't believe that this baby girl was dead. It didn't seem possible, nor did it seem like God could take someone this beautiful and innocent from this earth. My sobbing became louder, angry now at God, too.

Throughout my medical career, I'd had many patients pass away. It comes with the territory of being a doctor. Sometimes their passing was expected, sometimes it was sudden, but each time, it was tragically sad.

But this death was so different from all the others. This time, Emma was *mine*. Emma brought me so much joy in my NICU, and she was the link between me and the only thing that made me feel alive: Alexander. I didn't know where Emma stopped and Alexander started. I just knew that I still felt that the three of us were a family. A family filled with such grief and dysfunction, the ghost of our past here to haunt us once more.

After I had thoroughly cleaned Emma, I swaddled her and laid her back in her crib. I turned my back to her and shut off the lights as I made my way out to the nurses' station. By now,

I had wiped my tears and was focused on the very worst part of losing a patient, which was delivering the message to the family. The thought of telling Jason and Wendy that their only child was dead made me feel sick. They were undoubtedly at home sleeping right now, eager to rise in the morning with their coffee and their baby books and head to the hospital to play with their little girl. And, in delivering the news to them, it would be a reminder that they were, in fact, the parents of Emma. Not me.

I was also afraid to call Alexander. *Will he blame me for Emma's death?* I wondered. *Will he see me as an ineffective small-town doctor that didn't do her job? Or will he not even care about Emma's death?* I thought back to our conversation just the day before, and my heart dropped. Would he only be concerned about how it affected him professionally? Would he understand how I felt this was 'our' child? Would he acknowledge how devastated I was?

It wasn't even 3:00 a.m. yet, so I had a few hours to make my calls before the world started waking up. I decided to use some of my time to clear my head, and so I headed outside in the autumn air, the temperature now hovering around forty-five degrees. I knew I had only a couple minutes, but I wanted to be by myself, and to be in a quiet place. I sat down on a bench outside the hospital, adjacent to the Ronald McDonald House that overlooked a small pond. It was almost completely dark, except for the moon's sliver of light over the pond. Now away from the NICU, away from the noise of stretchers rolling across a tile floor and nurses typing on a keyboard, I began to cry uncontrollably. I was now crying for myself.

All of my nightmares were coming true.

How could Emma have left me? Did she really have to leave me, now? She was my baby, my thread to my past, my hope for my future, and she brought me back the man that I always carried a torch for. If Emma's life carried so much meaning for me, what did her death mean?

Without Emma, there was going to be a longing that could never be filled. I thought about my other babies in the NICU, born premature and now thriving. One day at a time, each baby was eating, developing, gaining weight, and becoming stronger. Why couldn't that have been Emma? Why did she have to die? And why did she have to die on my watch, as my patient?

As I was weeping, I began to associate Emma's death with the possibility of William dying. It was a horrible habit that many doctors fall prey to, having a patient's death play mind games with you, making you feel that your loved ones will also pass away, in a similar manner. For a moment, I began to think that when I returned home, I wouldn't be able to wake up William. I'd check his pulse only to see that he had died too.

I opened my eyes, trying to rid myself of that thought. I quickly stood up. Thinking about my own son's death was not getting me anywhere.

Knowing that I needed to call the parents—and Alexander—I headed back into the hospital. As I walked toward the NICU, the voice in my head rang out like a rallying cry. *Come on, Lauren. Just do your fucking job. No one cares if your heart has been ripped out.*

At the NICU nurses' station, I got down to business. I first contacted the hospital administration and the coroner, notifying them of Emma's death. I would soon have to produce a lengthy report detailing not only her death but the care and treatment I provided in the hours leading up to her death. This would take me the better part of the day, and before any words were on a page, I was already nervous that Covenant's administration was not going to agree with my treatment approach.

I went back into Emma's room and stared at Wendy's cell phone number, written on the white board in Wendy's handwriting. I pulled out my cell phone from my green scrubs pocket and dialed the number. Wendy picked up, her voice groggy, just like mine only two hours earlier.

"Wendy, it's Dr. Leonard. Wendy, are you awake?"

It must have been a mother's instinct, as she immediately knew the reason for my call. She started screaming. There was a piercing wail that she let out, and Jason must have grabbed the phone because he began yelling, asking over and over again if Emma had died.

I'd made these calls before, especially late at night, and I knew it was best not to get too detailed. Jason and Wendy didn't need to know the exact medicines she took, or how labored her breathing was at the end of her life. All they were cursed to have to know was that the light of their life, their focus and fight for the last eight weeks, and what they thought was their future, was now completely washed away.

"Please come to the hospital if you can, so that you can hold Emma a final time before she is taken to the morgue," my voice cracking while giving them instructions.

Now both parents were crying through the phone, but they abruptly hung up, no doubt in a hurry to come see their child one last time.

Putting my phone back in my white coat pocket, I approached Emma's crib slowly. I stood over her, kissing her forehead as I sang lullabies to her, all swaddled and perfect. It felt so odd to see her completely motionless. Usually newborns and infants, even those born prematurely, stir in their sleep and move around their incubator or crib. But Emma, now turning a light shade of gray, looked like a fake doll of a baby, as opposed to a human life.

Twenty minutes later, I could hear Jason and Wendy coming into the NICU because their cries were echoing through the hall. I heard them run toward the room. As they entered Emma's room, Jason dove toward the crib while Wendy was too frightened to approach. Jason scooped up Emma and held her upright to his chest, his head buried into her, proclaiming, "My baby, my baby, my baby."

Slowly, Wendy made her way to Jason. I wanted to provide the parents private time to be together as a family of three, for the last time, so I slid toward the door. I turned back to look at Emma, and said a silent final goodbye, my heart breaking for all of us inside of this nightmare.

*****

As morning came around, the sun began streaming into the NICU. We could hear the birds chirping outside, and the day shift nurses were starting to arrive. With each medical professional that entered the hospital, they all wanted time with me to discuss Emma's death. In a ninety-nine-bed hospital, each patient becomes well-known. Everyone loved Emma, and so I had doctors and nurses coming to me with words of sorrow, encouragement, and prayer. With each colleague that offered their condolences, I quietly nodded, wondering if they would have provided the same care and treatment to Emma that I did in her final hours.

Although common among doctors, we have the bad habit of Monday morning quarterbacking medical cases, especially patient deaths. We all wonder if those deaths could have been prevented, had we been the doctor to treat them. Emma was very sick from the start, but with each person that came up to speak with me about Emma, I knew they were secretly thinking that they could have kept Emma alive.

"Have you called Dr. Smithton yet?" Dr. Wang asked. She was still hanging around the NICU, helping with paperwork even though her shift was about to end. We were standing at the nurses' station, and I wasn't very pleased that she kept hanging around.

"No, I still need to call Dr. Smithton," I said indifferently. "He doesn't know yet."

"I wonder how he'll react."

I shrugged. I didn't want to entertain this conversation with my colleague.

"I've got to call Dr. Smithton," I said, "and I've got to write out the death report for the Covenant Medical board, *and* I'm sleep deprived."

"Those reports are the worst," she said. "Do you need any

help?"

I knew it was a final platitude before she declared that her shift was ending. And I knew I was unnecessarily mad at Dr. Wang. She'd been helpful every step of the way. She didn't kill Emma, just like I didn't. But in the moment, it felt satisfying to be angry at her.

"No," I said, trying to smile and keep my anger at bay. "Thanks, though."

As Dr. Wang left the NICU, I knew that if I wanted any privacy at all for my call with Alexander, I was going to have to retreat to my office. On my way, I ran into what felt like a parade of people, all wanting to speak with me about Emma's death. I wanted to scream. Steele's words about my three crises kept running on repeat in the back of my mind. *I lost Emma. I'm having an affair. My marriage is crumbling.*

I wanted to scream for everyone to leave me alone, to give me time to think. But instead, I just kept walking to my office, relieved to be able to shut my door behind me and be alone.

I worked on Emma's death report for hours and hours when I saw the clock in my office turn to 8:00 a.m. I knew it was time to call Alexander. I was surprised that he hadn't at least texted by now to see about Emma's condition given our conversation the night before. I decided it didn't matter what Alexander's intentions were because Emma was now dead.

I purposefully didn't have his number preprogrammed into my phone, so I dialed his cell number and waited for the call to go through.

"Hi," he answered after the first ring. "How's Emma today?"

I thought I would be able to open the call without becoming emotional, but I hadn't anticipated Alexander saying 'today.'

"She died," I said, my voice cracking.

"Oh my God, she did?"

Alexander's voice was quiet, like he had just received a punch to the gut. He kept exhaling, breathing heavily as he hung on to everything I was saying as I relayed what had happened hours before. Perhaps he was also slowly surmising that his link to me, and his link to his past, was being ripped away from him.

And I knew he had a lot riding on Emma's second surgery, professionally. Not only had he told me in our last phone call, but a couple emails here and there detailed how he was going to have a bit of a speaking tour for pulmonary pediatric surgeons detailing Emma's case. That is, if Emma would have lived. It's a bit difficult to give a TED Talk and halfway through the speech say, 'Well, actually, the patient died before I got to do the final surgery.'

To my surprise, Alexander didn't make it about him. He didn't lament that Emma was his golden ticket to the speaking tour, and he didn't seem angry with me. My heart started beating out of my chest as he asked me about the medications I gave Emma prior to her death.

"That's what I would have done, too," he said encouragingly.

I held my breath as I told him that I wasn't there when Emma expired. Because it was Alexander, I went through the long story of taking William to swim practice and coming home to put him to sleep and being woken up at 2:00 a.m. because Emma's vitals were failing.

I finished the story, including contacting Emma's parents and writing out the death report for Covenant Medical.

"Well," Alexander replied after a long silence, "we lost her, kiddo."

For what felt like the hundredth time that week, I broke down. It was supposed to be Alexander, and me, and Emma. We were supposed to be a family. It was not supposed to turn out this way, not this time. I had my dream life taken from me once, and now, it was being taken from me again.

PART II

OCTOBER 1994

CHAPTER 15

MY MOM HANDED ME MY PURPLE PLASTIC LAUNDRY BASKET, with each piece of clothing carefully arranged by color. I looked down at the artistic masterpiece of my clothes, now freshly washed, dried, and neatly folded. I smiled. Just forty-eight hours before, I had brought home a heaping pile of dirty clothes that smelled like a mixture of alcohol and sweat. And now, all clean!

This has to be the best part of coming home from college, I thought, *the laundry.*

Second only to fresh clothes were all the home-cooked meals my dad made me that weekend. He spent hours making his famous chili—which I think he just stole from the Cincinnati Skyline chili recipe—and he packaged up some chocolate chip cookies in a Tupperware container for me to take back to school and share with my friends. But I'm sure he knew I'd likely dig into the cookies on the drive back.

"Do you have enough gas?" my mom asked as she stood in the driveway, watching me load up my Saturn to head back to campus.

"You guys just gassed it up for me yesterday!" I laughed. That was another great perk of coming home: free gas.

"It was so lovely having you home, Lauren," my mom said wistfully. "I feel like you've been at college so long now. You know, I thought your freshman year was going to be the hardest for me with you out of the house, but I think this year is tougher than the first. I didn't expect you to stay in school past your first year, and so knowing that you are back now for a second year, well, it makes it more real," she shared.

Or should I say, overshared.

I wanted to roll my eyes at her, but that couldn't be the way I left after such a nice weekend home, with parents who idolized me, just for being me. I understood her sadness from me being away at school; I was all my mom had. I was her only child, and she didn't work. And because she didn't work, my dad worked nonstop, so my mom didn't get to spend much time with him. She was obviously lonely, and I felt guilty for adding to that loneliness, but I really wanted to get back to Columbus. As great as being home was, it was no comparison to the amazing life I found myself living at Ohio State.

"I'll be back for Thanksgiving, Mom. That's only five weeks away. Or maybe you and Dad could come to Columbus for a football game in a couple weeks! The Buckeyes are ranked 14th in the country right now!" I became animated as I told her all about my season tickets, and the traditions of game day, including how my friends and I baked muffins for each game-day morning tailgate.

I knew this was going to go over my mom's head, as she didn't understand the culture of Division I collegiate football at a Big Ten school. The football fan life wasn't just watching a sport; it was a religion. As my mom stared blankly at me while I carried on, I realized I needed to get back to school instead of standing in the driveway making her feel sadder. I shrugged and gave her a quick hug.

"Thanks for all your support, Mom. I'll call you guys when I get back to campus."

"I love you sweetheart," my mom replied wistfully, likely feeling the loneliness about to set in.

I hopped in my car and started my two-hour drive back to school. During my drive along I-71, I listened to the Counting Crows album over and over as I kept remembering the image of my mom's confused face when I brought up Ohio State football. It made me realize how much I had changed in the past year. She probably didn't recognize the vibrant young woman now before her.

I was nineteen and felt like I had really grown into who I was meant to be. I had never felt like I belonged before now. In grade school, I hit five feet and nine inches tall by the time I was eleven. Because I towered over all the boys—and all the teachers—I was seen as intimidating. Everyone saw me as an outsider.

And high school was such a disaster, shrouded in embarrassment over not making the cheerleading squad when my best friend did. When it came time to think about colleges, I knew I wanted to go somewhere that I could invent myself anew. I'd banked on the hope that if I went away to school, my luck might change. I could be a small fish in a big pond, and no one would have any preconceived notions about me. I could carve my own path.

That's exactly what I wanted, and so I made it happen. I luckily got accepted to Ohio State University, and the first week on campus I decided to put myself out there, rushing Alpha Chi Omega. It was a long shot, but I made it! I couldn't believe the night we received invitation cards and keys, mine saying that I was indeed a new sister of the sorority. When I read that card, it was the happiest night of my life. I knew I belonged.

And this year got even better as I got to move into the sorority house, which was certainly a considerable upgrade from a second year in the dorms. Living in 'the house' with all my sorority sisters felt like I was living a dream.

I had friends, they liked me, and I fit in.

I grinned as I stared ahead on the road and blasted the volume on my stereo.

*****

As I pulled onto the Ohio State campus, I knew I didn't want to go straight to the sorority house. I wasn't sure if he would be home, but I wanted to stop by my boyfriend's apartment to see him. We had gone an entire three days without talking or seeing each other, and I missed him so much my heart was about to break.

As I pulled into his apartment complex and got out of the car, he must have heard me because he opened his window from the third floor and yelled down, "Hey Lauren! I can't believe you're here! I'll be right down!"

I smiled and watched as he descended three flights of dirty apartment complex stairs, dodging empty beer cans scattered around from what I assumed was a party from his neighbors the night before.

As he came closer, I decided to be adventurous. I started sprinting toward him, with a huge smile on my face, and jumped into his arms, wrapping my legs around his waist.

"Alexy!"

He spun me around, my hair swinging, and I laughed as I closed my eyes so as not to get dizzy. I held onto his shoulders as he slowly lowered my feet to the ground, our bodies pressed together and our eyes locked.

"I missed you, babe," I said lovingly.

"I missed you, too," he echoed. He looked at me so adoringly, like I held all the keys to his happiness. "I spent all weekend studying for that organic chemistry midterm, and I'm sick of it. I'm ready to throw my chem book off my balcony," he said as he gestured back toward his apartment. And then, he added, "I thought about you constantly this weekend."

We kissed, and I was hoping he'd invite me into his apartment. We'd promised not to see each other this weekend so that he could focus on his midterm. I didn't want to tell him, but that was the only reason I went home to see my parents. I knew that if I stayed on campus, I'd pressure Alexander to come to the sorority tailgate and to the parties after the football game. I didn't want him to feel torn between having fun and having to study.

Alexander was deeply committed to his academics and his pre-med major. We'd met in a healthcare political science class the first day of school in late August, and right away, I was taken with how seriously he took his studies. I'd often joked with him about how he should have gone to Harvard, but one night, when I made the joke, he'd looked me in the eye and said, "I applied."

For Alexander, the stakes were high. He wanted to be a doctor, which I thought was so aspirational. I too was taking similar pre-med classes, as my guidance counselor in high school suggested I might want to go into medicine because I enjoyed helping people. But deep down, I knew I was going to have to change my major. I wasn't as committed as he was and nowhere near as smart.

Alexander came from a long line of doctors. His brother was currently in med school in California. His father was a practicing neurologist. And most impressively, Alexander's uncle was a doctor who completed his residency in Dallas, Texas and treated JFK on the day that he was shot and killed. I guess Alexander's uncle removed a bullet from JFK's head. That's the story Alexander told me, and he told it with such regard, like he had no choice but to carry on the family tradition.

"I don't want to take you away from your chemistry prep," I said, beating Alexander to the punch. My body was still pressed up against his, and I was hoping he would cave in and invite me into his apartment.

"I know. How about I call you on Tuesday after my exam?"

That wasn't what I wanted to hear. But I had to respect the diligent student he was, and these few days in between would just make my heart grow fonder for him.

"Sounds good," I replied cheerfully, trying not to show my disappointment and make him feel guilty. Not seeing him also meant I didn't have Alexander to distract me from my own studying for midterms.

As I got back in my car to leave, he bent down and through the window he gave me a gentle kiss. "It was so good to see you. You are so hot. How the hell am I supposed to focus on chemistry now?" he joked.

"Think of me tonight when you're lying in bed," I cooed flirtatiously.

We said our goodbyes and on my drive to the sorority house, I couldn't stop smiling. I had the most amazing, brilliant boyfriend in the world. I couldn't believe he was mine. Sure, I'd had boyfriends in high school, but this was someone I saw myself with for the rest of my life.

Back at the sorority house, I immediately hugged all my friends as I entered the front door and saw they were sitting in the formal living room, catching each other up about their weekends.

Over dinner later in the large dining room, sitting at a long table that sat twenty under a gorgeous chandelier, the conversation turned toward me and my weekend.

"Did you miss Alexander? Did he call you at your parents'

house?" my friend Claire asked.

Claire took an interest in my relationship with Alexander because she just couldn't believe I was dating someone shorter than me. Alexander was only 5'7", but if I slouched just right and wore flip flops and flats when I was with him, we looked the same height. Still, she teased me relentlessly that the only reason I was dating a guy shorter than me was because he was going to be a doctor and make lots of money. Anytime she said this, I smirked and rolled my eyes, although secretly I did daydream about us living in a big mansion. I imagined me supporting him around the house with a bunch of kids while he led a large medical practice.

"Yeah, he chose studying over me," I said with a sigh, half melancholic and half proud that the sorority sisters were hanging on my every word.

"Doesn't he know who he's dating?" Sarah joked.

I laughed. "He should know there are a couple guys over there that would love to hang out with me right now," I said confidently, pointing my finger toward the front door, a nod to the guys at the fraternity house across the street.

Feeling a quick jolt of guilt, I promptly changed the subject.

"Hey, let's do a movie night in the den," I suggested, still commanding the attention of all the sisters at the table. "Let's watch something fun."

"Your choice, Lauren!" Caroline, the most diplomatic sorority sister, declared.

"Let's watch that brand-new show, ER, I think Ashley taped it."

ER was a new obsession of the sorority house, about a bunch of doctors working in a hospital. We'd only seen the pilot episode, and ironically, the show made me excited for Alexander to become a doctor, but not myself, another reason why I was questioning if I should be majoring in pre-med.

We decided on watching that show and I made popcorn for all the girls. Around fifteen of us snuggled up together in front of the TV wrapped in blankets, with not a care in the world, just happy to have each other, and our futures.

CHAPTER 16

I COUNTED DOWN THE HOURS UNTIL TUESDAY at four o'clock sharp. That was the exact moment that Alexander would be finishing his organic chemistry midterm, and we could be reunited shortly thereafter. I'd anticipated spending the afternoon at the student memorial union studying with friends but decided instead to stay at the sorority house to wait for Alexander's call.

I had a plan for when he called. I was going to float the idea of him coming to a party hosted by our house and a neighboring fraternity. Our sorority didn't allow for parties at the sorority house, so all 50-plus girls usually walked just across the street to the frat to be able to drink. While Alexander wasn't in a frat, I was sure they'd let him in if I was with him. Plus, going to this party might be a good way for him to unwind from his midterm and all the stress he put himself under.

I was right on the money about Alexander calling. My phone started ringing at 4:28 p.m. I shared a room with two other girls in the house, but I had my own phone, which was really lucky considering some girls had to share one. I smiled even before I picked up because I knew Alexander was calling me the moment he got back to his apartment.

"Lauren, ugh, you're never going to believe it!" Alexander blurted out as soon as I picked up. He sounded mentally drained. "That test was so hard."

Although I should have been a good girlfriend and pumped him up, my heart dropped as I realized that next year, when I was a junior like Alexander was now, I would, in theory, have to take the same organic chemistry class. Already in my sophomore year, the pre-med classes were getting too difficult for me to comprehend, much less excel in. I found myself jealous of my sorority sisters who were majoring in merchandising, psychology, or communications. Their classes seemed so interesting and fun. And here I was learning science, but my heart was only half in it. If I was honest with myself, there was no way in hell I was ever going to graduate from pre-med. I didn't have the stamina, the intelligence, or the drive like my classmates did. I recognized how Alexander felt he was destined for medicine. I just simply didn't feel that way at all.

"Oh, Alexy," I purred. "I'm sure you did great! You're so smart. And you studied so hard."

"I thought about you like five times during the test," Alexander admitted, sounding like he was smiling behind his phone as well and purposefully changing subjects to get off the topic of his midterm performance.

"I know," I replied, hoping he would ask me to come over. "I miss you so much, too."

He didn't mention anything about us seeing each other, so I dove into telling him about the sorority-fraternity mixer that we were having tomorrow night. "Do you want to come with me?" I asked as I finished relaying the details.

"Tomorrow night, like Wednesday? A school night?" he asked incredulously.

"Well, yeah, but your midterm is over, and I think it would be good for you to relax," I said, trying to sell him on the idea. "It'll be fun!"

"Okay..." Alexander trailed off, sounding less than enthusiastic.

"Perfect, well, why don't you be at the sorority house at eight o'clock tomorrow night, and we can walk over to the frat house together," I instructed, hoping he wouldn't think that was too late. In reality, we would likely be the first ones at the party.

"Okay," he said again, this time with a little more energy. "It'll be great to see you."

After we hung up, I sat there in my bed, looking out my open window at the long, tree-lined street. The crisp October breeze carried the sounds of the frat guys playing football on the front lawn and the neighboring sorority houses practicing their cheers for the home game this weekend. I really loved this Greek life, but I also felt a bit of what I could hear in Alexander's voice, that we lived in two different worlds on campus. I was the social butterfly, and Alexander was the bookworm.

But it didn't matter to me. I loved Alexander so much, and I knew he was the guy for me, and we were making it work.

*****

Like clockwork, Alexander walked up the steps to the sorority house right at 8:00 p.m. He was dressed in khakis and a blue button-down shirt. He looked like he was going for an interview, not attending a fraternity party. Most of the junior guys wore head-to-toe Abercrombie & Fitch—plaid shirts and jeans— so Alexander was unequivocally going to stick out like a sore thumb. To make matters worse, he was wearing tennis shoes with his khakis—and not the cool kind of tennis shoes.

As I watched him approach the house from my bedroom window, a warm feeling came over my body and I felt even more in love with Alexander. I didn't care if the sorority girls didn't see in him what I did. I also didn't care if the frat guys made fun of him. Alexander was one in a million, and I loved that I could open him up to this cool college life that he didn't usually get exposure to. So what if he didn't look the part? I was going to be on his arm, and in my tight black pants and cropped striped thermal turtleneck, I looked the part for both of us.

I met Alexander on the sorority house porch, which was a massive wraparound with plenty of white wicker rocking chairs that were already occupied with girls sitting in guys laps. Alexander and I made our way to the corner of the porch, and I gave him a long kiss.

"I didn't know what to wear," Alexander said as our lips

parted, which I had guessed from his outfit choice.

"You're perfect," I said.

Moments later, a big group of girls and a few guys decided it was time to head across the street to the mixer.

"Let's party!" Caroline shouted as she led the way for all of us to start our evening.

As we descended the stairs on the porch, Alexander suddenly tripped and I watched as in what felt like slow motion, he toppled down the stairs. His khakis got dirty at the knee, and he looked up at me, mortified.

Paul, Caroline's boyfriend, stifled a laugh as he towered over Alexander. He extended his hand and said, "Hey man, you okay?"

Alexander took his hand, got up and dusted himself off, realizing that his khakis now had a rip in them at the knee. I grabbed his hand as we walked across the street. I squeezed his hand, hoping to somehow pass him a little self-confidence from my body to his likely bruised ego.

As we approached the fraternity house lawn, it was such a stark contrast from the beautiful sorority house we had just exited. The dichotomy of the beat-up, muddy lawn with beer cans strewn about and cigarette butts everywhere. I turned my head back toward my sorority house, the green grass and manicured shrubs, the white pillars with fresh paint.

We dodged the beer cans as we made our way to the door, having to wait to enter while the fraternity president checked off names from his clipboard list, one by one. I'd put Alexander's name on the list as my guest, so I wasn't worried, but Alexander seemed like he was holding his breath the entire time we waited in line. Finally, when we got to the front of the line and the president let us inside, Alexander visibly breathed a sigh of relief.

The fraternity house smelled of only one thing: alcohol. It was like we'd entered a distillery. We made our way to the makeshift bar in the large dining room. It was as masculine as could be: wooden walls, a wooden ceiling, and deer heads mounted above the fireplace. The music was already blaring, and Alexander asked me what I wanted to drink.

"Vodka soda!" I answered as I leaned toward his ear, trying not to yell.

When we got up to the bar, Alexander started making us drinks. I noticed his hands were fidgeting, and he made no eye contact with any of the fraternity brothers, who were trying to ask him if he was part of a neighboring fraternity.

I drank my vodka soda in about ten minutes as Alexander and I stood around. He wasn't really interacting with anyone, not even me.

"Sweetie, can you get me a refill?" I asked Alexander as I handed him my red Solo cup. He did, bringing himself back another drink as well. This time it was me breathing a sigh of relief, hoping that Alexander would enjoy the party with another drink in him.

Although I assumed Alexander would loosen up after a couple of drinks, I was finding that not to be the case. At all. At first, we were playing hacky sack, then dancing, then snooping around the fraternity house looking for snacks. The longer the night went on, the more he seemed like a fish out of water. I didn't know what I was doing wrong. I'd thought this party was just what he needed to relax and have fun.

"You hate it here, don't you?" I finally said, yelling into Alexander's ear again as we were back out on the dance floor.

"I don't hate it because I'm with you," Alexander yelled back diplomatically.

We went to a quieter part of the fraternity house and now, away from Nirvana blasting through the speakers, and with a couple drinks in me, I became a bit more brazen.

"You haven't talked with anyone, and you aren't having any fun," I complained like a child.

"Lauren, I don't get to have fun like this," Alexander retorted. "I wish I could cut loose, but I have my molecular genetics class at eight tomorrow morning, and you know I just got that new job at the student health center that starts next week. I wish I could blow off steam like this, but it's hard for me."

"Fine," I muttered, then shrugged. "So...what do you want to do?"

I could tell from the way he was being so attentive with me and always sliding his arm around my waist that it wasn't me that he had a problem with. Maybe he'd suggest we go to the diner around the corner.

"How about we go back to my apartment?"

"Of course," I replied as I touched his cheek with my hand. *Way better than the diner!*

We started weaving between everyone on our way out, the stuffiness and the smell of sweat wafting through the house. I waved to my sorority sisters and gave them a wink, a silent acknowledgment that Alexander and I were going back to his place.

Once outside it was such a beautiful autumn night, the contrast of the crisp air a heavenly reprieve from the musty, loud setting we had just left. Since Alexander lived less than a mile off-campus, we decided to walk to his apartment instead of taking the campus bus.

"Why don't you like to go to parties?" I asked as we strolled down the sidewalk. My ears were still pounding from being in the frat house with music that loud. "Putting studying on the back burner for one night isn't going to kill your academic career."

I waited for his reply, trying not to stare at his profile as we walked. Although thrilled he wanted me to go home with him, I still didn't understand why he couldn't enjoy being out and having fun.

"You know," I said when he still didn't open up, "those parties could be fun if you allowed them to be."

Instead of answering my question, he decided to turn the tables on me. "Lauren, you know you are so much better than that party, right?" Alexander said as we walked, turning his head toward me.

I stopped walking. "I like my sorority sisters and the Greek life is fun," I said. Alexander wasn't a fan of the Greek life, but I certainly had a right to enjoy it. Why would he insinuate a party was beneath me?

"You have no idea how much more you could be," he said, almost under his breath, staring me in the eye.

"Are you saying you don't like who I am?" I shot back, placing my hands on my chest, the alcohol helping me find my argument.

We stood there, turned toward one another, neither one of us moving. We were ready to have this fight and deeply committed to ignoring the position of the other person.

"I'm just saying that you don't need to wear tight black pants and cram yourself between sweaty frat guys and dance with your girlfriends every night. I know you think I'm just saying this because I'm jealous, but I'm telling you, Lauren, you are better than that. You are better than them. You're really special, and you're really smart. You don't think you are, but you are." And then he ended with the zinger, "You could be a doctor one day."

Deep down, part of me knew he was right. I was special, and I could be a doctor.

But I also knew he was wrong about the life I was leading. It was all too confusing, especially while tipsy. What I really heard was that Alexander didn't love me. That I wasn't as committed to medicine as he was, and that any girlfriend of his had to be just as aspirational as he was. It was all I could hear. If we were going to continue the night, I had to shake it off, and so we continued walking together, now in silence, me extending my hand for him to hold.

As we got to his apartment complex and Alexander unlocked his apartment door, he yelled, "Jordan?"

There was no response. I was immediately thankful to see that his roommate, Jordan, wasn't there. The only person that seemed more into becoming a doctor than Alexander was Jordan. They'd met in a physics class and knew immediately that they would get along as roommates. No loud music, no drunken nights, no bringing girls home. Except, I guess, for right now. There was a note on the kitchen counter from Jordan, that he was pulling an all-nighter in the library and that there was leftover pizza in the refrigerator.

With his roommate gone, Alexander and I brushed the chips off our shoulders, and we knew the great opportunity that was given to us: having the apartment to ourselves. We'd only had sex once before, about a month ago. We'd been dating about six weeks at that time, and I knew I wanted to give my virginity to him. It was so important to me that I have sex for the first time with someone I loved. Most of my sorority sisters had lost their virginity their freshman year or in high school, but I just didn't find anyone worth losing my virginity to. Yet when Alexander and I started dating, I couldn't wait, and sex with him felt so amazing. I finally understood what all the hype was about.

Alexander, unfortunately, had had sex before, with a girlfriend two years ago during his freshman year. She was still a student on campus, and I always feared running into her. I also feared that he still liked her. *What if she's prettier than me?* I wondered for the first time in a while. *What if she was better at sex than I am? What if Alexander thinks about her while he has sex with me?*

My thoughts started to run wild, so I decided that before we went into his bedroom, I needed another drink. I headed straight for his refrigerator, but as I opened the door, I quickly saw that there was only soda and pizza. I laughed to myself. Alexander's fridge was probably the only one on campus without a single drop of alcohol.

I made my way back to the living room, and Alexander was sitting on his futon, probably still unnerved from the fraternity party and our fight. I stood before him, and he looked up at me, and I knew from the look in his eyes that he wanted me.

The alcohol still keeping me brave, I straddled him on his futon, my black pants stretching to the limit, and we started kissing. He lifted me slightly and laid me down on the couch. He started to lift my shirt over my head.

"No, no, let's go into your bedroom."

He picked me up and carried me to his room, gently placing me on his bed. Alexander was so tender with me; he treated my body like a delicate flower. He undressed me slowly, and although he may have lacked confidence back at the frat house, he exuded so much assertiveness with me physically now. He began kissing me all over.

"Do you want to have sex?" he whispered in my ear, his voice low and determined.

"Yes."

Alexander got up out of the bed and undressed himself, never taking his eyes off me and my naked body. "Your body is like Cindy Crawford's," Alexander said cutely. I smiled as I watched him turn on a Janet Jackson song on his CD player and pull a condom out of his drawer.

As Alexander made his way back to the bed and climbed on top of me, and then into me, the rest of the world faded away. There was no organic chemistry midterm, or sorority house, or impossible major. Hell, there wasn't even college. There was just Alexander and I, and our undying love. I blocked out of my mind that we were two different people living two different lives at OSU. Tonight, we were one, as Janet Jackson's lyrics of "That's The Way Love Goes" echoed throughout his bedroom.

I was so in love.

CHAPTER 17

As the days turned cooler and the red leaves fell from the trees, I was in my collegiate element. Our football team was winning each Saturday, Alexander and I were spending all our free time together, and my sorority events took my mind off the fact that I was struggling in my classes. Thanksgiving was almost upon us, and Alexander and I decided to spend the holiday together at my parents' house.

I really wanted my parents to meet him. I'd already told them what a great guy he was and how I just knew that they were going to be so impressed by his intelligence. And then for Christmas, Alexander and I had already planned on me meeting his family and spending a couple days with them during the extended break. I felt so lucky to have a boyfriend during the holiday season, someone to experience all the traditions with.

And now that we were meeting each other's families, it made me more confident in how serious this relationship really was. I was so proud that I was going to be the first girl Alexander brought home to meet his parents. Hopefully, I would also be the last.

As we neared the middle of November, both Alexander and I fell under the weather. He seemed to be able to shake it, but without my mom there to take care of me, I was extremely fatigued for the better part of two weeks. I had all the classic symptoms of a bad cold. One night, I was too exhausted to go to his apartment so, being the sweet guy he was, Alexander showed up unexpectedly at the sorority house with a huge container of chicken noodle soup.

"Why don't you go to the student health center?"

We were standing in the commons of the sorority house, girls buzzing about around us. I looked horrible in my gray sweatpants and an oversized red Ohio State hoodie, my hair in a ponytail, not brushed in over forty-eight hours. He handed me the soup, and the smell alone was making my stomach turn.

"I don't know, Alexy, I just feel so shitty," I whined, "and I can't even go to my classes or the sorority events."

"Why don't I take you now to the health center to get checked out? I know all the good nurses and doctors," he implored.

For a moment, I thought Alexander might just want me to go get checked out so he could brag about his new job there. I wasn't sure if he was so eager to help me because he didn't like to see me sick, because he wanted me to be proud of his new job, or if he enjoyed medicine and the idea of treatment so much that this was going to be a 'fun night out' for him. At any rate, I decided that if I wanted to feel better, I should go get an antibiotic.

"Okay," I said. "I'll go."

Alexander seemed relieved that I agreed with his suggestion. A soft smile drew across his face as he put his arm around me. We headed out the door, having abandoned the soup he brought me.

We took the bus to the health center, which was our only health care facility on campus and mimicked an urgent care. Upon walking inside, it seemed we were the only ones there, a reminder that thousands and thousands of college kids were out living their life, and here we were in this gray, austere facility with posters all around detailing the deteriorating effects of drug use.

The workers behind the desk all came up to Alexander.

"Hey man, how's it going?" one of the employees said to Alexander as they gave each other high-fives. Looking at me, and then back at Alexander, the health worker said, "It's not your night to work, is it?"

"Um, no, this is my girlfriend, Lauren," Alexander said, gesturing toward me. "She's been sick for about two weeks. I think she's presenting symptoms of acute sinusitis, and I suggested she come get checked out," he explained for me. I was embarrassed that his co-workers were seeing me in my sweats, with no makeup and my hair pulled back. I made a silent promise to myself that at some point I would make sure to visit Alexander at work looking all cute and girly.

Since the health center had no other patients, I got all the attention and was asked about my symptoms as I filled out what felt like form after form. We were then led back to a patient room to see the nurse. As soon as we were alone together in the room, Alexander seemed in his element. He was upbeat and talking fast, explaining all about the health center's policies and which co-workers he liked best. He sat in a folding chair in the corner of the small patient room, tapping his feet on the floor while he hummed the song that had been playing in the waiting room. He smiled at me as I mentioned that he was probably the smartest worker here.

Within only a couple minutes, an older nurse with caked-on makeup walked into the room. She introduced herself as Dina, and then smiled at Alexander.

"So, you know this fella, huh?" Nurse Dina said as she gestured to Alexander in the corner. I will say he's one of my favorite students that works here, but how did he get a girl this pretty to date is what I want to know…." she said, laughing at her own joke.

I knew Nurse Dina was trying to put both Alexander and I at ease, and I laughed back and replied, "Usually I'm prettier than this!"

She picked up a clip board from the table and pivoted to asking me about my symptoms. I told her about my stuffy nose, and headache, and sore throat. She nodded and wrote down those words on the clip board. I ended by telling her that the worst part was being nauseous each morning into the afternoon.

Both the nurse and Alexander, in unison, exclaimed, "Nausea?!"

Their eyes now wide, they were silent, waiting for me to

answer.

"I've been nauseous for the past week, and I haven't wanted to eat, it just makes me sick to think about," I said, getting nauseous at talking about getting nauseous. "I'm thinking maybe it's due to the sinus infection? I think I have a sinus infection because I can't smell or taste, but I really just have no interest in eating thanks to the nausea."

I could tell that the nurse and Alexander didn't understand my symptoms. Nurse Dina now had a furrowed brow, and Alexander was leaning forward in his chair.

"When was your last period?" the nurse asked, staring me in the eye.

Embarrassed, my eyes shifted to Alexander. He looked like a deer in the headlights, and I knew where this was going. I didn't know my last period, but I knew that I wasn't pregnant.

"I'm not sure exactly when my last period was…sometime last month," I responded idiotically. "I don't really keep track that closely."

"Are you on birth control?" the nurse asked, asking the question to both me and Alexander.

We nodded. "We use a condom, every time," I said quietly.

What I didn't voice was that I'd had every intention of using two forms of birth control, like the birth control pill, but to be honest, I was afraid of the weight gain. I didn't let the number on the scale rule my life, but I had seen so many of my high school friends and my college sorority sisters balloon up once they took the pill. My doctor back home told me that wasn't even true, that birth control pills didn't cause weight gain, but I didn't want to chance it. I thought maybe Alexander and I could just use condoms. I'd talked with Alexander about it one night before we decided to have sex, and he seemed comfortable with it. But now, looking at him in the corner, I could read his mind. He was definitely rethinking our birth control strategy.

"I'd like to give you a pregnancy test, just to rule it out," Nurse Dina said, now saying the P-word aloud while simultaneously writing something on her clipboard. She looked up at me again, this time with a softer tone, and said, "Lauren, why don't you provide me a urine sample, and we'll have the results in about five minutes. And then we can treat your cold symptoms."

Mortified, I hopped off the exam table and followed her to the hallway bathroom. She gave me a cup, a wipe, and detailed instructions on how to provide the urine sample. As I shut the door behind me in the bathroom and peed awkwardly into the cup, I could not believe this was happening.

I am not pregnant, I told myself, my heart pounding in my chest. *Alexander and I use birth control. We don't even have sex that often. This is all a misunderstanding. I just have a cold. I just need antibiotics, then I'll be fine.*

I twisted the lid on my sample, cleaned off the cup so it looked presentable, opened the bathroom door, and handed the sample to Dina. Again, she looked in my eyes and with her bright red lipstick, she smiled and said, "Thanks, hun. Head back into the room and I'll be there in a minute."

I went back to the patient room and climbed back onto the exam table. Now alone with Alexander, he started peppering me with questions.

"Do you think you're pregnant? Did you ever feel the condom breaking in you? When you kept telling me you weren't eating this week, was it because you were that nauseous? Has that ever been a symptom for you before when you had a cold? Did the nurse say when we would know the results?"

He finally ended his barrage of questions, and instead of answering, I decided I needed to change the narrative.

"Alexy," I said quietly and deliberately, "I am here for medicine for my cold, and in a few days, I'm going to feel so much better. And in less than a week, we're going home to my parents' house for Thanksgiving, and I think you'll love the Thanksgiving dinner my dad is going to make."

Alexander let out a big sigh, seeming to relax as he sat back down in his folding chair and rested his head against the wall. We started talking logistics about Thanksgiving and what time we would leave the Wednesday before. I was just about to ask him which pie he liked best when the nurse came into the room, this time without her clipboard. She carefully turned her back to us and shut the door. She did a 180 again, turned to face us, and clasped her hands together at her waist.

"I have big news," she said, trying to be enthusiastic but falling short. "Lauren, your pregnancy test is positive. You're pregnant."

I was speechless. I couldn't find any words to come out of my mouth, but my jaw was agape, and I turned my head to Alexander, who now looked white as a ghost. He seemed so small, sitting on that folding chair in the corner, his shoulders now hunched and looking down between his legs. Neither one of us said anything. It was too difficult to talk and do the math in our head about what this meant for the rest of our lives.

And so, Dina filled the silence by talking about what a positive pregnancy test means, like we were idiots.

"Lauren, you'll want to make sure you get healthcare during this pregnancy. You need to schedule an appointment with an OBGYN for the seven-week mark, based upon when you think you may have conceived," she instructed.

I sat there, stunned, with my heart beating so fast that I could feel my ears pulsing. I was starting to sweat, and my oversized Ohio State hoodie felt like it was cutting off my circulation.

"Do the cold symptoms still mean I have a cold, in addition to being pregnant?" I asked, confused.

"It's possible," the nurse replied. "I'd like to hold off on any cold medication for you though, since you are pregnant."

Alexander looked at Nurse Dina and nodded, his first attempt at body language since we heard the news. Alexander then glanced off into space, no doubt calculating how he was going to live the life he had planned for himself while also being a young father.

Once we had all the printouts and the pregnancy test report, we headed back to the lobby of the student medical center, in complete shock. The same co-workers that were shaking hands with Alexander when we came in were now, with this new medical report, not even making eye contact with him. As we left, the nurse and attending doctor told Alexander that they looked forward to seeing him on his shift tomorrow, and he nodded robotically.

Once outside, the cold breeze hit us both hard, and I started shivering. Alexander took off his beanie and put it over my head.

"I need my babies to stay warm," he said with a small smile.

All at once, I started sobbing, outside on the frigid November night, in the middle of the Ohio State campus. Other students walking by could see and hear me, but I didn't care. I was *pregnant*. I didn't know if this meant that my life was over or that my life had just begun. I just knew that in eight months, I was going to do the most important thing I'd ever do in my life, and that I had the man I loved by my side to help me do it.

Alexander started to wipe away my tears. "Why don't we go get pizza?"

My stomach flip-flopped at the thought of pizza, once my favorite food. I didn't have the heart to tell Alexander that I was too nauseous, so I agreed. He put his arm around my waist and leaned his head into mine, silently reminding me that everything was going to be okay.

CHAPTER 18

A WEEK LATER, MY COLD WAS GONE, my nausea was lifting, and Thanksgiving was upon us. To say that I was 'thankful' was an absolute understatement. In a week's time, the shock wore off for both Alexander and me. We were having a baby, and I was getting more and more elated by the day. Alexander and I were spending each evening together, harboring our little secret and telling each other what fantastic parents we'd be. I hadn't told anyone at school yet, and I kept up my normal routine, participating in all the sorority events and going to classes. Besides abstaining from alcohol, my life looked similar to before I was pregnant. But I couldn't shake that I was withholding this big secret from all my sorority sisters, and I knew that in due time, I wouldn't be living in the sorority house anymore. It was difficult to keep up my friendship with all the girls knowing that soon enough, I would want to move out.

I was looking forward to being home in Jacobs for the holiday. I yearned to sleep in my childhood bedroom and eat my dad's home-cooked meals and introduce Alexander to my hometown life.

Alexander and I decided that with him coming home for the holidays, we should tell my parents. I was six weeks pregnant, and it was killing me that I hadn't disclosed my pregnancy to them. I contemplated calling them from school to give them the news, but I wanted it to be in person, and I wanted Alexander with me when I did it.

I think in some masochistic way, Alexander wanted to be thrown into the fire, standing by my side when I delivered the news to my parents. He'd told me that he assumed they would be upset and that he wanted to be there for support. But I knew my parents so well. I wasn't afraid of their reaction; they would be extremely supportive. They might not be thrilled initially, but I knew that telling them over Thanksgiving would be much easier for me, and that's all I could think about. I wouldn't have to keep a secret from them, and they could show Alexander that he didn't have anything to be afraid of. *My parents are great people,* I thought.

As we were closing the trunk of my car and ready to head to Jacobs, Alexander offered to drive for the two-hour trip. At first, I thought he was being a gentleman, but halfway through the drive, he asked me to quiz him from a worksheet he had in his backpack. It was again for his organic chemistry class, and even though I could see both the questions and the answers, the content made absolutely no sense to me.

If my heart hadn't been in my studies during this, my sophomore year, it sure as hell wasn't a focus now that I was pregnant. I daydreamed about finishing my college classes for the rest of 1994 and then not enrolling for the spring semester. The baby was due in June 1995, and so although it was *possible* for me to take a full course load next semester, I just didn't see that it would be *probable*.

I chose not to mention these thoughts to Alexander during our car ride, instead focusing on his quiz sheet. As I read off the questions, I could tell he didn't have a firm grasp on this material, certainly not like he usually did. I felt sorry for him every time he gently punched the steering wheel, trying to recall the various compositions of carbon-containing compounds.

"Why don't we take a break from the quizzing? We could talk about the baby a little bit," I suggested.

"Okay," Alexander said as he watched me put the quiz sheet back into his book bag. I felt a bit guilty as I had been pulling him away from his studies each night to talk about the pregnancy, my symptoms, and our future. Was that why now he had trouble getting through his chemistry worksheet?

"I know there is a lot that hasn't been decided yet, but I've really enjoyed our talks about the baby this week."

"Yeah, I'm excited," Alexander said as he looked over at me. "I know that it isn't going to be easy, and we've both had to rise to the occasion, becoming adults overnight."

Certainly, Alexander was already so mature, but his commitment now was to being emotionally available for me and less absorbed solely in his studies.

"I like becoming an adult overnight. It makes me feel closer to you, since you're so mature." I smiled while looking at him. "I know my social life with the sorority is going to come to a halt."

We both understood the sacrifices that we were going to have to make.

"To me, it's worth it," I continued. "We are a team, we believe in one another, and we are going to make it, as a young family of three." I looked over at Alexander for affirmation.

"Yes, we are," he said as he grabbed my hand.

As we exited the highway and merged onto the winding roads near Jacobs, I stared out the window. The trees were barren now, a warning for the upcoming cold months. I loved college, but I also missed the feeling of my hometown.

"Have you thought of a name for the baby?" I asked, turning to Alexander.

"Alexandria," he said softly, smirking.

"Actually," I said excitedly, "that was a name I had too! But not for our first child. I kind of want four girls, and I want to name them all long-syllable girl names and then call them short-syllable boy names as nicknames. So, I want Samantha, Alexandria, Josephine, and Victoria. And then we would call them Sam, Alex, Joe, and Vic."

"Wow, you've really thought a lot about this, haven't you," Alexander said, surprised, now turning his head toward me and then back to the road.

I blushed. I couldn't tell if he was referring to my thoughts on the names or my thoughts about us having four children together. The fact was that I'd been thinking of this moment for my entire life. Although I didn't purposefully get pregnant, I somehow felt like this pregnancy was meant to be. Why did God choose me to have a baby, now?

There has to be a reason, I thought. *This is all meant to be. Little Sam will be the biggest blessing of my life.*

✶✶✶✶✶

We'd only been home an hour with my parents when I got antsy to tell them about my pregnancy. My dad was sitting at the kitchen table with Alexander, making small talk. He was asking Alexander all about his classes, impressed with his course load and his part-time job at the student medical center.

"With all your studying and your job, do you have any time to go to the football games?" my dad asked. I smiled. They were weaving in and out of topics, and my dad was now onto sports. Alexander was mimicking my dad's temperament during the discussion, agreeing with everything my dad said and nodding with every point my dad made.

My mom and I were in the kitchen, prepping for the Thanksgiving meal the next day. We were rolling out the dough for the apple pie crust, and as my mom leaned in to sprinkle a little sugar on the dough, I almost whispered to her that I was pregnant. I felt guilty keeping this secret from my parents for even one hour, and I just wanted it out in the open.

"Rob, honey, do you want one can of apple filling and one can of raspberry filling?" my mom called. "Or do you want to stick with just the apple?" Then, turning her gaze to Alexander, she said, "And sweetheart, do you like apple pie?"

Both my dad and Alexander looked up at us in the kitchen with our aprons on and smiled, confirming they liked any type of pie we might make for them.

While my mom started opening the cans, I couldn't help but stare at Alexander. This scene felt like a Norman Rockwell painting. Everyone home for the holiday, making a home-cooked meal, happy to be together. I could tell my parents were already smitten with Alexander and in awe of his brilliance.

I was so overjoyed to be home, partaking in all the Thanksgiving traditions I'd grown to love, including helping bake the pies. And to top it off, I had a baby growing inside of me, a baby that was going to bring so much joy to the four of us and add another generation to the family.

*****

That night, after dinner had been served, my mom suggested that we 'retreat to the living room for coffee and dessert.' This was a great deal of pomp and circumstance, definitely aimed at Alexander. Traditionally, we never sat in the formal living room, and my mom had never before used the word 'retreat.' We usually sat in our den, which had wood paneled walls and a couple of brown suede sofas. The living room had no TV and no comfy couch but looked prettier. Maybe my mom sensed a big discussion was about to take place.

As Alexander, my parents, and I all sat in high-back chairs

in our living room, coffee in hand and dessert bowls in our lap, I smiled at the formality of it all. Not just my mom trying to be fancy, but the fact that most of my college friends were all in their Ohio hometowns, like me, likely on their way to their local bar for 'blackout Wednesday.' And yet here I was, listening to classical music from my mom's cassette player while I sat in a formal room I wasn't even allowed to enter as a child.

Even though Alexander was devouring his ice cream and berries, I could tell he was nervous. He knew that at any moment, I could go and announce my pregnancy. And so, I decided to put him out of his misery and use this opportunity, with the classical music as a calming influence, to share the news.

"Mom, Dad," I said, "Alexander and I are really excited to be here for Thanksgiving."

My parents smiled at me, oblivious to the fact that this was the opening to something bigger.

"Well, the pleasure is all ours, sugar," my dad replied as he scooped up another spoonful of his mint chocolate chip ice cream.

I decided I had to say it now and say it rather fast, so that my parents didn't interrupt me again. "And…we also wanted to come home for Thanksgiving to let you know we have great news! I'm pregnant. I know it's a surprise, and we weren't expecting it, but Alexander and I are very excited!" My voice rose at the end, hoping that my parents would consider my pregnancy to be a high note too.

I looked over at Alexander. He was looking down into his empty bowl. I looked back to my parents, who were now also looking at Alexander, staring at him like a predator who got their daughter knocked up.

My parents were speechless, and I knew I had to make this right. I had to make my parents see that everything was going to be okay. If I believed it, I could get them to believe it, too.

"Alexander and I took a few days to come to terms with it too," I said, nodding my head empathetically. "But we realized this is the biggest blessing in the world. I was meant to be a mom, and a young mom. Alexander was meant to be a father and a doctor. I look forward to being back on campus for the spring semester, not taking classes but working as a secretary in the student memorial union and helping Alexander with his studies."

That part about being a secretary was made up, but I hoped it would calm any financial fears that might be bubbling up in my parents' heads.

I was waiting for my parents to answer, but it was almost as if they were waiting on additional information before they could make their conclusion. And so, I gave one last rallying cry and said, "God knew what He was doing when He brought Alexander and me together. God knew what He was doing when he gave us this opportunity to have a baby."

Alexander, now surely feeling like he needed to cement his position, lifted his head to look at my parents. "We feel God is guiding us," he said. "And I love your daughter, and I am committed to becoming a father, and taking care of Lauren, and becoming a physician to provide for us."

Of course, it was Alexander's statement that did it for my parents. They hadn't spoken in what felt like eons, but with Alexander's tiny overture, my parents both lit up and congratulated us. My mom's eyes teared up as she called herself a grandma and came over to hug me. She was careful not to 'press on the baby' during her hug, and my dad shook Alexander's hand.

"You guys are going to have a long road ahead. Having a baby is tough, but you two are wise beyond your years, and love will get you through," my dad said confidently. "You know that both your mom and I will be there in any way we can to support you."

The four of us went in for a group hug, and I felt like the pieces of my life were fitting neatly together, just like a puzzle. I had it all. I had a boyfriend I loved. I had two wonderful, supportive parents. And most importantly, I had a new purpose for my life—to be a mother. I knew I could do it, and as I embraced my family, I was confident that the four of us would make the most amazing team.

My heart was exploding, and my destiny was here.

CHAPTER 19

"SWEETIE, CAN YOU COME HELP ME WITH THESE BAGS?" my mom yelled from the kitchen.

I was sitting in the den with my dad, watching football to pass the time until Alexander was done studying. After the game and his studying, we were going to go out to eat for our last day home on Thanksgiving break, as we were all now sick of the Thanksgiving leftovers.

"Just a sec!" I called out as I stood up from the couch. "Do you want anything from the kitchen, Dad?"

"Oh, no, I'm fine. Thanks," he replied, staring straight at the game on TV.

I walked into the kitchen to find the door to the garage open and my mom nowhere in sight. I poked my head into the garage and saw her head down in the trunk of her car, parsing through bags.

"What did you need, Mom?" I asked, walking over to her. The concrete garage floor was cold even through my thick socks and so I stood on my tip toes.

"Oh, Lauren, you'll never guess what I found!" my mom said proudly. She put her hands through the openings of what looked like a million plastic bags, and then she held them all up. There was a big red K on them, the telltale sign she'd been at K-Mart. It was one of the few big box stores we had in Jacobs. Before I had a chance to say anything, she handed me one of the bags. "Go ahead, look!"

I opened one of the bags and found myself staring down at a dozen shades of pink. "What's all this?" I asked, glancing up at her with a smile.

"Oh, I just couldn't help myself!" she laughed. "Baby clothes! Lauren, I bought practically everything they had. I know we don't know yet, but I can just sense that the baby is going to be a girl!"

I grinned, and as her words settled into my heart, tears started welling up in my eyes. I opened my mouth, but I couldn't say anything.

"Oh, honey, what's wrong?" she asked, reaching out and touching my shoulder. "What happened? Are you feeling nauseous again?"

"What?" I asked, feeling a tear stream down my cheek. "No, I'm fine. I'm just..." I paused, trying to find the right words to explain why I was standing in my parents' garage and crying. "I'm just so happy, Mom. I'm just so happy to be having a baby.

Thank you for the baby clothes."

She wrapped me in a quick hug, all the plastic bags enveloping me with her arms. Then she ushered me back inside the house. "Let's not have this happy girl catch a cold out here. Let's go inside and show your father what I got."

I hurried back inside the house, goosebumps prickling my skin. Behind me, I heard my mom's car trunk shut as she came in behind me. I headed back to the den, where my dad was still watching the Ohio State game.

"Dad, look what Mom got," I said, looking at him with a knowing smirk, pointing to the bags that my mom was carrying.

He finally tore his eyes away from the screen. "Uh-oh," he said, giving me the same smile back, "what did she find this time?"

I laughed.

"Just open the bags and see!" my mom said as we shoved them into his lap. "There's a lot in there." My dad practically groaned as she added, "It was all on sale. Don't you worry; it was all on sale!"

"How much did you buy?" my dad asked, half amused and half concerned as he started pulling out frilly dress after frilly dress.

"Oh, probably just every piece of newborn clothing they had for girls," she said casually.

"And how do you know it's going to be a girl?" my dad asked legitimately, taking his gaze from the pink frilly velvet dress to the TV just as Purdue was scoring a touchdown against Ohio State.

"Oh, I just have this feeling!" my mom said, looking at me

and winking.

"I feel the same way, Dad! And I want to name the baby Samantha and call her 'Sam' as a nickname. Isn't that cool?"

My dad didn't seem to have a position on the name, as he was now fully lamenting the touchdown scored against us, so he just nodded in agreement.

"I think it's a lovely choice," my mom said as she gave me a second hug in less than five minutes.

We picked up all the clothes my dad had in his lap and moved everything over into the dining room, where we could neatly arrange the clothes by sleepers, dresses, and onesies. As I looked at the mass of newborn clothing I now had for my baby, my emotions started rising in me again. I felt my stomach flip-flop and I didn't want to tear up again in front of my mom.

"I better go check on Alexander," I said as my mom continued laying out the clothes.

He'd been studying for almost two hours, and I hadn't heard a single noise coming from my childhood bedroom. When I knocked on the door to my room (a gesture which felt odd) I could hear Alexander talking to himself. It was muffled, but I heard him say, "You got this. You know this material."

"Hi, babe," I said as I peeked my head inside my room. Alexander was facing away from the door, sitting at my white wicker desk that I used in high school.

"Oh, Lauren, I didn't hear you there at the door," Alexander said, turning around. "I was actually just studying for my organic chemistry class," he said blatantly, as if I didn't already know that.

I opened the door further and walked in, sitting down on

the side of my bed. "Why don't you come watch the OSU game? Take a little break. The fourth quarter is about to start."

"Well, I don't know. I think I should study a bit longer," Alexander said, looking down at the desk. "I only got through my worksheet, and I was planning on making flash cards." He held up a bunch of blank 3x5 index cards.

"Sweetie, it's the holidays. You promised me you would be with me and pay attention to me and the baby," I said rather dramatically, considering he wasn't ignoring me. He was just studying.

I thought Alexander was going to plead with me, perhaps make me feel guilty for making *him* feel guilty. Instead, he nodded, placed his index cards back on the desk, closed his textbook, and got up to follow me into the den to watch the game. As we approached the dining room, he put his hand on the small of my back. It felt heavenly. But he seemed to stop in his tracks when he saw all the baby girl clothes, neatly laid out on the dining room table.

"Don't worry," I whispered, "just an excited grandma." I smiled at Alexander, but between the studying and the baby dresses, he didn't smile back.

*****

After a full weekend at home, and almost a full drive back to OSU, I was exhausted and I think Alexander, God bless his heart, was ready to be back in his academic environment. I couldn't believe how frigid it now felt. The wind seemed to seep in through the tiniest of cracks in my Saturn car. A faint whistle and a draft on the driver's side gave way to Alexander trying, unsuccessfully, to fix it while also trying to keep his eyes on the highway.

"Don't do that babe, you're going to get us in an accident," I said as he gently punched the driver's side window with his left hand, his right hand on the wheel accidentally swerving us into a different lane.

"Sorry, it's just so fucking cold in here," he muttered. Alexander wasn't usually one to curse, but I shrugged.

"Why don't we finish the discussion about the baby's name," I offered, trying to get him to stop focusing on the window.

He put both hands back on the steering wheel and his shoulders seemed to relax. "So, Alexandria is completely ruled out?" he said, this time seriously.

"Well, I think let's have that be our second child's name. I really want to name our baby Samantha and call her Sam for short. You like that, right?"

"And if it's a boy, we'll name him Samuel, and then call him Sam?"

I let out a big sigh. *Such an intellectual,* I thought. This baby was unquestionably going to be a girl. I didn't care to even entertain boy names. I knew I was having a girl. I didn't know how I knew, but it had to be a mother's intuition.

"So, you like the name Samantha for a girl? And calling her Sam…you like that, right?" I asked again, leading the witness.

"Samantha Smithton," Alexander said slowly. I looked over and saw a small smile trace at his lips. "That's a beautiful name."

I hadn't put the first and last name together, but oh my God, was it a beautiful name. Just hearing our daughter's name come out of Alexander's mouth made my heart fill with joy.

Since the baby name felt like an easy win, I decided I would broach a tougher subject, which was our living situation. It was no surprise that it would prove impossible for me to live in the sorority house while I was pregnant. As much as I had loved the girls and the house, I felt out of place knowing that I couldn't drink, I couldn't go to parties, and I couldn't partake in the once-fun activities of staying up until 2 a.m. eating raw cookie dough and gabbing about celebrities. Even just a few weeks ago, I thought that was my life, and I'd reveled in it. But last week, I was handed something far greater. I was given a gift, a purpose, a baby. Living the Greek life didn't fit into my new world or the journey I was about to embark upon.

I'm beyond all that now, I thought. It felt like overnight, I'd matured in a way my sorority sisters hadn't, and I didn't want to live in that environment anymore.

"So," I continued, "while we prepare for Samantha Smithton's arrival, I think we should move in together, in your apartment. It's a two bedroom, which is perfect, and I'm thinking we could help Jordan look for a new place to live for the spring semester."

"You want to move in with me?" Alexander blurted out. The way he said it made it sound like we were practically strangers.

"Are you thinking we should live apart while I'm pregnant?" I tilted my head to the side for emphasis. Had he really given this no thought?

"Well…I guess I had figured that you would stay in your

sorority house through the spring semester, because if you're due in June, we'll be out of school early May. And we talked about you giving birth in Jacobs, right?"

I started grinding my teeth. Alexander was changing the subject on me, talking about me being in classes next semester. I was quiet for a moment, searching for the right way to explain to Alexander that I didn't want to enroll in the spring semester. Meanwhile, he took my silence as permission for him to continue talking.

"I think if you stay in your sorority house, and I stay in my apartment, it might be easier, and then we could get our own apartment in the fall with the baby. Maybe I could re-lease my same apartment in the fall, and Jordan's bedroom could be the nursery."

"Do you not want to live with me and our growing baby?" I asked, anger rising in me. My cheeks grew hot as I glared at him. "I want to start my life with you, Alexy. I don't want to live in the sorority house because I'm not a part of that life anymore. The girls will all be drinking and partying and staying up late. That won't be good for me or Samantha!" I exclaimed. "Besides, I thought you didn't like me being a part of that Greek life."

Alexander nodded, and I could tell he was doing the math in his head about me moving in with him right away and what that would mean for his roommate Jordan.

"Also, Alexy," I persisted, "I don't know if I want to take classes in the spring. With the pregnancy, and the pre-med rigor, I think maybe I should take a semester or a year off. I can get a part-time job to help pay our bills. And then, when I do re-enroll, we may be somewhere else other than OSU for your med school, and so maybe I'll take general classes, and maybe I switch to a different major…something more manageable with me being a mom."

I knew I'd said a lot there, and some of it had been rambling, but I was so nervous that Alexander wouldn't support me in my decision to take time away from school. I just knew that for me, it was going to be too arduous to be pregnant and take classes. *Besides, this way I can devote more time to helping Alexander with his studies*, I rationalized. *And I can keep the apartment clean, and I can cook each night.* Well, maybe not the last one. I didn't know how to cook anything but popcorn.

But what came out of Alexander's mouth next was not what I had anticipated.

"I don't want the baby to keep you from becoming a doctor," Alexander expressed honestly.

I sighed. I knew I wasn't getting through to him and that I was going to have to do all the legwork on my own. I was going to have to embarrassingly tell all the sorority sisters that I was moving out. I was going to have to help Jordan find a new apartment on short notice. I was going to have to work with my guidance counselor to pause my enrollment at Ohio State. And I was going to have to search for an OBGYN in Columbus to make our seven-week appointment.

I felt ready for my new life, and I was prepared to uproot the old in search of the new. I could handle it. I just didn't foresee my biggest obstacle being the man I loved.

CHAPTER 20

My body wrapped in a towel and my hair freshly blow-dried after taking a shower, I made my way into my bedroom at the sorority house, happy to be alone. Most of the girls weren't back at the house yet, either because of classes or studying for finals at the library. I finally had a moment by myself in my room, and I knew what I needed to do this morning before my OBGYN appointment later in the day.

I needed to call Steele.

I hadn't seen her over the Thanksgiving break, and I had been dying to tell her my big news. I knew Steele had a light schedule on Tuesdays, so now was the perfect time to call her.

Picking up the phone, I dialed Steele's number and climbed into my bed next to the window. She answered after a few rings.

"Hello?"

"Hey, Steele! It's Lauren."

"Lauren!" She always sounded so happy when I called. Her voice felt like home. "How are you? How was Thanksgiving?"

"It was good," I said. I didn't want to be rude and dive right into my news. "How was yours?"

"Oh, you know," she replied. "My mom made her big dinner, and I ate too much pie. Sorry I didn't get to see you. My mom said you called but I had to head back to Kent State early to study. I really want to hang out with you over winter break!"

"That's okay, it was actually really good to spend time with my parents. I brought Alexander home with me."

"That's right! I forgot about that," Steele said with a laugh. "How was it? Super awkward?"

"No, I mean," I stammered, staring out the window and twisting the phone cord around my finger. "It was…well, I have some news, Steele. Are you sitting down?"

There was a pause on the other end of the phone.

"Steele?"

"Okay, now I'm sitting down," she said. "What's your news?"

"It's not bad, I promise," I said, and I could feel myself smiling. Any nerves I had about telling my best friend melted away as I imagined her meeting little Samantha in the summer. I imagined her being in the hospital with me, and us going to the parks in Jacobs, pushing the baby in the stroller. In my heart, I knew my best friend would be there for me no matter what, and now, I was bursting at the seams. "Steele, I'm pregnant."

There was another pause, then Steele yelled through the phone. "Oh my God, you're pregnant? Oh my God, Lauren!

How? Well…I know *how.*" She laughed, and I did too. "When? When did you find out?"

I filled Steele in on everything that had happened—getting sick, taking the pregnancy test at the student health center, my parents' initial reaction, and even the name that I picked out.

"Wow, Lauren, that's amazing," Steele said. "I know you're going to be a great mom. Like, I know you're young, but you were meant to be a mom."

"Thanks, that means a lot. I'm going in for my seven-week appointment this afternoon."

"So that means, what, the baby is due in the summer?" I could practically hear her doing the math in her head. Steele was always so sharp.

"Yes!" Telling Steele hadn't been hard—she was so supportive, always the eternal optimist, always leaning into the good of situations, and never judging me. "And actually, I've decided I'm taking some time off of school, starting in the spring so I can prepare for the baby."

"Really?" Steele asked. "So, a semester before the baby and then probably a semester after the baby. Do you *really* want to take a year off school, Lauren?"

Unfortunately, she didn't seem to be the glass-half-full type when it came to me taking a sabbatical from college. I sighed.

As I gazed out the window of my bedroom and focused in on a neighboring sorority in their front yard raking leaves, I realized I had now heard the rallying cry for me to stick with my studies from almost everyone close to me in my life. But try as they might, I wasn't hearing what they were saying.

First up were my parents, who were now coming off their high of finding out they were going to be grandparents. In sobering up to the fact that their baby was going to have a baby, they'd called me and urged me to get as many classes in as I could before the baby arrived.

My college guidance counselor also asked if I was 'truly sure' I wanted to refrain from enrolling in spring classes. As I sat in her office a couple days ago, she kept sharing with me that she'd also had a baby in college and that course loads were tougher after having a baby than while pregnant.

And then there was Alexander, who obviously wanted me to stay in school. He was still pushing the 'you could be a doctor, Lauren' narrative that went in one ear and out the other.

And now from Steele, I received the same sentiments. Talking to her on the phone in my bed felt so nice, but this wasn't how I'd imagined this conversation going. I'd thought Steele might be the one person who saw it from my perspective.

"There's a girl here at Kent State who is pregnant, and she's actually due in April, in the middle of the semester. She's asking her professors to take her finals early!" Steele exclaimed. "You know, to make sure she gets her credits for each class."

"That sounds miserable," I mumbled.

Steele started laughing. "Oh, Lauren, I love you. I'm so excited you're having a baby. I didn't expect to be an honorary auntie so soon, but you're going to be a great mom. Keep following your heart. You know, I always knew there was something special about you and babies. Remember in high school when—"

Abruptly, my sorority roommates walked into the bedroom.

I hadn't even heard them coming up the stairs. I hung up the phone. *Shit, I just hung up on Steele.* Would she call me back? Probably, and that would only lead to questions from everyone. Gently and quietly, I lifted the phone off of the receiver to prevent any calls from Steele.

I stared at my roommates. Luckily, they were oblivious to my freak-out.

"Hey Lauren!" Katy said as she and Lindsay plopped down on their beds. "Why did you scratch your name off the list for the philanthropy event tonight at the Columbus soup kitchen?"

"I have a doctor appointment," I said casually. "Remember when I had that sinus infection a few weeks back? They want to see if it ran its course and if I can get off the antibiotics now."

"Let's hope," Lindsay said. "You haven't been able to drink in forever because of those antibiotics."

I was glad the sorority sisters hadn't seen through my ruse, and it was obviously effective considering they were making correlations between my lack of drinking and my being sick and needing antibiotics. I felt bad for lying to my friends, but it was necessary.

In reality, I had my seven-week doctor appointment late this afternoon, then Alexander and I were going to go out for pizza to celebrate. Today was our first real doctor appointment since that night at the student health center when we found out I was pregnant. At this appointment, we were going to meet the OBGYN, listen to the baby's heartbeat, maybe even get an ultrasound picture.

I knew that I had to quit lying to my sorority sisters. It was becoming too much, plus, my God, I had just hung up on Steele! I thought about calling her back, but my roommates were still lingering in our room. Steele was away at Kent State and had such an active social life that she surely wasn't waiting by the phone for me to call back this second.

*****

A few hours later, I drove to Alexander's apartment to pick him up for the first OBGYN appointment. The doctor was on the other side of Columbus, about as far away from OSU as you could get. I actually found the doctor through my guidance counselor. Even though I was nervous about the appointment, I was mostly just excited. I couldn't wait to hear the heartbeat and see the ultrasound. I was going to see my baby for the first time and have the experience with Alexander by my side.

As Alexander came out from his apartment and hopped in my car, I asked him to get out the map from my glovebox to look at the highways in Columbus and where this doctor's office was. He gave me turn-by-turn directions, while I gave him a play-by-play breakdown of what would take place at the seven-week appointment.

"We won't be able to feel the baby move," I said, "as that comes later in the second trimester." That was obvious, but I didn't know what exactly Alexander had anticipated with this first appointment.

Unfortunately, though, Alexander seemed more interested in talking about a game plan for me to continue taking classes while I was pregnant.

"I was thinking, Lauren, about the spring semester, and there are some elective courses I need to take. They can be anything, so I was thinking maybe we could take them together. We could take some home economic courses to prepare for the baby, and maybe a history class, and a public speaking class, and maybe—"

I'd heard enough. I was so sick of the relentless pushing of me to continue my education. Why didn't everyone see that I wasn't afraid of taking classes and being pregnant? I just didn't have any desire to continue my education anymore. My focus was the baby, the nursery, being a mom, staying healthy, and yes, not being overwhelmed by classes. Why did everyone act like taking a break from school was some kind of misstep? Like it was the biggest mistake I could make?

"You know, why don't we talk about that later?" I suggested, feeling like the parent of a child who couldn't focus on the task at hand. "Let's focus on the appointment now."

Luckily, we arrived at the doctor's office without getting lost, and as we walked from our car to the office, I leaned my body into Alexander. I thought he would put his arm around me, but he didn't, making it seem to him like I lost my footing and somewhat fell into him.

As we entered the doctor's office, Alexander seemed more eager to be in another medical setting than to be with me. We checked in with the receptionist. As we made our way down the long hallway to our patient room, Alexander looked all around, nodding at all the medical equipment and eyes widening when he heard a doctor or a nurse on the phone talking about a medical prognosis.

"Lauren, go ahead and hop up on the table," the nurse instructed. Then, she proceeded to explain to us exactly what I had prepped Alexander for. This appointment was to meet the doctor, get a heartbeat on the baby, and get a glimpse of the fetus through an ultrasound.

"I'm going to step out for a moment while you change out of your clothes and into this hospital gown. Keep the opening in the front," the nurse said with a wink. "When I come back, I'll get a quick heartbeat and then the doctor will be in."

I felt so excited that this was all happening, and even Alexander was smiling.

As I sat naked under my gown, my stomach still completely flat and not at all showing, I realized what would happen to my body over the next seven months. I thought about the huge belly I would get, and how if I was like all the other pregnant women I saw, I'd probably gain weight in my arms and legs and face. I imagined myself with a big bowling ball stomach and a backpack, lugging textbooks from one OSU building to the next. *No thank you,* I thought.

The nurse knocked on the door before entering and quietly turned on the equipment. For the heartbeat, she took what looked like a microphone instrument and explained how she was going to insert it. "This is going to feel cold. I'm inserting this vaginally," the nurse said. "I'm sorry!"

I felt the cold instrument inside of me and started to grow a bit embarrassed, especially since the nurse wasn't saying anything. Alexander was now trying to play half doctor and half detective, mulling over each and every movement on the screen. For my part, I sat back and tried to relax, thinking about what middle name we were going to select to go between Samantha and Smithton.

The nurse pressed a button by the door, but still didn't say anything. The button created a doorbell-like sound, and ten seconds later, the doctor appeared.

A tall man in his sixties, completely gray with sun damage on his nose, walked up to me and stuck out his hand. "I'm Dr. Hawkins," he said gently. "Our nurse is going to take a look one more time, so you will feel cold pressure again."

"It's nice to meet you, Dr. Hawkins," I said as I tried to look at Alexander. I was lying down, and with that thing inserted in me and Dr. Hawkins and the nurse basically on top of me, I could barely see Alexander unless I scrunched my chin into my neck. But both Alexander and Dr. Hawkins were looking at the TV, which showed a lot of white, gray, and black circles. It was hard to know what we were supposed to be looking at.

"Has the office been busy today?" I asked both Dr. Hawkins and the nurse, trying to make small talk to fill the silence in the room.

"Lauren, I'm going to have you sit up," Dr. Hawkins said, completely ignoring my question and placing his hand on my shoulder to help me sit upright as the instrument was abruptly pulled out of me.

As I sat up, the nurse left the room and Dr. Hawkins turned off all the equipment. It seemed like he was done examining me, and I looked at Alexander to understand what was happening.

Alexander, though, just stared at Dr. Hawkins.

"Lauren, I'm afraid I could not find a heartbeat for your baby."

I didn't know what that meant. I was confused. How could there be a baby inside me without a heartbeat? Was I earlier along in the pregnancy than they originally thought?

"Doesn't...doesn't a baby need a heartbeat?" I asked.

Dr. Hawkins nodded, and repeated, "Yes, unfortunately I could not find a heartbeat for your baby. Your baby does not have a beating heart, which means your baby is not living anymore." Now turning directly toward me, Dr. Hawkins looked me in the eye and said, "I'm sorry. You had a miscarriage."

A chill came over my entire body, goosebumps coating my skin as I immediately felt lightheaded. "A miscarriage?"

"Sometimes this happens," Dr. Hawkins said. "It's unfortunate, but it's also quite common."

My hands started shaking. *Sometimes this happens,* I thought. *A miscarriage.* I didn't know when, but I started crying. Alexander walked over and grabbed my hand and squeezed it once, but in all my crying he let it go. *Our baby is dead.*

The doctor launched into an explanation of what would happen to my body and what this miscarriage meant—or didn't mean—for future pregnancies. His clinical explanation made something in my chest feel tight, and I started sobbing uncontrollably.

"There has to be a mistake," I begged. "Please, can you try just one more time to find the heartbeat! *Please.* Let's just try it again." I couldn't lose Samantha, not before I even got to be her mom. "Please, there has to be something you can do. Alexy, maybe you can find the heartbeat."

"Lauren," Dr. Hawkins said slowly, "I'm sorry, but there's nothing we can do now except keep you healthy as your body completes the miscarriage."

I was crying and shaking my head no.

"Lauren…" Alexander said, looking up at me. I could barely see him through the tears in my eyes. "Let's hear what the doctor has to say, okay?"

The rest of the doctor appointment seemed to be a complete blur. With my crying and rocking back and forth, holding my stomach, Dr. Hawkins focused his talking points on Alexander. The few things I heard were scary changes in the body including bleeding, remaining tissue in the uterus, and increased back pain from the miscarriage.

The two men kept talking about what was to come, while I sat there alone, naked under my gown, crying on the exam table. Dr. Hawkins turned to me and patted my shoulder, likely giving the same number of taps that he gave to the scores of women that come in every day only to find that their baby was now gone. How many other women got the same horrible news in this office? How did any of them heal their broken hearts? I couldn't imagine ever putting mine back together.

"Again, I'm so sorry Lauren, but the good news is that you are young, and you were able to get pregnant, so you will likely get pregnant in the future." He stopped for a moment and then continued, "Do you have any questions for me?"

My mind started racing, and a million things bubbled up.

Why is this happening? Why did God choose me to have a baby with Alexander and then take it away? Why did I get so close to living my dream life, and now it's gone? Is this my fault? Did I do this? Is Alexander going to be mad at me? Is there any way to get my baby back?

But I knew he couldn't answer those questions, and there was only one thing I wanted to know before we left.

"I have one question," I said, answering Dr. Hawkins through my sniffles and wiping my eyes. "Can you please tell me if my baby was a boy or a girl?"

"Oh," Dr. Hawkins said with the hint of a laugh, "it's way too early to have known the sex. Usually, parents find out at their twenty-week appointment. You were only seven weeks."

CHAPTER 21

I woke up the next morning in Alexander's bed, wearing the same clothes that I had on at the now-fateful doctor's appointment. I sat up and looked around the room. What time was it? Was Alexander even in the apartment? It was so quiet.

My eyes searched around the room for a clock; there wasn't one on either nightstand. I looked out his bedroom window and the sun had barely risen, so I gauged that it wasn't even 8:00 a.m. I thought about what I had missed within the time I found out I was no longer pregnant: I missed the soup kitchen sorority philanthropy event, I missed the Thursday night ER TV show tradition that the sorority sisters had started in the den, and I was sure the girls were wondering why I hadn't come back to the house last night and why I never even called.

And I was likely going to miss my classes for the morning. I shrugged. It didn't much matter. After all, I was just trying to get through the next few weeks to end the semester and then school would be over for me.

My heart sank. It *did* matter. I had no baby anymore, no overarching reason to not be in school. I buried my face in my hands and started to cry. I had just lost my baby, and I was now realizing that I was losing the future I had planned, too.

After the doctor had told us there was no heartbeat on the ultrasound, a blood test confirmed it. I looked down now at my arm and tore off the Band-Aid where the blood was drawn. I had a bruise. One of the only physical markings that represented what had happened to me yesterday.

I didn't remember much of the appointment after the doctor delivered the news. Alexander had taken me back to his apartment and let me cry, holding me and letting it be all about me. We'd sat on his bed together for what felt like hours, and I wasn't sure if I asked him even once how he was doing. I was just so devastated. I'd vacillated between utter despair and numbness, until the numbness finally won, and I drifted off to sleep for the night.

But now it was the morning, and I had to face my reality again.

I heard the door open and looked up to see Alexander walk into his bedroom. He was holding a glass of milk. I rarely drank milk, but he sat down next to me in bed and handed me the glass.

"Here you go, Lauren," he said softly. "I think taking in some calcium will help with any remaining tissues in your uterus."

I had no idea what he meant by that, but I put the glass to my lips and took a sip. I didn't love the taste, but I drank a little more anyway. Alexander sat on the bed and rubbed my leg. I knew he was waiting for me to give him an update about my emotional state. But when I stayed silent, he tried, rather unsuccessfully, to cheer me up.

"Do you remember that one time you spent the night?" he asked with a bit of a smile. "You remember we did our pushup competition? I can't believe you did fifteen pushups. I think we'll keep training you and before you know it, you'll be at twenty."

"Can I train by doing them on my knees?" I asked, referring to the modified pushups but really just asking the question to appease him while he attempted to entertain me.

"Um, sure," Alexander said as he rubbed his chin and smiled, pretending to mull it over. "I just need to keep training you because I like looking down your shirt while you attempt your pushups." He leaned his shoulder into my shoulder, giving me a bit of a flirtatious nudge.

I laughed. It was the first time I'd laughed in what felt like forever, and it was the first time in a long time that I thought about my body being sexy. For almost two months, I'd either felt extremely sick or pregnant, but definitely not alluring.

With my laugh, it seemed like Alexander was now comfortable asking me some harder questions.

"So, do you think you'll tell your sorority sisters about the pregnancy and the miscarriage?"

I hesitated. I didn't know, and this felt so unfair that not only was I not going to have a baby, but I was going to have to unravel everything that I had orchestrated the past few weeks.

I was going to have to tell my parents, Steele, and my guidance counselor. I was going to have to decide about going back to school in January. I was going to have to pretend that I wanted to live the Greek life of going to parties and staying up late.

I was beyond it all now. Even if I no longer had the baby, I knew my maturity had surpassed the limited existence I was living before. Still, I didn't see a way out.

"I don't think I will tell them, actually. It's private, and I think it will be easier for me to live in the house without the sorority girls knowing," I answered diplomatically. "It'll be so sad to tell my parents and Steele. They were all so thrilled for me and this new life I was going to lead. I bet they'll be heartbroken about the miscarriage."

Alexander nodded, rubbing my back.

"What about your parents?" I asked after a brief silence seemed to stretch on. "When will you tell them about the miscarriage?"

He slowly looked up at me, reminding me of a puppy dog that knew he did something wrong and was going to get reprimanded. Alexander paused for a moment, likely trying to weigh in his head whether he should take the truthful or untruthful route. I tilted my head to the side.

"I actually haven't told my parents about your pregnancy," Alexander admitted as he got up from the bed. He walked to the window to pull back the curtains and crack open the window for some fresh air.

"What?!" I said, jumping from the bed and matching his stance.

"Well, you know that pregnancies often end in miscarriages, and in theory, we should have kept this private for another five weeks until your second trimester," he said, his voice a little shaky like he was about to get yelled at.

"What?!" I repeated, my hands on my hips.

Alexander turned toward me, his shoulders hunched. "You know my parents are so focused on my studies. They would have freaked out about the pregnancy news." Alexander was tapping his fingers against his leg, being vulnerable but likely wishing he wasn't.

I shot daggers across the room with my eyes. "So you just pretended like Samantha didn't exist?" I exclaimed, throwing my arms in the air. My throat tightened as my eyes welled up with tears.

"Lauren, I supported you when you wanted to tell your parents, and when you wanted to shop for baby girl clothes, and when you wanted to name the baby. I supported you in everything you wanted these last few weeks," Alexander replied as if he should have received a medal.

"Exactly, Alexander," I retorted. "And I supported *you* weeks ago when you asked me to leave your apartment early one night so that you could call your parents and tell them about the pregnancy news. And I supported you the next day when I asked how the call went and you said that it went pretty well! So, I guess I supported a liar," I finished, throwing my hands in the air again.

"Please, Lauren, sit back down in the bed with me. Let's talk about this," Alexander said as he himself curled up in bed by his headboard. He propped his legs up by his chest and hung his head. "I'm sorry, I don't know what to do. But I'm actually relieved that we aren't having this baby. Think about it, Lauren. This baby would have taken us away from school, our classes, our downtime, our families, our med school prospects. Aren't you at least relieved that you can go back and live at the sorority house and go to all the football games?"

I couldn't believe what I was hearing. I didn't dare sit with him in his bed. How could the father of my child be happy that our child was now dead, gone forever, gone before we even got to know her? I walked around to his side of the bed and stood there, towering over him, pointing my finger in his face.

"I am disgusted with you!" I yelled. "You didn't love our baby enough to even tell your parents. You didn't deserve to be Samantha's father," I said, my tears falling fast as I cried through my words. "You'll always put being a doctor above everything else, even children. You'll become a great doctor, but that's all you'll ever be."

He stared up at me, tears now in his eyes, perhaps silently acknowledging that I was right. He didn't say anything, and I was not about to let him defend himself. I wanted his heart to break the way mine was breaking, to feel the anger and pain and betrayal I felt. I promptly turned around on my heels, grabbed my purse, and headed out the door.

As soon as I stepped outside his apartment door, my feet felt cold. Looking down, I realized I'd forgotten to put on my shoes. I headed back into the apartment, but Alexander was still inside his bedroom. I snatched my shoes from where I'd left them near the front door and saw Jordan come out of his room. He gave me a quiet smile, likely having heard word-for-word our argument, now a member of the small circle that knew I was pregnant and also that I was now not.

Stoically, I made my way to my car, but once I closed and locked the door, I couldn't control my emotions. I leaned on my steering wheel and sobbed, the type of cry where you start hyperventilating. All I could see was how, in a matter of twenty-four hours, my entire life had started slipping away. How that might also include Alexander now. I knew I was angry, but I could also see the writing on the wall. He had a one-dimensional path: become a doctor. That path didn't include me, but rather his white coat, as his partner.

Even in my daze, I didn't want to stay too long in Alexander's apartment complex parking lot. I was afraid people would hear me crying in my car and alert Alexander. Before I went back to my sorority house, I was going to have to pull myself together. I didn't want to share my trauma with the girls, and I knew my only 'story' could be that I was arriving home twenty-four hours later in the same clothes I left in was because Alexander and I went out for a date night, got drunk, went back to his place, had sex, and I blew off my morning classes. There was no other story to tell. It felt so fake and phony—so wrong—but sadly, the sorority sisters would love it and eat it up.

As I started my car, Christmas music came on the radio. My stomach turned, thinking about the Christmas dress my mom had told me she got for Samantha for next year. I knew that I had to call my parents. I didn't trust that I would be alone in my sorority bedroom long enough for the conversation, so as I drove home, I looked on every street for a pay phone. Finally, I found some next to our OSU supermarket, but they were in use. I came across one adjacent to the football practice field, so I got out of my car. I fished for quarters in my purse and found a few to feed the pay phone. I dialed my parents' phone number and held my breath.

"Hello?" my mom said after the first ring.

Hearing the voice of your parents when you, their child, are distressed is one of the most surrendering experiences. All at once, I felt like a baby myself, wanting to be in my mother's arms. I immediately burst out crying, and through my wailing and sniffles, I explained to my mom about my miscarriage.

"What?!" my mom shouted. "Oh my God, Lauren, oh honey, oh my God," she said as she was now crying herself.

We talked about the mechanics of the miscarriage and how the doctor couldn't feel the heartbeat. I told her that after the appointment I was so emotionally exhausted that I slept forever, and that when I woke up, Alexander and I got in a fight because he didn't tell his parents about the pregnancy. I started shivering as the early December wind whipped across the practice field and into the phone booth. I could hear the wind carry the sounds of football coaches whistling to end scrimmages. I looked over at the players, so focused. I wondered if I would ever be focused again.

My mom didn't seem to listen to anything I was saying. She was crying and talking about keeping the dresses she bought for Samantha.

"You know, Lauren, this family is cursed," she finally said. "I was cursed with Nicholas, and you have been cursed with Samantha."

My mom was referring to my baby brother, who died of SIDS. I was only a year old when he was born, and he died a few months later in his crib during a nap. I knew my mom always held this position, that she was cursed for losing Nicholas. I never really saw it that way, but now having lost Samantha, I understood how she felt.

I stood there in the Ohio winter wind, a healthy nineteen-year-old with a bright future before me. Deep in my soul, I knew I could bounce back from this miscarriage. And I knew this wasn't what a mother should be telling her daughter during this sad time. I knew I was supposed to receive more emotional support and guidance. I knew it all.

But for just a moment, I closed my eyes and took solace in knowing there was someone else out there who had lost a child, and that as family, we were fused together in this terrible fate.

CHAPTER 22

"Don't think about him!" Katrina, my sorority sister, yelled into my ear as she swayed her hips on the makeshift dance floor at the fraternity house.

I smiled and took another drink of my vodka soda. I looked at my plastic cup, red like Christmas, wrapped by my perfectly manicured fingernails, also painted Christmas red. I glanced down at my red corduroy skirt and green tights and realized that with finals mostly over, and my baby now gone, I had all the time in the world to drink and let loose during the holidays.

But it sure didn't feel that way. My friend Katrina was attempting to cheer me up; I'd confided in her earlier that Alexander and I were 'fighting.' What she didn't know was that we weren't speaking because I was still angry that he felt relieved about the miscarriage. I was also still fuming that he felt I was 'too much' for him. He actually said that to me, a couple nights back, on the phone. "Lauren, maybe you are just too much for me. Maybe I just don't know how to be with you.'"

I sighed. The last couple of weeks had been so hard. My relationship was up in the air. I still hadn't enrolled in classes for the spring semester. I was still keeping this huge secret from my entire sorority. That was why I'd decided that I might as well spend one of my last nights on campus drinking and being with those that accepted me for being me. Here, at the frat house, I wasn't 'too much' for anyone.

As the music changed from one song to the next, Katrina walked off the dance floor. I started following her, but someone grabbed my hand. I turned around, spilling some of my vodka and watching it splash on the dance floor. One of the senior and most well-known fraternity brothers, Chad, smiled and leaned his head down to me. He was around 6'4", and it felt so lovely to have a guy tower over me.

I always have to slouch around Alexander, I thought. *Just another way I'm too much for him.*

"Hey, Lauren, I like your holiday get-up. Very festive," Chad said, his voice deep as he slid his hand around my waist. My lower back felt a jolt of pain the way he pulled me toward him. My body was still sore from the miscarriage, and the pressure of his hand around my waist was making it worse.

He was being flirtatious and although he was grinning at me ear to ear, my heart was breaking all over again. I didn't want to be with Chad. The last thing I wanted was to have this sub-plot enter my story.

"Thanks, Chad," I mumbled as I took a few steps away from him, arching my back a bit to stretch it. Slowly, I turned away from him and headed off the dance floor in search of Katrina.

"Whoa, Lauren, wait up!" Chad called as I took a huge gulp of my vodka, finishing off the drink. He pointed casually at my red cup. "You want another one of those?"

I looked at my empty cup. I didn't know what I wanted in that moment. I didn't even know what I wanted to be doing in the spring. But what I did know was that I wanted to be drunk right now.

"Sure," I replied.

He gently took the cup from my hand, walked over to the bar, cut the line in front of everyone, and filled my drink up with straight vodka. I watched as he dropped two maraschino cherries and a drop of Diet Coke in the drink for good measure and headed back my way.

"Here you go," he said with a smile.

I took another massive gulp and could barely swallow. It was like drinking rubbing alcohol. It went straight to my head, and my body felt warm and tingly. The music was blaring again, and Chad just stood there, smiling at my aggressive drinking.

"I've had a hard day," I yelled up in his ear, standing on my tiptoes.

We were still on the side of the dance floor. After a moment, Chad leaned down and asked, "Do you want to dance? Forget about finals?"

"No, I'd rather go somewhere quiet," I said. I actually just wanted to sit down. My back was aching from all the standing, and sharp pains kept shooting down my leg. This wasn't the worst it had been, but Alexander had mentioned during our call that I should take a pain reliever, and now I wish I would have taken his advice.

Chad kept the smile on his face and led me up to his room. Since he was Vice President of the fraternity, he had his own bedroom, a true luxury in the Greek life. As I walked toward his room, I wondered if I re-enrolled in school for the spring and stayed at the sorority, would I someday have my own room too? Was that my path for the next couple of years? Did I want that?

His room was near the end of the hallway, and I strolled inside, eyes fixed on a Green Day poster over his headboard. Chad followed me, shutting the door behind him. I turned around, and he immediately lowered his head and kissed me. At first, I didn't realize what was happening. The room was still, and it took my brain a moment to catch up. But then, when the kiss didn't feel like Alexander, my mind registered that something was happening that *definitely* shouldn't happen. I put my hands on Chad's chest, pushing him back. He didn't say anything at first, just kept smiling. I stared up at him, silent too. What was I supposed to say?

"You're so cute, Lauren," he said, his broad shoulders framing his perfect jaw line as he smiled. "The cutest girl here tonight."

I should have liked that attention. Chad was popular, tall, and handsome. Instead, I took another gulp of my drink, set it down on his dresser, and walked out of his room. I felt sorry for myself, and Chad's words just made me miss Alexander. I didn't want to be with some frat guy. I walked downstairs to the corner of the bar, where Katrina and a few other sorority sisters were.

"Lauren!" Katrina stared at me wide-eyed as she lowered her voice and whispered, "Did Chad just take you up to his room?!"

"Where's my coat?" I asked Katrina, tears now in my eyes. She pointed to the commons area. Hurrying, I grabbed my coat and walked out of the house, the cold December night taking my breath away.

I stood outside, the quiet and the cold a stark contrast to the sweaty, loud, boisterous party I was leaving behind. I knew I had to see Alexander, but there was no way in hell I was going to be able to make the walk to his apartment in this cold. I was unsteady on my feet in my heels, and as I attempted to walk down the sidewalk, I got dizzy. Luckily, before my foggy brain had to make any decisions, the campus bus pulled up to the bus stop right outside of the fraternity house.

Perfect, I thought. *It's only a five-minute ride straight to Alexander's apartment on this bus route. Go see your guy, Leonard.*

I got on the bus and showed my OSU ID card, the harsh bus light making me squint. The bus accelerated before I could sit down, and I swayed back and forth as I made my way toward the back of the bus. As I got about halfway back, I could feel eyes staring at me. I looked up. It was Alexander. I plopped down next to him.

"What are you doing?" Alexander asked quietly.

"What are YOU doing?" I said, louder than him, staring straight ahead.

"I'm coming back from studying at the library," Alexander

replied, patting his book bag that laid on his lap. "What are you doing?" he asked again, this time turning his head toward me.

"Well, I'm actually on my way to your apartment, Alexander, to see you. To talk to you. To try to make you love me again."

"I do love you," Alexander whispered.

We were quiet for the rest of the quick ride, and we stayed silent as we walked the three sets of stairs to Alexander's apartment. I was stumbling as I tried to climb the stairs, so Alexander took my hand to help me steady my steps.

Once we were in his apartment, I plopped down on his futon. Alexander stood at the door, his book bag still in hand.

"Chadwick Kensington tried to kiss me tonight," I said, hoping to start a fight. I had enough booze in me to go for a knockout, so this was my opening punch. "He's Vice President of the fraternity."

"With a name like that, I'm surprised he's not President," Alexander quipped as he walked into the kitchen and opened a bag of potato chips. He popped one in his mouth.

"Oh, you think you're SO MUCH BETTER than everyone else, don't you?" I yelled as he came back and sat down with me on the futon. "Alexander Pierce Smithton. Such a common, working-class name," I said sarcastically, rolling my eyes.

Alexander was quiet, and I knew that at any moment, whatever response he gave was going to be the actual round one knockout.

"Lauren." Alexander sighed as he turned toward me. "This is too much. I don't know what to do."

"I get it, Alexy! I'm too much for you!" I cried as my hands flew up in the air.

"No," he replied. "This." He pointed at himself and then me, and then back at himself again. "We are too different, Lauren. We want different things, and it's too much to have all of it. You're getting hit on by senior frat guys while I'm some dork in the library studying. I'm working so hard to become a doctor, yet I'm getting you pregnant. And we lost the baby, and I…I can't fix that." He paused, clearing his throat. "This is too much…all of it… and I don't know what to do."

I wanted to yell at him again. I'd been angry at him since that morning after the doctor appointment. But seeing him, sitting with me on the futon, trying to be vulnerable with me… it softened me. My head started to clear up, and I put my hand on his knee. "We will get through this," I said, trying to hold back my hiccups. "We will be okay. I'm sorry I yelled at you, Alexy. I'm sorry." I reached over and gave him a hug, but his body was stiff.

As I pulled back away, Alexander slowly shook his head, avoiding eye contact with me. He watched as I rubbed his leg, and I could see him wince. He looked like he was in pain, like his heart was literally breaking.

"I think we have to break up."

I didn't reply. I couldn't find the words to combat this devastating proposal. And perhaps worse, I couldn't find a reason to fight again for our relationship. I did want to figure it out, to be there for Alexander and to work through it, but there was that writing on the wall again. There was no way I was going to be able to compete with Alexander's sole-focus of becoming a doctor. There was no way I was going to be able to convince him that I preferred him to the Chadwick Kensingtons of the world. And there was no way to put our innocence back in the bottle once the genie delivered us, albeit briefly, a baby.

"If that's what you want," I said, my eyes filling up with tears.

"It's not what I want, Lauren, it's not," Alexander pleaded as he shook his head, now looking me directly in the eye. "I just can't keep doing this. I...I don't know what else to do. I *have* to focus on school. I don't have a choice."

I'd heard this argument over and over from Alexander. I was always the one trying to make the relationship work, craving some attention from him, craving a place in his life in between his textbooks. He couldn't love me the way I wanted—needed—him to.

And now, there was nothing left to say.

I got up off the futon, the alcohol again rushing to my head, and I headed for the door. I opened it, then looked over my shoulder.

"Bye Alexy."

Alexander, sinking into the futon, looked so small. "Don't forget to schedule that appointment with the OBGYN to check the pregnancy hormones again. Remember the doctor—"

I closed the door behind me.

The December night was even colder now, and I walked to the bus stop, got on the bus, and headed back toward the sorority house, knowing that soon, it wouldn't be my house anymore.

CHAPTER 23

THE CHURCH BELLS RANG OUT in our small Presbyterian church in Jacobs as my parents and I headed toward the front doors. Christmas Eve mass was ending, and everyone around me was in a celebratory mood. I'd decided to dress up in a red and black buffalo plaid holiday dress, dovetailing the Seattle grunge music fashion with a reverence for my church. My parents and I had been sitting up front close to the altar, and as we made our way slowly up the aisle, I saw Steele and waved. She mouthed 'Cute dress' and gave me a thumbs up.

I'd been home now a few days, having moved all my things out of the sorority house and back into my bedroom in Jacobs. My sorority sisters kept asking why I was packing up everything, including my lamp and my desk supplies. I continued giving non-answers, basically lying to my sorority sisters, even as we hugged on our last day on campus before the winter break. "See you in 1995!" my roommate Katy had said to me. Little did she know, I was never coming back.

Maybe it was the miscarriage, or maybe it was my own embarrassment, or maybe it was even my lousy grades. I just knew that I couldn't go back to that house, to that campus, and I didn't have the strength to tell my sorority sisters to their face that I was running away. I pushed the thoughts from my head as the frigid air outside the church stung my face.

As my parents and I walked across the parking lot, I held onto my dad's arm. It had snowed while we were inside, and with the temperature dropping, the ground was icing over.

"Lauren!" Steele called from behind me. I turned around and slipped. "Whoa, Lauren!" Steele said as both she and my dad caught me right before I fell.

I felt like a fool and started blushing. "Hi, Steele."

"Merry Christmas, Leonard family!" Steele said, so bright and cheery. "Lauren, let's get together. I have my mom's party tomorrow on Christmas night," she said as she gestured to her mom, who was talking in a small group in the parking lot, "but maybe we can go shopping together on the twenty-sixth? We could attack those after-Christmas sales."

I hesitated. Steele knew about my miscarriage, and that in coming home, I had no plans for the rest of my life. In her small way, she was trying to breathe me back into life. We always used to go shopping together in high school, and I remember once, after I didn't make cheerleading, she took me to the mall. She bought me a necklace and treated me to TCBY frozen yogurt in the food court.

"Okay," I said with a hint of a smile.

"Awesome!" she replied and gave me a hug. "Don't worry," Steele whispered in my ear as she leaned in close. "The holidays are always the hardest, aren't they?" I nodded, and as Steele pulled away, she said, "Merry Christmas, Leonard family! See you in a couple of days."

My parents and I carefully traversed the rest of the snow and ice, making our way home. On the car ride, my parents tried to make conversation with me.

"I know it's still over a month away, but I can't wait for the Super Bowl," my dad said. "I've already got the entire menu planned out."

"And it even fits in with this new low-fat diet I'm trying, Lauren," my mom said. "Maybe you want to try it with me. We can eat as many bagels as we want."

As my parents chattered on in the front of the car, I gave noncommittal answers, trying to be the daughter they wanted me to be. I could see right through both of them, though. They were filling up the silence, trying to fill up my time, trying to filter out the noise in my head that kept reminding me that I no longer had Alexander, or school, or my baby.

As we pulled into our neighborhood, my dad changed topics from Super Bowl dip recipes to everyone's Christmas decorations.

"Lauren, what's this trend nowadays with white lights on Christmas trees and houses? In my day, it was only colored lights. Look at that house," he said as he pointed to the house adjacent to ours. "Where's the originality?"

I laughed. "Well Pops, maybe you should decorate for the whole block!"

"Maybe I'll do that next year…only if you help me," my dad replied, undoubtedly trying to silently approve of me living with them for as long as I needed.

As we pulled into the garage, my mom announced that she was going to get the mail. I headed into the house. I was going to go straight for the French silk pie in the refrigerator, a Leonard family Christmas Eve tradition. As I started to cut myself a rather large piece, my mom came up to me, a serious look on her face.

"This was in the mailbox," she said.

I looked down and took the letter from her, the pie knife still in the other hand. The letter was addressed to me, in Alexander's handwriting. The return address was his apartment at OSU, and it was postmarked only a day ago. *Wow, he's staying at school to study through the break,* I thought.

"Don't read it if it's going to make you upset," my mom warned. "It's Christmas Eve, sweetheart. Everything is harder during this time."

"Steele just said the exact same thing to me," I murmured. My mom nodded, and we both stared at the letter in between us. "I'm going to read it now," I said definitively. "I have to."

My mom jumped into hostess-mode. "Do you want me to make you a cup of cocoa? Honey, why don't you read the letter in the formal living room?" Then she shouted to my dad, "Rob! Go make a fire in the living room!"

The three of us walked, single file into the living room, and I clutched the letter in my hands. My dad bent down on his knees near the fireplace, and my mom started fluffing the pillows on the chairs, trying to give me a beautiful, cozy space. I would always associate this living room with telling my parents I was going to have a baby, and then six days later not having the baby anymore, but I tried to push the thought away.

I sat down in the chair near the fire, my parents now gone, with the letter in my lap. My heart started to beat wildly. I was going to hear from Alexander, only I couldn't answer him back in real-time. *That's the problem with letters,* I thought. *They are so one-sided.* My hands were now shaking, but I flipped the letter over and tore open the envelope.

Dear Lauren,

I wanted to write you a letter. I have a hard time expressing my feelings, and I thought writing you might be the best way to explain how I feel. The last few times we've spoken, you've been so angry at me, so maybe with this letter, I can speak without you getting upset.

I want you to know that I really loved you. I know we aren't meant to stay together for the rest of our lives, but the time we spent together was the happiest point in my life. There would be times when we would be in the car and I would look over at you and wonder how I got so lucky. You are truly out of my league, with both your personality and your beauty. I always knew this, and it's been hard to even keep up.

I know you loved me too. Thank you for accepting me as I was. Thank you for supporting me with my pre-med major and for trying to give me a life on campus. As you can see, I'm just not cut out for the college life, in terms of parties and tons of friends.

I'm so sorry that you lost Samantha. You would have made a wonderful mom. I'll think about Samantha for the rest of my life and honor her memory.

The only thing I really know about myself is that I am on a path to become a physician, just like my dad and grandpa when they were my age. And what comes next for you is hopefully happiness. I know one day you are going to do amazing things. Please don't get angry, but the world needs you as a doctor, Lauren. I've listened to you talk about it, I've seen you in classes, and I have so much faith in you. I know you don't believe in yourself, but I believe in you. You were made to be a doctor, maybe even more than me. You're more natural. Imagine how lucky your patients would be to have you with them when they are ill. You deserve to be a doctor. I know you can do it, and I hope one day I see that you have.

I know you're probably mad at me by now, so I'll end this letter. But I wanted you to know how much I loved you, and if I see you on campus, I'll be friendly and wave and be instantly reminded of your unparalleled beauty.

Thanks,

'Alexy'

My throat felt tight, and my vision was becoming blurry from my tears. I placed the letter in my lap and buried my face in my hands. I started crying so loudly that my dad yelled from the den, "You okay in there, sugar?"

"I'm okay," I yelled back through tears.

I removed my hands from my face, tears running down my cheeks. I stared out the window, looking at the fresh snow,

Christmas carols playing from the kitchen and the fire crackling beside me. It was such a peaceful setting on such a traditionally joyous day, and yet I was in complete anguish.

Alexander's words gutted me. I'd held it together since I saw him last at his apartment when he broke up with me, but now, weeping, the significance of everything I'd lost hit me like a pile of bricks. The heaviness enveloped me, and my body felt weighted down.

What nineteen-year-old loses a baby, a boyfriend, and a college life all within the course of a month? I thought. How much grief could I endure? When would it get better?

I looked back out the window, at the white moon, the neighbor's white Christmas lights, and the white snow, the purity of the idyllic setting I was in. A car drove by with a father and mother in the front seat and kids sleeping in the back seat, the family undoubtedly on their way home from Christmas Eve celebrations. That wouldn't be my life anytime soon—no Samantha, no Alexander. No sorority sisters or parties.

There was nothing left of who I used to be.

*****

"That's a cute top," I said to Steele as she held up a striped tank top that was on clearance. All the summer clothes were on deep discount considering no one was buying tanks for thirty-degree weather.

We were browsing clothes in The Limited, the nicest clothing store in the small Jacobs mall. I realized that the last time I was in this store, around six months ago, pregnancy had never even crossed my mind.

"Let's try on all these clothes now, before we go eat lunch," Steele suggested. "I want to eat my Panda Express in peace without worrying about getting bloated."

When she said the word 'bloated,' it reminded me of my miscarriage. The doctor had said my stomach might retain water, and now that I was a few weeks past miscarrying, my body was slowly starting to feel normal again. No more cramps, no more back pain, no more bloat.

I followed Steele around the store, trying to focus on our fashion options. We tried on some jeans, and she even made me try on a New Year's Eve sequined dress, which was so short I started laughing. I came out of the dressing room and modeled for Steele.

"See!" I said, still laughing. "This is what happens when you're 5'9"! This dress is way too short."

"You poor baby. You and your long legs, it must be so hard for you! To look that hot in a dress. I feel so sorry for you!"

I laughed again and for a moment, I thought about buying the dress and making Steele plan a fun New Year's Eve for us. But I thought better of it, went back into the dressing room, and changed back into my corduroys.

As we made our way through a couple more stores and then up to the food court, Steele went straight for the Panda Express while I went for the Sbarro Pizza. Like my mom, I was a carb girl, and thanks to my mom's new diet, it was all I'd been eating for the last few days. I ordered my pepperoni slice and a large Diet

Coke, then met Steele at a table by the carousel.

"How are you feeling, being out like this?" Steele asked, probably wondering if it was a bad idea for us to sit so close to the carousel, full of moms riding with their babies, taking pictures with their disposable cameras to lock in the moment.

"I'm okay," I said. "I'm glad I decided not to go back to school this spring semester. There's no way I could go back to the sorority life...or risk seeing Alexander on campus. I need time to heal."

"I understand."

I tore off a small piece of pizza crust, popping it in my mouth as I said, "Also, Alexander wrote me."

"What? What do you mean? Like a letter? Do you have it?" Steele asked eagerly.

I fidgeted. I'd been carrying the letter everywhere, trying to feel closer to Alexander. I pulled the letter out of my purse and handed it to Steele. She looked me in the eye, silently asking permission to read it. I nodded, my fingers tapping my legs. Steele pulled the two pages out of the folded envelope and started to read it. I sat there in silence, trying to calm the nervous energy in my body by watching the kids run to pick out which horse they wanted to ride on the carousel.

After a few minutes I saw Steele's eyes tear up a bit, then she refolded the letter and placed it back in the envelope, handing it to me.

"Wow," was all she said.

I sighed. "You know Steele, I think the thing that gets me the most is when he said he loved me, like past tense. I know it's over, but to see your relationship written down in the past tense is a tough pill to swallow."

Steele nodded. "How did you feel when he wrote that part about you being a doctor?" she asked as she took a bite of her egg roll.

"I think it's classic Alexander, trying to see something in me that isn't there."

"What if it is there?"

I smirked and rolled my eyes, thinking it was ridiculous that Steele was now on Alexander's bandwagon to make me become a doctor. But then Steele leaned forward and looked me dead in the eyes.

"Lauren, what if there was a reason for everything that happened to you this month?" she said. "What if you took all this trauma and everything that you lost, and you harnessed it into something incredible? What if Alexander was onto something and what if you allowed yourself, just for a minute, to think it too? If Alexander believes in you and I believe in you, maybe you could find it within yourself to believe in you too?"

PART III

OCTOBER 2016

CHAPTER 24

IT WAS A BEAUTIFUL LATE-OCTOBER SATURDAY, and the town of Jacobs had laid claim to the most colorful willowy trees, various shades of dark red, burnt orange, and mustard yellow. We watched the leaves fall, one by one, as a group of thirty was gathered at a small cemetery on the east side of town. Today was Emma's burial and getting out of bed felt like an acceptance of her death. It felt wrong.

Emma had been dead for three days, and her parents had decided to have an outdoor memorial for her. Feeling that her body had been put through so much during her short life, they'd arranged for Emma to be buried versus cremated. And they arranged a proper funeral, as Wendy and Jason Webinson wanted to honor their daughter, and so their family, a few friends, and a few members of Emma's medical team were invited to this gut-wrenching event.

The sun was shining with a tame wind, and through tears, many of Emma's family stood up to read poems, Bible passages, and tell stories about Emma. Of course, every story included Emma in her hospital crib because she never had a life beyond Covenant Medical Hospital. In fact, she had only been in three rooms in her entire life: the operating room when she was born, another operating room during her surgery, and her NICU room. I guess some could say that Emma barely had a life at all. But what she did for so many of us during that time made her a legend.

Of course, I didn't get to share with the group what Emma meant to me. I wouldn't get to stand in front of Emma's friends and family and tell them that this little baby brought back the man I once loved. I didn't get to cry over Emma's casket and tell her that because of her, I felt alive again, and because of her, I had fallen in love with her surgeon. I didn't get to tell the group that because of Emma, I got to show my value and worth as a professional to the one person that inspired me to become what I am today. Instead, I had to sit there, like the stoic physician, nodding and whispering between hugs that Emma's little body could not withstand the physical trauma, and that now, she was no longer in pain.

Wendy stood to speak and opened a piece of paper. She took in a deep, shaky breath.

"My dearest Emma," she started. "I remember the day that you were born. We were so worried about you and your health. And yet, the day you were born was the happiest day of—"

All of a sudden, a series of helicopters started approaching in the distance. They were flying so low that even though they were far away, they drowned out Wendy's speech. Some of the guests even put their hands over their ears. We all looked up. The helicopters came closer now, flying almost directly overhead. I could see American flags and presidential seals...the campaign. Our minds shifted from honoring Emma to thinking about the election in only ten days. Ten days and it would all be over; our small community would once again be at peace. Or, without Emma, would anything be peaceful for this group ever again?

We tried to wait out the helicopters passing overhead, but one helicopter kept hovering in the distance, causing enough noise to prevent Wendy, or anyone else, from giving a tribute. There were no microphones, and the continued sounds of the helicopters turned our feelings of grief into feelings of disgust. Everyone was glancing at one another, unsure of who should make the first move. But we all just wanted to leave.

"We'll all meet back at Wendy and Jason's house!" Wendy's dad tried to yell over the noise.

We made our way to our cars. As we did, the helicopters created a wind tunnel, and many of the women had to hold down their dresses and skirts. Ashley, one of Emma's favorite nurses, attended the burial and we drove together. I had picked her up from her apartment.

"Those helicopters were insane. I wonder if there's a rally around here today," Ashley said as we finally had a moment of silence in my Prius. "It's hard to keep track of it all."

"It's so disruptive," I agreed. "They had to see that they were flying so low over a cemetery, and we were gathering for a burial. I mean, Emma deserves better."

Ashley nodded, and though I wanted to fill the grief-filled silence, I couldn't bring myself to make small talk.

After the quiet ride to Wendy and Jason's house, I parked my Prius, and we walked to their front door. Many of the burial guests had already arrived, and they were staring Ashley and me up and down as we rubbed our shoes on the floor mat in the foyer. We made our way from the front hall to the living room to hug Wendy, then to the kitchen to make ourselves a plate for lunch.

Traditionally, I would have thought that the guests were throwing daggers my way, blaming me for Emma's death. That often happens when a patient dies; the family blames the doctor. It's even more prevalent when the patient is a baby because the death of an infant is so horrific and jarring that people do anything to make sense of it, and an easy way to make sense of a death is to blame the caretaker.

However, the stares today were more likely for Ashley, who didn't recognize it, but she was quite literally the most beautiful girl on the planet. I always joked that if she weren't a nurse in a small Midwestern town, she'd have to be in Paris walking the Givenchy runway. Tall, blonde, lean, and a great dresser, today she wore a black sweater dress with a black leather jacket and black booties. I told her she looked funeral chic as I picked her up, her laughing that Emma would have loved trying to grab at her leather jacket zippers.

Ashley and I stood in the kitchen, remarking on how great

all the food looked.

"This was donated by Jason's work, his accounting firm," Wendy's mom said as she waved her hand among all the Italian dishes. "Lasagna, rigatoni, salad...oh! Make sure you get some garlic bread, too. I just took some out of the oven."

"Thank you so much, this looks delicious," I said. I grabbed a plate and paused, then looked right at Wendy's mom. "I...I think we met once before. I'm Dr. Leonard; I was one of Emma's physicians. I'm so sorry. Emma was so special."

"I know who you are," Wendy's mom said in an accusing way.

A lump rose in my throat. I could feel tears welling in my eyes. I swallowed and nodded.

Ashley and I quickly made our plates and headed to the dining room, thankful to be the only people in it. I felt more comfortable being away from the other guests.

"Do you think she blames us?" Ashley whispered as we sat down. She laid her napkin in her lap.

I shrugged. "I think, Ashley, that I still blame myself, so maybe she has a right to blame me."

Ashley sat there, pushing a lasagna noodle around her plate and avoiding eye contact. I knew what she was thinking. Was she supposed to let what I said be a fleeting comment, or was she supposed to comfort me? I didn't blame her; what was she even supposed to say to that? I berated myself for even admitting it out loud.

"Dr. Leonard...it's not your fault," Ashley finally said. "You were constantly monitoring her bloodwork and her feeding schedules, and I've never seen you spend so much time with one patient. You were always holding her—"

"I loved Emma very much," I interrupted, my head starting to pound from the stress.

Ashley looked down, not having yet touched her food, and nodded. "I know we aren't supposed to do that," she said. "Love our patients, I mean, but I could tell how Emma was so special to you. She was a special baby."

All of a sudden, I had no appetite. I sat there quietly, not knowing how to engage in a conversation in which there was so much more than met the eye. What was I supposed to do? Detail my own trauma, my affair, my failed marriage? But then, Ashley gave me an opening.

"I don't think I ever asked you, but why did you decide to become a neonatologist?"

I smiled. Usually, I gave the standard party line, that there was no better patient than an infant because they couldn't talk back and their bodies healed quickly. I would always deliver those lines so effectively. But today, having seen Emma in a casket, anything less than the truth felt like a betrayal to her.

"My trajectory to becoming a doctor, and landing in neonatology, was grounded in trying to turn pain into progress," I started. "When I was in college, I was studying pre-med, a suggestion from my high school guidance counselor. I'd excelled in science classes and took an interest in medicine in high school. I was about halfway through undergrad at OSU studying medicine when..." I paused. "I got pregnant. I was actually really excited, Ashley. My boyfriend was also in pre-med, and I thought that I would become a young mother and follow his career. I lost the baby, though, early in the pregnancy."

"I'm so sorry," Ashley said, trying to make eye contact with me.

I looked up at her, a young girl herself, wondering if she too, had ever had a miscarriage. It felt wrong to ask her, although I knew how common it was, and how talking about it could be cathartic. Still, losing Samantha hurt so much, even now, and I didn't want to have to engage Ashley in that pain.

"It took me a while to get back on my feet," I admitted. "I lived with my parents for almost two years after that, working at Covenant Medical as a receptionist, and then I transferred to Kent State. My best friend was finishing her undergrad there and had just gotten accepted to their grad school education program. While she did her grad school program, I finished my undergrad. But I kept up the pre-med major and graduated. I couldn't believe it, but when I focused on my studies, I actually excelled."

Ashley nodded. "That's great that you were able to get back to school."

"I think I wanted to escape the perils of my life by becoming a doctor, if that makes sense," I conceded. "Becoming pregnant at such a young age like that was so blindsiding, and the miscarriage had this ripple effect of breaking up with my boyfriend and dropping out of school. When I finally got back on my feet, I thought going all-in on becoming a doctor, just diving into my studies, would be less invasive than trying to have a life. I just accepted that my life took those sharp turns, and I decided to focus on the one thing I could control, which was doing well in school."

I took a drink of my water and breathed in slowly, realizing that with every passing day, the stories of our past get even more complex, more layered. In a year's time, would Emma's death become part of my past? Would it be one more story to tell?

I decided to keep talking. "And I did med school a little slower than most too, choosing neonatology because I think, in some half-romantic and half-sick way, I was trying to make up for losing my baby, for having the miscarriage and having my life fall apart. I think…" I paused, attempting to find the right words. "I think I thought the loss of my baby had to make sense. I had to be able to point to something to say, 'This is why.' And the only way for it to make sense was to let it drive me to help save other babies."

I'd never told any of my colleagues this. I wasn't even sure why I was telling Ashley. But if I was honest with myself, it felt good to say it out loud. And Ashley, working in the NICU, surely understood, at least in some small way.

I shrugged. "Maybe I couldn't have saved my own baby, but I could sure try to save those that came across my NICU." And then choking up, I added, "And here I am, having let another baby die."

"That's not true," Ashley said, shaking her head. "Do you ever wonder what your college boyfriend would think about you being a successful neonatologist and using the miscarriage as inspiration for your area of medicine?"

I smiled, knowing that the one unutterable piece of this story included that the boyfriend was Emma's surgeon. And that his belief all those years ago in me becoming a doctor was what catapulted me through those lonely nights studying. The idea that someone out there thought I was good enough. That one day I could show Alexander that I had 'made it.' And finally, when that day did come with our patient Emma, she felt like a reincarnation of Samantha. Emma gave us, fleetingly, a glimpse into what life could have been for us.

All of this, of course, couldn't be spoken aloud.

"I would hope he would be proud of me," I answered, this time not making eye contact with Ashley.

As we ate, Ashley and I continued to talk, sharing stories about Emma, then talking about next week's work schedule, plans for Halloween, and finally, election predictions.

After we had finished eating, we walked back into the kitchen. Wendy's mom was taking yet another loaf of garlic bread out of the oven.

"Girls, take some food home to your families!" she called. "I have Tupperware in the corner, make yourselves something to go!"

We politely declined, never making eye contact with Wendy's mom.

Wendy came into the kitchen next, and she teared up at seeing Ashley and me again. I felt confined, running into Emma's kin at every turn and was a little jealous that Wendy got to own all the pain of being the mother to lose Emma. In some disastrous way, I wanted to relive my past trauma, being the mom and losing a child. I wanted to have proprietary over Emma. But as I saw the pain on Wendy's face, I snapped out of it, recognizing that my miscarriage could not have carried the pain that Wendy was now experiencing. Often when I thought about losing Samantha, I thought 'It could always be worse. Other people have it worse.' And here, I was right.

"Thank you for all you did for Emma," Wendy said to us. We gave an awkward group hug, then Ashley and I headed straight for the door, relieved to leave the scene and distance ourselves from the grief.

But my heart didn't let me leave my grief at their house. A few minutes into driving Ashley home, I started crying.

Ashley turned to look at me. "Oh, Dr. Leonard, it's so hard, I know."

"At least you were with Emma in her last few hours of life," I said, still mad at myself. "I spent her last hours at a fucking swim practice. This morning, I was even blaming my son's nightly activities in my head, Ashley, because he had swim practice while Emma was struggling to live. And you fucking called me!" I shouted, my words echoing in my Prius. "You fucking called me on our drive home from practice, and I didn't call you back. I was trying to be with William and now, look, Emma's dead."

Having this breakdown in front of my employee was unprofessional, but at this point, I figured I had already gone past the point of no return. The dam was breaking whether I wanted it to or not, and I had no way of stopping it.

"Lauren, I promise you, no one could have done anything to keep her alive," Ashley said gently. "Her white blood cell count dropped so rapidly. She had so many issues. You did what you could, but it was out of your hands."

I knew Ashley had no shot at actually making me understand that Emma's death was not my fault. She only had half the tragic story, innocent to the knowledge of my affair with Alexander, how I had compromised Emma's care by recklessly sleeping with her other doctor. Ashley didn't know the domino effect that I created. If I hadn't slept with Alexander, I wouldn't have been so upset. If I hadn't been upset, I wouldn't have needed to go to William's swim practice and ground myself by watching him swim and talking to Steele. If I hadn't been at swim practice, I would have worked that night and would have been in the NICU.

I would have been in Emma's room.

I could have saved her.

But instead, I pushed that first domino, I thought, *and a million pieces fell, and now she's dead.*

Chapter 25

I PULLED THE SHINY BLUE PANTS out of William's closet as he was stirring in his sleep, knowing I had only a few moments before he would be popping out of bed this morning. I tried my best to gather his entire Superman costume, wanting to lay the Halloween costume out to add to his excitement when he woke up.

A few moments later, William sat straight up in bed. He turned toward me, grinning as he asked, "Today is Halloween, right?"

"You got it, kiddo!" I exclaimed, trying to match his enthusiasm but feeling silly for having such high energy this early in the morning. I took a sip of my coffee and set it back on his dresser.

"Principal Dan is going to let us have a Halloween parade

in the gym!"

As someone who had always hated Halloween, I tried not to dampen his excitement. Instead, I nodded and smiled. William had a fun day ahead of him, with the parade, classroom party, and then trick-or-treating.

"Okay, buddy, here are your pants, and here is your puffed out chest with the 'S' on it," I said as I patted the inventory of his costume, showing William the various pieces he would need to put on. "And wait, where is your cape?" I said, turning back toward the closet to see if I had forgotten to pull it out. "You were wearing it yesterday in the basement."

"I'll go get it!" William yelled. He jumped out of bed and ran out of the bedroom, descending the basement stairs like a herd of elephants.

Today was going to be a busy day. William's school had an early dismissal, and then trick-or-treating began later in the afternoon for our neighborhood. William would likely have a bucket full of candy by 6:00 p.m. And then Billy and I, shockingly, had a date.

Neither Billy nor I were fans of Halloween, but we both took the day off work to celebrate this holiday that our son reveled in. When our Google calendar informed us that both Billy and I had the same weekday off, I basically coerced Billy into going out after trick-or-treating. He had been ambivalent, but I reminded him that the bar downtown had an Octoberfest beer thing and he agreed. Then, I called my parents to come watch William for the night—and limit his Halloween candy intake. Before Billy could take back agreeing to the date, I let him know that my parents would watch William and spend the night.

As William came back into his room, cape now in hand, I started to debate dressing up myself today. It felt foreign to me to actually *want* to participate in this way. Maybe it was because I was never the creative type that could design my own costumes. Or maybe it was because as a little kid I was always so tall, never fitting into any of the kid costume sizes. Or maybe it was because as an adult, I had to decline so many Halloween parties because I always had shifts at the hospital. For so many years, I'd considered Halloween a lost holiday.

But this year, Halloween fell on a Monday, and being off work felt like a new start. Today was the first day in a long time that I felt any type of promise for myself. The anguish of the affair and the heaviness of Emma's funeral, only days before, had created so much chatter in my brain and chipped away at my heart until it started to feel like it was breaking into two. Finally, today was perhaps a new beginning for me and Billy.

"Should Mommy dress up for Halloween?" I asked William as he started putting on his blue pants.

"Do you want to wear my old fireman costume?" he replied seriously. I was laughing as Billy came into William's bedroom. "Dad! I'm changing into my costume now!"

"Can I see those muscles? Can you do a Superman flex for me?" Billy asked as he showed William how to do a bicep curl pose.

"Billy, my parents said they would be here tonight around 6:30," I said, trying to remind him about our date without being blatant about it.

As excited as a married woman might be for a day off together to enjoy her child, Halloween activities, and a night out, I still found myself feeling like a fish out of water. *What the hell are Billy and I even going to talk about?* The election was in eight days, and Billy was inundated with his work's State of Ohio polling technology contract. I doubted he had much to discuss beyond his job. I certainly had a lot on my mind, but absolutely none of which I was prepared to tell Billy. A pit formed in my stomach at the thought of tonight's date. I was indeed going to reveal the affair to him at some point in the future. Maybe not tonight, but I owed him at least the truth.

"All right," he said apathetically, not looking at me but instead focusing on helping William into his Superman vest.

Soon, Billy and I had William dressed as a superhero and Billy took William to school.

I had some time on my hands this morning, a rarity, and so I made the decision to break out of my Halloween-hating mold and try to look for a costume to wear tonight. Having no originality, the only place I thought I might have any luck was Target. So off I went, stopping first at Starbucks like any self-respecting Target shopper, and allowing myself at least one to two hours of blissful distraction.

As I made my way to the Halloween section at Target, I turned into my old self again, lamenting at just how gross the holiday was. Skulls, black makeup, coffins, and the like. *Remind me again why people enjoy this holiday?* I thought as I sipped my venti extra hot cinnamon dolce latte. As I rounded the corner and saw all the Halloween family costumes, my heart sank. Most adults appreciated Halloween not just to see their kids dressed up, but because they got to wear themed costumes with their spouses as well. Halloween, for so many families, was a lighthearted day, a time to come together.

I sighed. Billy and I were always missing out on things like this. Whether it was seeing pictures of matching Halloween costumes at Target and later on Facebook, hearing my neighbor talk about her trip to an all-inclusive resort with her husband, or the nurses asking me for nights off to go to concerts with their significant others. My marriage had none of that. I typically ushered these thoughts out of my mind, rationalizing, for instance, that I was too busy to coordinate costumes with my husband or that he'd never want to wear a costume with me. But at every turn in my life, and literally every turn down the Target aisles, there was another glaringly obvious example of what was missing from my relationship with Billy.

Why couldn't we have at least some of those things?

As I started looking at costumes for myself, I saw adult Superman and Superwoman costumes that mirrored William's. *Perhaps we could all go as the same superhero,* I thought, touching the plastic packaging. What was the worst that could happen? And instead of the worst, what if Billy laughed, wore his costume, and we all got a picture and I posted it to Facebook? Could this be our chance to be a normal family?

"If you want to make your marriage work, just buy the fucking costumes," I muttered under my breath. They were $39.99 per costume, but I shrugged. It would be money well spent if it put Billy in a good mood for our date.

Smiling, I laid the costumes in my shopping cart. I went over to the women's clothing section and bought a blue sweater to go over my costume for when Billy and I went out for drinks. Then, I made my way to the men's section and bought Billy some red sneakers to wear with his costume. I laughed as I looked at the cart full of superhero-colored gear. No wonder people liked Halloween. *This is actually kind of fun*, I thought.

I glanced at my phone and saw I'd only been gone for about an hour. Billy would be back from the school run by now, but I could take a little more time to wander around Target. Leisurely, I strolled around the store until the last of my latte was gone, then made my way to check out. My cashier, a girl in her early twenties, seemed like a Halloween enthusiast.

"Wow! Matching costumes! That's so cool," she said as she started scanning my items.

"Yeah, my husband and I are taking our son trick-or-treating, then he and I are going out for drinks," I said. "Are you doing anything?"

"My boyfriend and I are going as ketchup and mustard. It's going to be great." She grinned at me as she reached for the red sneakers. "I bought red and yellow felt, then found this YouTube tutorial about how to sew everything. It's all based on body length, which was kind of weird, but it's been fun."

"Oh wow," I said as I pulled out my credit card. "That… sounds like a lot of work."

"Yeah, and I still have to go home after my shift and make the hats!"

"Well…good luck," I said as I picked up my bags. I hoped

she didn't notice me change from chatty to awkward. I had no idea how to talk to her about *making* costumes or anything else related to Halloween. "Enjoy tonight."

"You too!" the cashier replied.

I took the receipt from her, left the store, and placed the costumes in the trunk of my car. I removed the costumes from their original wrapping and laid them perfectly flat. Staring at them, I realized that I was looking forward to tonight with Billy. This was me, trying. I was getting out of my comfort zone. I was pushing him to go out to dinner, I was pushing myself to wear matching costumes, and hopefully, we would both rise to the occasion and enjoy the night, and each other.

*****

"TRICK OR TREAT!" William shouted as our neighbors came to the door with a basket full of mini-Snickers bars.

William was in his element, running from one house to the next, collecting as much candy as possible. He wasn't trick-or-treating with any other children, which I self-consciously took as other parents not wanting to spend time with me and Billy. There were couples getting together with their army of kids to trick-or-treat all around our block. It was just that my family wasn't a part of it. Maybe it was because I was usually MIA during Halloween and they didn't think to invite me. Or it could be because Billy had little personality around big groups of people. Who knew?

Just focus on how happy William is, I reminded myself.

William had also been my little negotiator and closer for the matching superhero costumes. When I brought the costumes home, I'd laid them out on our kitchen table so that they would be the first thing William and Billy saw when they came home from school. Sure enough, William was ecstatic that his parents were going to dress up like him, and it was hard for Billy to say no to a kid squealing with delight that his daddy was going to wear his same costume.

"I haven't dressed up for Halloween since I was a kid," Billy had said to me as we were in our bedroom changing into our costumes.

"It's fun to try something new; maybe we could start doing it every year," I'd suggested, trying to make my voice sound flirtatious and not demanding.

Billy didn't respond, but he didn't complain about the costume, the sizing, the red shoes, or the fact that I suggested we wear our costumes—at least the superhero tops—to the Octoberfest bar downtown. And I loved the way I looked in my costume. As I'd stood in front of our full-length mirror, I'd decided to curl my hair and put it in a high ponytail to play up the sporty part of Superwoman. I put on my knee-high boots that I'd barely ever worn, making my costume look even sexier. I actually felt…confident.

Turning around, I saw Billy in his costume, and the horrible twinges of guilt crept in. I was harboring a horrible secret from a person that agreed to wear a matching costume, but I'd decided to push all the shame, guilt, and despair out of my mind and focus on making the most out of tonight.

We'd now been trick-or-treating for almost an hour, with William's 'Trick or Treat' getting louder and louder with each house. I could tell that other couples we ran into were surprised to see us—and to see us dressed up together.

"Billy, hi man, how's it going!" Caleb, a lawyer that lived down the block, said as we passed him and his kids. "Great night to be out, right?" he said, referring to the unseasonably warm weather for the last day of October in Ohio. "Hey man, feel free to stop by tonight. I just installed a flat-screen outside in my gazebo, and I'm going to light the fire pit and watch Monday Night Football."

Billy didn't respond, almost like he hadn't even heard anything Caleb said.

"It's Vikings-Bears, it should be a good game," Caleb followed up. He glanced at me, his brow furrowed, probably wondering why Billy didn't respond.

Billy just shuffled his feet, barely making eye contact with Caleb or myself. My cheeks started burning. I didn't want to speak for my husband, but I had to do something.

"Thanks, Caleb," I said, trying to make my voice casual. "Actually, Billy and I are trying that Octoberfest brew at O'Malley's tonight."

"Oh, fun!" Caleb replied, obviously surprised given his tone and raised eyebrows. "Well, enjoy!"

As we continued along, walking down the sidewalks of our neighborhood, we kept running into neighbors whose eyes widened as they saw us. I got asked so many questions…how did I get my hair to curl like that, where did I get the matching costumes, shouldn't I be at the hospital, and my personal favorite, "I've never seen you and Billy together before! Are you sure you're married?" this one old lady at the end of the block joked.

"I don't think I would be in this costume if I wasn't married," Billy replied for me.

It made me laugh, even though it was a knock to the costume and perhaps a knock to the staleness of our relationship. How could everyone in the world see it except for Billy?

Soon enough, it was time to go home. My parents would be here soon. It wasn't tough to drag William away from trick-or-treating as he knew he was about to enjoy all his candy, plus he idolized his grandparents and loved spending time with them.

When we got back to the house, my parents were already there. As we walked in, they scooped up William and fumbled with their iPhones to get a picture of all of us in our matching costumes.

"I can't get the camera to turn around. All I can see is myself," my mom said.

"Grandma! Just hit the circled arrows in the corner!" William said.

"Oh, there it is! William, you are so smart. Okay, everyone say 'Cheese'!" my mom said as she took the picture and sent it to my phone.

My parents asked William what he wanted for dinner, which of course he answered with his favorite: 'Ohio-style' pizza. He even asked me if he could go out to eat in his costume.

"You guys have to wear your costume too the whole night!" William demanded of us.

"Sounds good, sweetheart, we will," I replied as I bent down to his level. We hugged, our puffed costumes barely allowing us to wrap our arms around each other.

As my parents and William headed out the door, I went into the bathroom to reapply my makeup. I saw out of the corner of my eye that Billy had come into our bedroom and was changing into his favorite ten-year-old jeans.

"Are you keeping on the Superman vest?" I asked, thinking of what we'd literally just promised our seven-year-old. "We gotta wear our costumes, right?"

"Honestly, Lauren, that Octoberfest beer...I don't even think it's going to be any good," Billy said, not at all answering my question but apparently trying to get out of our date.

"You don't want to go out?" I asked.

"I thought maybe we could just stay here."

"Is it because you want to go over to Caleb's and watch the football game?"

Billy exhaled a laugh. "No, I'm just not in the mood to go out."

"You don't have to wear your costume," I offered, my heart racing. "Let's just go out for one drink, then we can come home. One hour, that's all. Please?"

He shook his head. "I'd really rather just stay home," he said. "I need to catch up on emails, and I'd like to watch TV and wait for William to come back."

I looked over at him in the bedroom then back to myself in the mirror in the bathroom. In mere seconds, I went from having gorgeous hair, a cute costume, and a sparkle in my eye to sliding down onto the bathroom floor, my eyes black with tear-stained mascara and my cape and tights ripped in a fit of fury.

"Lauren…Lauren…Lauren!" Billy called as I went from silent, to emotional, to manic.

I sat on the bathroom floor, weeping and pounding my hand on our remodeled tile. I'd kept up the cheerfulness most of the day and really gave it my best shot at being a married couple, but here I was, coming up short yet one more time. Now, I felt like an imposter in this stupid costume.

"Are you okay? Lauren, are you okay?" Billy asked.

I hugged my knees to my chest, rocking back and forth. It had been wrong of me to think that Billy was going to follow through with our date. It was wrong of me to expect Billy to be a normal husband, and it was wrong of me to require anything of Billy considering that only a month ago, I'd cheated on him. I was in this perpetual purgatory, where I had no in and no out. I fell onto my side, using a bath towel as my pillow as I wailed.

I continued to weep as Billy stood there in the bedroom, not knowing what to say or what to do. That was part of our problem. We never advanced in our relationship because Billy didn't have social skills. His lack of communication was why we didn't have real conversations about our real problems. If I was going to have a dialogue with Billy, I was going to have to lead it, just like I always did.

"You don't love me," I said to Billy between tears.

Billy was silent as he stared at me.

"Billy, I'm so unhappy. I just want us to love each other again. We don't do normal couple things. We don't spend time together.

We don't have sex. We don't even talk with one another!" I cried as I laid in a fetal position on the cold bathroom tile.

"We aren't newlyweds anymore, Lauren."

Was that his sole argument? That love and passion inevitably fade as a marriage ages? He sat down on our bed, staring at his hands in his lap.

"I just want it to be how it used to be, Billy. We loved each other once," I said.

It was true. We did love each other once. We met when I was in med school at the University of Toledo College of Medicine, and my anxiety was reaching an all-time high. I'd decided to get into a young adults group that met on the weekends at the Presbyterian church, to take my mind off studying and my upcoming boards. Billy had joined that same group at the church a couple of months before me. His sister had made him join, driving her to each event as her car was perpetually in the shop. Billy grew up in Toledo, and by that time, he already had a good job there in IT.

Billy and I started talking one night in the parish basement as we all played cards. He was a bit bolder back then, a bit more confident, or perhaps he hadn't yet understood how he could shield himself from me. Nevertheless, he had more life in his eyes back then, and he'd asked me out one night. Very quickly, I knew he was someone that understood me.

As we started dating, he'd listened to me drone on and on about med school, petting my hair while I laid in his lap talking about how difficult my tests were and listening while I gave detailed descriptions of each of my patients and their prognoses.

As we got closer and our relationship developed, I was able to be honest about my desires to move back to my hometown of Jacobs and work at Covenant Medical. Billy had supported this, saying there were IT jobs everywhere and that he could work from anywhere.

Billy and I got married two years after we started dating, and I remember being so happy on our wedding day, knowing that I had a best friend for the rest of my life, someone that understood me, supported me in my job, and even supported my wishes for us to move away from his family so I could be closer to mine.

Now, curled up on the bathroom floor, I thought back to those first days of meeting Billy. When he was a different person. Or maybe he was the same person, and I just saw what I wanted to see in him, to fit into who I wanted him to be.

"Don't tell me that you want it to be how it used to be, Lauren," Billy said, his voice raised. "Do you understand how much I do to support this family? You come in here with a matching Halloween costume and expect a round of applause. You aren't here most of the time. I pick up the slack around the house. I shuffle William everywhere. I have a big job too. I'm sorry if I say I'm tired and don't want to go to some fucking bar tonight, but it's a little dramatic for you to say it's because I don't love you."

"But you don't," I persisted.

Billy didn't respond.

"I slept with someone," I said, the words coming out of my mouth as I sat upright, giving Billy the decency of being able to look him in the eye while I killed his reality of the faithful wife he was married to.

"What?" Billy asked as he turned toward me with a face of disbelief.

I started sobbing again. I couldn't believe I'd said it, but the guilt of Billy commenting that I was never home had bubbled up to the surface. He had meant, of course, that I worked all the time. But when he said that, I'd thought back to the night Alexander and I were at the hotel.

"I slept with someone," I repeated. "Last month, I had sex with another doctor, Alexander, that guy I used to date in college. I've been trying so hard, trying everything I can think of for so long to make this marriage work, and I did the wrong thing and had an affair," I said, very plainly stating the obvious. "I'm sorry."

Just then, the door to the garage opened, and I heard my parents walk in the house. William and my mom were laughing and my dad, likely having seen both our cars still in the garage, yelled into the house with a joyful cheer, "Well, the pizza place closed early for Halloween! I guess we'll do pizza delivery!"

All at once, Billy rushed into the bathroom and shut the door behind him, bending down and holding onto my arms. His eyes moved wildly, looking me up and down, taking in my ripped cape and torn tights and mascara raccoon eyes.

His eyes slowed when they reached mine. Still holding my arms firmly against the side of my body, Billy leaned toward me and said, "Don't do it again."

Then he got up, threw on a sweatshirt, and walked out of the bedroom, closing the door behind him. As he did, I could hear him say, "Sounds great, I'm hungry for pizza."

PART III

CHAPTER 26

THE NEXT MORNING, AROUND 5:00 A.M. before the sunrise, I
heard my parents leave the house. They had slept last night in
our guest bedroom on William's side of our long ranch-style
home. My parents, now in their mid-sixties, usually woke up at
the crack of dawn. Today, they woke up even before dawn and
had likely slipped out before William could wake up. If William
saw them this morning, he would beg to spend the day with his
grandparents and whine when we insisted he go to school.

As I heard them leave through the front door, I got out of
bed and went into the living room and started to text my mom.
As I did, I saw the picture she had texted me of the three of us
in our superhero costumes. The picture looked so...happy. The
smiles on our faces, William flexing in a muscleman pose, and
Billy's arm around my shoulder. The picture felt like fraud, and

I stared out the window, thinking about the difference twelve hours can make.

I decided to dial my mom's cell instead.

"Hi honey, we just headed out. We had so much fun with William last night," my mom said as she answered the phone.

"Hi Mom, yeah, I heard you guys leave. I just wanted to thank you for coming and—"

"Are you feeling any better? Billy said you weren't feeling well last night…do you think it was all the Halloween candy?"

My throat got tight, and tears started welling up in my eyes. I wanted to confide in my parents so badly about the hell I was going through emotionally. I wanted to be their little girl with a big problem, one that they could solve for me.

"No, not the candy," I lied, the weight of the world pressing down on me. "I think I had the stomach flu. I'm feeling mildly better this morning."

"Okay, sweetie, well take it easy," my mom said, her voice gentle. I squeezed my eyes shut as tears forced their way through. "Go back to bed, I hope you get some rest."

After I hung up, I went back into the bedroom, finding Billy already awake and getting out of bed. I stopped in my tracks at the bedroom door, not knowing if I should enter our bedroom and talk with him, attempting to pick up where we left off on the bathroom floor last night.

"Good morning," I said sheepishly.

"Good morning," he replied mechanically, without looking at me.

"How are you feeling this morning, with what happened last

night? Do you want to continue the conversation?" I asked.

"No," Billy said with a bit of a fake laugh.

He didn't give any indication of how he was feeling, and I knew I was not going to get any emotion out of him. *Just like always*, I thought. I'm not sure what exactly I wanted…did I want Billy to erupt in anger? Yell and scream and knock over a lamp? It would have shown passion, and it would have shown, in some twisted way, that he loved me. I think I was hoping for at least some dialogue, but I knew better than to think that Billy, overnight, would have found his way to become a conversationalist with his wife.

"Do you think we should start therapy?" I asked, again grasping at straws but trying to hold onto any way that we could talk about what happened with the affair and talk about ways to claw back our marriage. "I could get some great referrals, and we could Skype with the therapist. We don't have to go to someone here in Jacobs if you're worried about that," I said, trying to anticipate why he might be unagreeable to marriage counseling.

"You had an affair. I don't think a therapist will be able to change that."

"No," I agreed, looking down at the floor. "But maybe therapy could help us get back to a place where we could be a real couple again. A place where we could be happy together."

"Before last night, I didn't have a problem in this marriage, Lauren," Billy replied bluntly. "It sounds like *you* need therapy to straighten yourself out, and then maybe you'll be a better wife and happier in this marriage." He walked into our bathroom and pulled his face wash from the drawer.

I couldn't believe how simplistic he saw our relationship. And how, if there was an issue, it must be *my* issue. Yes, I was the one that cheated, but was I at fault for everything that was wrong in our relationship? So much of our broken marriage was not fault-based at all. We both had demanding jobs, we both had parental duties, we both had household responsibilities...all of that got in the way of having a healthy bond. That's nothing new. Every married couple on the planet needs to find ways to combat the perils of life in order to stay together. The difference with us was that any recognition of our perils was a blame placed on me.

"You can go to therapy and let me know what you learned," Billy finalized, ending the conversation abruptly as he turned on the shower and closed the bathroom door.

*****

At the beginning of November, I found myself starting not just a new month but a 24-hour shift. I sat at my desk. I finally had time to demand-plan the proposed census numbers for the NICU for the next few months. My mind was anywhere but work, equal parts pissed off and numb at what had transpired between Billy and me this morning. I thought being in the office would be a pleasant distraction, but my loneliness was overwhelming me instead.

I thought back to the summer. How I'd sat in this same chair and was so nervous to call Alexander to ask him about Emma's surgery. Back then, my life seemed so simple. I was a different person back then, more confident, more at peace. Now, I was upside down and making wrong choices at every turn.

Alexander had texted me a couple of days after Emma had died, asking how I was doing. I couldn't tell from the text if he truly cared or if it was a way for us to get together again. I was dealing with Billy's response to my affair, yet I was also curious and confused about Alexander and his intentions for me. *Does Alexander want to continue the affair?* I wondered, toying with the pen on my desk. *Is it just about sex for him? If so, is he upset that we only slept together the one time? Does he think about me during the day? Is he mad at me for Emma's death?*

Just as I'd done several months ago, I decided to google him. I debated searching him on my work laptop but thought better of it. I opened the Google web browser on my phone and typed in, "Alexander Smithton, Doctor, Ohio, Cleveland." A bunch of hits came up, and I toggled between the web results and the images. The images were mostly him in his white coat, standing in front of the Cleveland Clinic buildings with rows of other doctors.

I googled, "Smithton, Alexander, Doctor, Cleveland, Photography, 2016" to see if I could find any additional images. When I did, I found pictures of him from a photographer's website at a benefit. It was the Pediatric AIDS benefit at Cleveland Clinic, and there was an image of Alexander in a tux with a beautiful blonde that looked at least five years younger than him. She was gorgeous, wearing a purple eyelet dress and a bronzed tan.

I scrolled further down and found a more recent image from June 2016. It was of yet another benefit. This one depicted him speaking from a podium. I clicked on the image, taking me to the photography website. It was the Ronald McDonald House gala, and Alexander apparently spoke at it, as the image showed him with a champagne glass in his hand, toasting a crowd from the stage. Next to that picture was another picture of him with a small group. It looked like three couples, and he had his arm around the woman next to him. She was another stunning blonde, with a mega-watt smile and her hair in beachy waves. She was shorter than him but still wearing high heels, her petite frame complimenting him perfectly. I looked again at the date of the picture, Saturday, June 20, 2016.

I'd first reached out to him in June. *Was he dating this girl at the time?* I wondered. *Are they still dating?* My stomach started turning, and I could feel myself getting physically sick. I thought back to us having sex and wondered if he had had sex with this girl the night before or the night after. It was too much, and I grabbed my wastebasket from under my desk and vomited. My body was having a physical reaction to the trauma of my life, and in some way willing itself to live out the lie I had told my mom only hours before about having the stomach flu.

As I sat there, staring at this picture, my body exhausted, overwhelmed, and at its breaking point. I realized that I had now made a mess so big that I had no idea how to clean it up. How to clean it up logistically or how to clean it up inside myself. How would I heal a broken heart? How would I fall in love with Billy again? How would I fall out of love with Alexander?

I picked up the phone and called down to the NICU.

"Hi, Ginelle," I said as the nurse's station seemed abuzz. I could hear the click-clacking of fingers on keyboards and nurses talking in the background. "I'm up in my office working on the census projections, and unfortunately I'm not feeling well. I'm going to head out without coming down into the NICU, so I don't pass any potential virus. I'll be on call so please Skype or call with any medication changes or new orders needing to be written," I instructed. I then quickly called the pediatric physician on call and asked that he oversee the NICU for a couple hours.

I got up and looked in my mirror on the other side of my office, adjacent from the Monet painting. I looked haggard. I sighed. There was somewhere I had to go and someone I had to see. I sat back down at my desk, picking up my phone and shooting off a quick text. My heart started pounding out of my chest.

(Me) Hey, do you have time to meet tonight?

(Alexander) It's my shift for pediatric rounds until 5:00 pm, then I'm free after that. Would love to see you.

(Me) Perfect, I'll come to Cleveland.

He texted me his address and I googled it. It was downtown Cleveland, and I assumed that the PH by his condo number stood for 'Penthouse.'

I placed my laptop into my work bag, took off my white coat, and changed into the Lululemon leggings and tunic stored away in my workout bag. I had packed it the week before, an attempt to work out in the hospital gym that obviously never materialized.

I made my way out of the hospital and to the parking garage.

For the second time in only a month, I was being untruthful to both my workplace and my husband about being on my 24-hour shift. I knew this was another wrong turn. But at this point, I felt I had nothing left to lose. I couldn't focus on my job. I couldn't get through to Billy, in any capacity. So, I latched onto the one guy that did want to speak with me and headed north toward Cleveland.

I knew I needed to see Alexander, and we needed to get to the heart of what we went through, all those years ago.

CHAPTER 27

"Excuse me, ma'am. Ma'am. Ma'am, who are you here to see?"

A doorman ran up beside me as I attempted to open the glass exit doors in Alexander's lobby multiple times to reach the elevator bank. I had arrived at Alexander's condo building in downtown Cleveland and walked right past the front desk, my mind scattered as I tried to plan for the conversation we were about to have.

"Oh, I'm sorry," I said, embarrassed. I turned toward the doorman. "Um, I'm here to see Dr. Alexander Smithton, I think he's...I think he's on the top floor."

"Certainly, ma'am. If you'd like to take a seat in one of those chairs, I'll call him."

I sat down in the modern swivel chair in the lobby as instructed, watching the doorman pick up the phone behind his desk to call Alexander.

"Hello, Dr. Smithton. Hi, this is Eddie the doorman. Good evening, sir. There's a woman here to see you..." Eddie paused, covering the receiver with his hand as he turned to me. "Ma'am, what's your name?"

"Dr. Leonard," I replied, giving myself some street-cred and hopefully showing the doorman I wasn't just another one of Alexander's girls.

"Dr. Leonard is here in the lobby...oh okay, certainly, sir. Have a good evening."

"You can go up now," Eddie said to me as he hung up the phone. I finally had access beyond this lobby.

I stood up and Eddie programmed the elevator for the Penthouse. I took the long ride up, and the elevator chimed as the doors opened. There was a wide hallway with only one door. *Jesus Christ,* I thought, *Alexander has this entire floor.*

I checked my hair and makeup in the gold-framed mirror next to the elevator. I'd attempted to freshen up in the car ride to Cleveland, but I certainly didn't look good. There was no amount of makeup that could cover up on the outside the way I felt on the inside.

I was about to knock on the door when Alexander opened it with a soft smile and a gentle hello. He was wearing nice pants, a button-down shirt, and dress shoes, looking much more put together than my casual Lululemon outfit and my hair in a top knot.

My attention was immediately drawn from him to the soft jazz music coming from his condo's entrance and the expanse of the condo itself. It was a two-floor residence with a winding staircase and a panoramic view of Lake Erie. It was breathtakingly gorgeous, a mix of the blue water below and the city skyline above.

"Oh my God, Alexander, this is incredible," I said, my jaw agape as I walked into the residence and looked around. I immediately felt out of place, not fancy enough to be privy to such an elegant home.

"Thanks. It's really serene, right?" Alexander said as he gave me a quick tour of the marble kitchen, the all-white living room, and the masculine dining room. It was one big room, with the amazing view complementing the sleek, modern furniture and flowing white drapes that descended two floors and added to the grandeur of the home. There were fresh flowers in the kitchen (green hydrangeas) and about fifty candles of different sizes unlit in the hollow fireplace below the massive flat-screen TV programmed to display a painting.

Once the sheer awe wore off a bit, I realized it was highly unlikely that Alexander actually outfitted this condo. At first, I thought that perhaps he bought it furnished, but then my heart sank, knowing that it was quite possible that the interior design was at the hands of one of the girls I saw today in the Google images.

"Yes, it's very serene, it's just...." My voice trailed off. My brain started to see dollar signs, and I calculated that the money Alexander must make was staggering. I always knew he was successful but, my God. This was next level, even for a doctor.

"Would you like a drink?" Alexander asked, my thoughts

still preoccupied with my surroundings. I didn't look him in the eye once.

"Uhm, sure," I said. I needed to relax a little bit if I was going to start this conversation.

Alexander walked across the kitchen, up two steps into the dining room, over to what looked like a wine cellar, and grabbed a wine and an electronic wine opener. As he made his way back to the kitchen and opened the bottle, I was immediately anxious that he might spill this red wine on his lustrous bone-white marble. He was careful as he poured the wine in his-and-hers tiny decanters, then poured the decanters into wine glasses. It all felt so highbrow, and I tried my best to center myself and focus on why I came here.

"Thanks for meeting with me tonight," I said as I took the glass of wine in my hand. The sun was setting more and more each minute, creating a purple skyline that made for an even more spectacular view.

"Sure. I've missed you," he replied, toasting my glass delicately, probably trying to feel out what tonight was going to be.

"Umm, Alexander, uh, so…" I said, stammering as I was trying to find the right words, us standing in the kitchen awkwardly. "If it's okay with you, I'd just like to talk with you tonight."

Alexander looked confused, but he nodded. "Would you like to sit down?"

Grabbing the wine and stretching his hand out, he guided me toward the dining room, and my eye went straight to the massive modern chandelier with circular beams that illuminated the entire condo. I felt inadequate sitting down at the table, not dressed well enough, nor smart enough to carry on the intellectual conversation that this room deserved.

"So, what's on your mind?" Alexander said as he sat back in his chair, crossing his leg over his knee and taking a sip of his wine.

Already, this was such a welcome departure from Billy, who didn't want me to speak at all, much less share my thoughts or perspective. I tried not to compare the two men, but the differences were obvious and just for a moment, I forgave myself for falling in love with Alexander.

"Well, for starters, I googled you today and saw a lot of pretty blondes by your side in gala pictures," I blurted out, smiling a bit. Was I trying to flirt with him, or trying to get him to go to confession?

"Ah, I see," Alexander said, leaning forward uncomfortably, probably regretting inviting me over.

"Did one of them design this place?" I asked, looking around again.

"Katherine, yes."

I took a deep breath. This conversation was going nowhere. This wasn't what I wanted to talk about. I needed to explain to Alexander why I was here. I started to open my mouth to speak, but he beat me to it.

"They're with me for the conquest, Lauren. What, you think they're with me for my height and my hair?" He smiled briefly as he rubbed his balding head. "Since I've gotten divorced, there's a whole new crop of women who are younger, more beautiful, more charismatic, more brilliant, more determined. They see me as this eligible bachelor, and each woman pours herself into trying to be the one to give me a family, and give me children, and give me a lovely home," he said, raising his arms to the space around us.

"It is lovely," I said.

"They think they can reel me in like some fish who is unhappy in the water and would prefer to be on land, gasping for breath." He was silent for a moment and then he added, "They all think they can save me, make me more whole, and be the one to change me."

"Well, I can certainly relate," I said, "I was the first to attempt that."

Alexander laughed. "Yes, you were. But back then it was real. Our lives were still out ahead of us. You loved me for me, Lauren."

So many lost years that had escaped were now sitting between us, the pain on our faces matching the distressed mahogany table we were sitting at.

"It's been difficult for me, seeing you again after all this time, sleeping with you, and even seeing those girls on Google and being in your condo now," I said honestly. "I think, throughout the years…well, I became a doctor to please you, in a way. I mean, somewhere along the way it became about me and my goals and my desire to serve and to heal. But Alexander, all I ever wanted was to be enough for you." I started choking up, feeling tears well up in my eyes.

I suddenly felt like I was nineteen again, the girl who succeeded more at sorority parties than measuring up to Alexander's expectations. I bit my lip to force back the tears.

"Lauren. Lauren, you were *always* enough for me," Alexander said. The earnestness in his voice made me believe him this time. "That was the problem. You were always enough, and you were ten steps ahead of me. You were so smart, so popular, and I was no match for you. I always knew you'd be a wonderful physician. I remember yelling it to you over loud music while frat guys flirted with you at those college parties."

He looked out his window, and I wondered if he had made peace with himself, being the titan he now was, or if he felt he was still that kid, coming up short compared to those popular fraternity brothers.

I wanted Alexander to really hear me though, that his impact on my life was far-reaching.

"Well, you willed my life to be what it is today," I said, giving him the nod as to why I became a doctor.

"And you mine," Alexander said, this time more matter-of-factly.

"You always knew you would become a doctor," I said casually as I took a sip of my wine.

"Yeah, but do you remember what you said to me when we were in college?"

I shook my head. Alexander took a big gulp of his wine, as if the alcohol would help him deliver his lines.

"You stood in my apartment bedroom, and you said, 'Alexander, you'll become a great doctor, and that's all you'll ever be.'"

"I'm sorry I said that."

"You're sorry you said that?" Alexander, now visibly angry, retorted.

"I shouldn't have said that." My chest started pounding. "That was wrong of me. I'm sorry."

"Lauren, you're not the only one that shaped their life around what happened to us in college. The only woman that really loved me and really wanted to be with me for me? And wanted to be the mother of my child despite everything going against us? Well, she told me that I'd never be anything more than my profession. I *never* forgot that. It's led me to today, where all I have is my career...my surgeries, my speeches, and this fucking palace. So...you were right."

"No, that's not true," I replied, trying to make him understand. "You're more than your job."

"Is that why you called me in June?" he said. We both knew that I never would have reached out if not for his surgical expertise.

We sat there in silence for a few minutes, both of us taking the last sips of our wine and Alexander getting up to pour us both another glass. I was shocked by his revelation, that he'd never forgotten my words. I was astounded that through all these years, we had, until this point, lived out each other's proclamations of one another.

"Do you think Samantha would be proud of us?" I asked, looking Alexander in the eye, saying the name of our daughter for the first time since I walked out his campus apartment door close to twenty-two years ago. My heart ached at the thought of our love back then.

"You know, Samantha was my only child," Alexander murmured. "I never conceived another child after that. She was the closest thing to a legacy that I will ever have."

"You would have been a great father," I said.

Alexander didn't reply, but he gave me a warm smile, his eyes unlocking a sadness that had spanned decades.

"I miss Samantha," I said. "She'd be in college now. When Emma was born, and we both had to care for her, it was like we were living out the life I had always wanted for us...you and I... and our daughter. It's like having that exact same love, twice."

Alexander reached over and held my hand. "As a doctor and as a person, you know that it's never the same," he warned gently.

I sighed. "I know."

And I did know, deep down, that it was never really the same. We'd cared for Emma, but she wasn't ours. She wasn't Samantha, and neither Alexander nor I were the people we'd been as college students.

"So, what comes next, Lauren?" Alexander asked, releasing my hand.

This conversation was right turn after right turn, and I felt myself continuing to steer correctly.

"I loved you once, Alexander, and I found myself falling in love with you again this summer. And even though I'm married and shouldn't say it, I fantasized about us being together, forever. I still do. Reclaiming that love that was stolen from us. Reclaiming that time that was stolen from us. Reclaiming that daughter that was stolen from us. Taking our love and making it work this time."

Alexander held my gaze. "But?"

"But I can't see you anymore," I said. "Please know, you've won. I fell in love with you, and I'll go to my grave loving you and longing for you. I sculpted my life's work to satisfy you. I miss you so much that I Google you just to feel closer to you." I laughed a little, and Alexander smiled. "It's been over twenty years, and I can still feel the fabric of your college futon. But... but I have to live with myself, and I can't keep up this affair with you. And I can't chase dead baby after dead baby trying to win you back. And I can't try to blend our entirely different lives."

"Yeah." Alexander nodded. "Sometimes, love lasts, but from afar."

"Twice," I said.

He smiled and closed his eyes. "Twice."

We talked a bit more, the vulnerability seeping out of us, the acknowledgment that neither one of us were, in this moment, attempting to fight for each other. Recognizing that the young love, our history, our affair, and the eternal what-ifs were sustainable enough for us.

It felt as if our souls finally allowed the last two decades to carry us to tonight and have our love come to light. The sun was down now, and the gorgeous lake view had vanished and been replaced with what looked like a black screen on the windows.

"Well, I better start heading back to Jacobs," I said. It was time to start piecing my life back together, one decision at a time.

We stood up, and with our wine glasses still in hand, we

walked toward his front hallway. Right then, a loud boom came from behind us. We both turned around toward the massive windows to witness three fireworks, one right after another, in red, white, then blue. They lit up the sky, a reminder that even if the world had stopped for us, even if our hearts had never moved past 1994, that there was a whole country out there continuing to move forward, new thoughts and new ideas and even a new president soon.

As we watched the fireworks together, the aching to give into my desires took hold, the romanticism of the sexy interior now competing with the serendipitous fireworks. We turned back around toward each other. I was afraid we were going to embrace, which would lead to us kissing, which would lead to sex.

"Let's...not hug," I suggested.

Alexander laughed. "Fair enough."

"You know," I said, "as easily as we are leaving one another right now, we could be growing old together."

Alexander nodded, knowing that I believed our love to be the eternal kind, the kind that would last forever, outlasting even us. Then, for the second time in my life, I said my final goodbye to him, walking out of his home and out of his life.

CHAPTER 28

THE MINUTE I PULLED ONTO THE HIGHWAY RAMP, heading south toward my town of Jacobs, an immediate rush of relief washed over me. For the first time in a long time, I was finally proud of myself. I could feel myself starting to make right turns instead of wrong turns. The first right turn had been that conversation with Alexander. The second was heading back to toward Jacobs and toward my life.

The relief I felt was relief in knowing I had made my peace with Alexander and Samantha, and that they both hopefully knew how much I loved them. But more than relief, I was also stunned that I was actually walking away from something that made me feel alive. And the equally stunning quality of Alexander, that he was letting me. The only girl, according to him, that ever really loved him…and he let me walk right out of that door. Did he really love me as much as he said? The complexity of our relationship and our love felt so overpowering that if it took me twenty years to come to terms with what happened to us in college. It might take the next twenty years to unpack what happened to us when Emma brought us back together.

It was only 8:30 p.m., and I was, in theory, only halfway through my 24-hour shift. I quickly called the NICU, and Ashley picked up.

"Hey Ashley, it's Dr. Leonard," I said. "I'm feeling much better. I'll be back in about an hour. You know, give me a quick update on the babies and then, if you've got the time, I'd like to review my proposed 2017 census plans with you and get you familiar with that process."

"Oh okay, well tonight has been pretty mild," Ashley started. "Only Tristan is having difficulty with his sucking, but I see in the notes that you prescribed the occupational therapist."

She went through all five patients. Then, I spent some time explaining to her about the financial side of the NICU occupancy, and how each quarter the hospital asks the leading physicians to forecast a census to understand not only occupancy demands, but how much revenue will likely be coming into the hospital.

"Hold on, let me grab a pen and paper, I want to take notes on this," Ashley said, and I smiled, realizing that perhaps I was making an impact on not just the babies, but also my team.

We continued talking for a while, and then as we ended the call, I kept thinking about the five babies that were currently in our NICU, and how my treatment for them worked. I saw each baby growing stronger and developing. Week after week, month after month, year after year, I cared for sick babies, and they got better. They went home. They grew up. I had a true impact on these babies, but also on the parents, and hell, maybe even the community. Just because Emma died didn't mean that the other babies this year were inconsequential. I healed tiny humans. And Alexander too, in a more obvious way. Alexander took the worst of life's tragedies and created surgical miracles.

Would all these babies have been saved by us if we would have had Samantha? Was I meant to miscarry her? I had wondered that for so many years, and in talking with Alexander tonight, her father, I still didn't know the answer.

Why can't we definitively know why things happen? I wondered as I leaned my head back against my seat.

The straight vertical lines on the highway, both yellow and white, hypnotized me, and I could see new lines drawn left-to-right across my dashboard, my mind flooding with the image of a chart I used to use. While in residency, when we needed to assess a patient's need for medications, we'd often use a 2 x 2 matrix chart, four boxes in a big square indicating risk and reward.

And tonight, on my drive, I again saw the lines: the straight line left-to-right across my dashboard, low risk on the left, high risk on the right. And then the vertical yellow line on the left side of the road. Low reward on the bottom, high reward on the top.

That bottom left box, low risk and low reward…doing nothing…perhaps that's what I had been doing for so many years in my relationship with Billy. I let myself make excuses in the beginning. I let us fall out of love—well, Billy did too. It was so easy, though, and by letting our relationship deteriorate,

I could protect my heart from Billy crushing my dreams of what I wanted our life to be. Whenever I could feel the risk increase, and I could feel Billy's rejection, I would just work more. I lived like this for so long, obviously without any reward.

And I knew I was beyond this box now. I needed something greater.

The bottom right box, high risk and low reward. That was what I had just done, having the affair with Alexander. I used alcohol as my crutch to be bold, to drown out the right path. I used my fantasies to ignore my real problems. I was so risky, giving myself to a man while I myself was unattainable. And what made it risky was not just that I was married, but that I knew Alexander was also unattainable. I was told twenty years ago in a letter that for Alexander, medicine came first, and tonight he doubled down on that philosophy. It didn't matter that he loved me. He only had one single path and so in choosing this path, my reward was always going to be low.

The box on the upper left, low risk and high reward. This one was the mirage. This was the night out at the bar with Billy. Or Billy booking us tickets to Cancun and surprising me, or me waking up and making Billy pancakes in the morning. There was little risk here, with us already being a couple, already married, already in position to work on our relationship and fight for the love that we once possessed. The reward would have been so high. The risk would have been so low. But this box was an illusion. It didn't exist. Or at least, Billy never allowed me to penetrate it.

And then, finally, the box that was always the North Star.

The box on the upper right. High risk, high reward. This was where I needed to journey. This was where I had to confront all my fears to exude courage and determination.

This box was me, striking out on my own, getting divorced and building my life back. This was me looking terror in the eye and boldly stating, "I'll survive."

I realized that given everything I had already been through in my life, I could survive this divorce from Billy. I could survive the gossip that would be spread about me, that I chose my career over my marriage. I could take it because I knew my truth. And I could survive the narrative that Billy was better off without me or any other hurtful accusation that came my way.

I could even survive what this meant for little William. I wouldn't lean into the narrative that I was ruining his life, failing him. I had to believe that I could push through that risk, push through a custody arrangement, push through what William would ultimately think of me. And I knew that my fears for William underestimated his power. In the face of adversity, I would guide my child, and he would excel. He would be resilient, and he would thrive.

I could survive what I was about to embark on, to allow myself that high reward. The reward of being proud of myself, of looking at myself every day and being comfortable in who I was. The reward of not tiptoeing around the house, or around my personality, trying to stifle who I was. The reward of shattering everyone's preconceived notions of me and still holding my head high. The reward of peace, of stillness, of loving myself.

Being a divorced single mother, a small-town doctor, and,

most important of all, finally happy.

I moved into the right lane and turned on my blinker, exiting the highway for the ramp that would lead me back to Jacobs.

Another wave of calmness washed over me, and I had made my decision. Everything in my life had brought me to this moment. My past had intersected with my present, and it was now catapulting me toward my future. And I was ready.

EPILOGUE

FEBRUARY 2019

"We're out of time for today, would you like to schedule another appointment?"

I'd just finished a cathartic therapy session, talking mostly about my fears of the upcoming massive expansion of Covenant Medical and my expanded role within it.

"You know, you're really doing great," my therapist added. "Today is Valentine's Day, and you seem so happy. I'm very proud of you," she said through head nods.

I booked my next appointment and as I headed home, listening to my podcast, I started to smile. My therapist was right. I was happy. I hadn't even thought about the fact that I was single on Valentine's Day. I simply didn't let that noise inside my head. I was just happy that I was on my way to see my son.

As I pulled into my driveway, I got a text from Billy. *On*

our way. It was my night with William, and what I had imagined would be an ugly custody battle a couple years back turned out to be rather anticlimactic. William was able to spend ample time with each parent, and it warmed my heart that I actually saw him more now than when I was married. I was more of a mom now than ever before. *Sometimes life works that way,* I thought.

Inside the house, I started preparing dinner. Since the divorce, I learned all new talents, including how to cook. I wasn't very good, but William seemed to eat whatever I made with little complaints. Tonight, William and I were having spaghetti followed by a chocolate dessert in honor of Valentine's Day. I pulled a chocolate cake mix out of the cupboard and started adding the mix, eggs, and water into a bowl. I reached into the drawer to pull out a spatula.

"Alexa, how long do you bake a chocolate cake for?" I yelled into the living room.

I didn't hear Alexa's answer because the doorbell rang. I rushed to the front door and opened it.

"Happy Valentine's Day Mom!"

William shoved a school-made Valentine's Day card at me. He smiled as he asked, "Do you like it?"

Billy stood at the door, smiling at William. He was dressed up in a button-down shirt and nice pants. His car was still running, and I saw his girlfriend, Sarah, in the front seat in a red blouse. I realized they must be on their way to a Valentine's Day dinner, and I waved at her gently. She smiled.

"Mom, do you still have that Valentine's Day candy?" William asked.

"I have something better for you. I'm making us a chocolate cake!"

William ran right past me into the house, and Billy's gaze followed him. "See you next time," he said quietly to William as he waved and then began walking back to his car.

I shut the door and walked back into the kitchen, admiring the house as I did so. It was so clean, and I loved the way I had decorated it a year back. I took in a deep breath, smiling as I watched William, now in the kitchen, grab the spatula and attempt to stir the cake batter.

"Happy Valentine's Day sweetheart," I said as I kissed the top of his forehead. "I love you so much. You okay with spaghetti tonight?"

"Can we eat the cake first?" William asked seriously.

I laughed. And then I kept smiling as I stared at William. I was so happy to be here in this moment, to be me, and to be living the life I was living. It wasn't easy, and it wasn't a straight line, but I had gotten to a place where I knew who I was, and I could appreciate everything I had in my life. Gratitude swelled up inside of me, and my heart burst with pride as I knew I was where I was meant to be.

"Sure, sweetheart," I said. "Let's have the cake first."

Acknowledgments

In 2017, for months on end, I stared at the four walls of a hospital room. The only people I had contact with for 16 hours a day were medical professionals. As they continuously walked in and out of the hospital room, I wondered, *Do they have lives beyond their jobs? What are they going through right now outside of work?* Over those months, *Never the Same Love Twice* was born.

This book would not be possible without the incredible medical community that I got to know. Thank you for being nothing short of angels.

Thank you also to my amazing literary team, including my editor Hannah Bauman, who gave me the confidence to take this novel to print. Thank you to my beta readers, my parents, my sister, my friends, and colleagues who inspired me along this journey and encouraged me to write these characters and this story with authenticity.

Lastly, and most importantly, thank you to my son, Prescott, for being nothing short of a miracle, the reason I am me, and the reason for this novel.

Made in the USA
Monee, IL
19 November 2021